LE............ACE

DETECTIVE REBECCA ELLIS BOOK 4

ROBIN MAHLE

INKUBATOR
BOOKS

Published by Inkubator Books
www.inkubatorbooks.com

ISBN (eBook): 978-1-83756-271-8
ISBN (Paperback): 978-1-83756-272-5
ISBN (Hardback): 978-1-83756-273-2

1

Summer air settled over the suburban street, clinging to homes bathed in darkness. Porch lights spilled pools of amber that cut through the shadows. The strong scent of lush pine drifted into windows left open.

Gone were the distant rumbling of cars, the laughter of children playing outside, and the smell of barbequed meat on backyard grills. To him, it was as though the entire world slept.

This was when they were most vulnerable. Lying in their beds, half-covered in weightless sheets. The whirl of fans blowing a gentle breeze onto bare skin, giving rise to tiny goosebumps. Believing they were safe inside their idyllic neighborhood.

This was his time now.

Dressed in dark clothes with his head shrouded by a thick hood, he felt his body heat climb under the heavy attire. From the shadows of a hedgerow that lined the home's front garden, he spied the cameras. One at the front door, one at the garage. A sense of safety offered, which was anything but guaranteed.

Piece of cake.

He made himself small and kept low to the ground as he blended into the night, moving to the front window left ajar. Beneath the window lay a row of evergreens trimmed flush and easily straddled by his long legs. Gripping the bottom of the windowpane with gloved hands, he pushed upward, inch by inch, until he made enough room to climb inside.

His burly arms steadied his weight as he raised his right leg over the hedgerow and slipped it through the opening and into the room. A delicate balancing act, as he placed his weight on his right leg and braced with his arms to bring over the left.

He was inside.

The dark room disoriented him for a moment until his reflection in the television appeared thanks to the scant moonlight diffusing between the curtain panels. As his eyes adjusted, he began to make out shapes. An L-shaped sectional sofa. A square table in front of it. A brick fireplace under the wall-mounted television.

A hall lay feet ahead with a staircase positioned to the right of it that led to the second-floor bedrooms. Stairs could be tricky. They creaked and squeaked and made all manner of noises in these older homes.

The sound of his breath broke through the stillness. Sweat dripped down his back under the hoodie, and his pulse raced. *Calm down.* His rubber-soled shoes softened each guarded step as he moved onward, fingers outstretched, searching for unseen obstacles until he reached the banister.

One careful foot placed on the first step, and he climbed, slowly, quietly, until he reached the top landing. A short hall, then three closed doors to his right. He pointed his finger at each one as though playing a game that would dictate his next move. Who would be first?

He aimed for the door on the far left that was open just a crack. A child's room—one who feared the darkness. Whether it was a boy or girl made no difference to him. He knew why he was here and what needed to be done.

He pressed his index finger on the edge of the door and gently pushed it open. Light curtains floated with the breeze that came in from the window on the back wall. A low dresser lay underneath it. A twin bed with a wooden head and footboard rested in the center of the room. Night tables flanked either side, each one with a stick lamp on it. Above the headboard appeared a saying of some kind, though the words were too dark to read.

And the boy—sleeping.

Colors were impossible to see, but the shape of the boy was well defined under the sheets. A tiny thing. His little arms at his sides above the covers. His head turned, exposing a puffy cheek. His chest rose and fell with each breath.

The hood he wore acted like blinders as he stood at the end of the bed, and he drank in the boy with his eyes. Five? Maybe six. An angel.

The boy rustled his little legs under the sheets. Surprised by the movement, he stepped back, ready to bolt if the child opened his eyes and let out an inevitable scream. Instead, the boy settled.

Now, his toes peeked out from under the sheets. Perfect little toes that would get cold with the window open.

He reached out and gently pulled down the sheet to cover them again.

"Daddy?" the boy muttered, his eyes still closed.

"It's okay, son. Go back to sleep," he whispered, caressing the boy's soft foot.

"Okay, Daddy. I love you. Night, night." He turned on his side.

"I love you too." He let go of the tiny foot.

Time was against him, and he'd already wasted too much of it. He stepped toward the nightstand and examined the photo that lay on top of it. The light was too dim to make it out fully, but it appeared to be the boy and his parents. He laid it facedown. A Hot Wheels car was inches away from the frame, and he took it, slipping it into his jacket.

A final look at the child and he stepped out of the room, quietly pulling the door back to its original position.

Standing in the middle of the hallway, he eyed what he was certain was the parents' bedroom door, wondering how they hadn't realized that an intruder stood here right now, willing to go to extraordinary lengths to accomplish his goal. They were oblivious, thoughtless, selfish people.

A small turn of his foot and he started toward the door until a sound, something like a cough, echoed from behind it. His entire purpose was to get inside. To see them. To make them feel fear.

Don't get caught.

His options narrowed in an instant, fearing the man inside that room would awaken. Would this be enough? Would his point have been made? That depended on whether they noticed someone had been here. Would they notice the displaced object? The missing toy? Would they sense the violation of their sanctuary?

With only seconds to decide, the logical option was to abort, sooner than he'd hoped, but the groundwork had been laid. It would have to be enough this time.

But this is just the beginning.

———

DETECTIVE REBECCA ELLIS climbed the steps to the second-floor Criminal Investigation Division of the Bangor Police Department. Her blond, stick-straight hair, which usually brushed against her shoulders, was pulled back in a small ponytail to help keep her cool on this warm summer morning. Wearing a gray short-sleeved blouse and dress pants, she entered the detectives' bullpen and glanced at Euan McCallister's desk, which was next to hers. Yep, still empty.

Detective Gabby Lewis, who'd already arrived this morning, tossed a nod her way. The forty-year-old mother of two teen boys had worn her long braids high on her head today, as it was set to be a scorcher. "Morning, Becca. You have a good night?"

Ellis shrugged. "About the same as the night before. You?" She carried on to her desk and set down her things.

"The boys are finishing up with school this week, so things are about to get real at the Lewis house."

"I don't envy you, Gabby," Ellis joked. At almost thirty-five, she had no kids. No husband—anymore—so commiserating with her teammate was awkward at times, though both women took it in their stride.

Ellis had begun to feel her age over the course of this past year. Ever more challenging and troubling cases had fallen into her lap. Her father—Bangor Ret. Det. Hank Ellis—was still recovering from a stroke. And her brother, Carter, had been sent to drug rehab, where he remained, though according to her, he deserved to be in prison.

As Ellis prepared for a meeting with Unit Commander

Sergeant Abbott, she noticed the rest of the team trickle in as it struck eight a.m.

These guys had come from all over, and somehow, they had landed here in this small police department. Was it fate? Maybe. Because a thread ran through each of them, connecting them to one another in a way that had only begun to reveal itself.

But, for now, Sergeant James Abbott waited. Ellis circled around her desk to head back into the hallway. The sarge was always in earlier than anyone else, so she felt confident he'd be sitting in his office, drinking a cup of black coffee, and getting up to speed on their current investigations.

His door was open, as always, and Ellis rapped her knuckles on the frame. "Sarge?"

Abbott stood in front of the whiteboard with a marker in his hand as he updated the investigations board. "Becca, come in. Good morning."

"Morning, sir." She meandered inside. "I wanted to see how things were progressing with Euan's leave of absence."

Abbott removed his reading glasses, revealing his kind brown eyes. He was a substantial man with thinning hair and a bulbous nose. Damn close to retirement at sixty, everyone knew he'd hang on for a few more years.

As the unit commander of the Criminal Investigation Division, he assigned cases at his discretion. No specialty units in this small outfit. Everyone did just about everything, at least as far as the detectives were concerned. Abbott had been on the force for more than twenty years and had worked with Ellis's father for a while. Though Hank had a closer relationship with Lieutenant Abe Serrano, who was the top of the top brass at Bangor PD.

Abbott returned to his chair, setting down his coffee mug

over the top of an existing water ring on his desk. Several were scattered around, and the wooden finish was in pretty rough shape. Abbott was tight with the department's budget, so he often did without. But never his people. "You know that's not my call, Becca. That's up to the lieutenant."

Ellis walked over to a nearby chair and leaned over it with her palms clutching the back. "Sarge, it's been six weeks. That was the agreed-upon timeframe. No one's talking about it anymore. Everyone on social media has moved on to whatever the hot topic is for the day. Even the journalist who created this mess."

He laced his fingers over his full waist. "I hear you. Let me talk to the lieutenant. We'll see how things go. Maybe I can talk some sense into Fletch—"

"Last I checked, sir, Fletch doesn't run this department," Ellis cut in.

Abbott raised a brow. "Watch yourself, Becca."

Her gaze retreated. "Sorry, Sarge. I'm just..."

"I know. We're all just..." He trailed off. "We have the staff to manage without Euan a while longer. He's getting paid. He's not going to lose his health benefits or anything else. You know why we had to do this. I know you do."

Ellis sighed. "Yes, sir. I do. I just know that he's ready to come back to work."

"I'll bet," Abbott replied, holding his gaze on her a moment. "I hear you two have been spending a fair amount of time together."

"We're friends, Sarge. That's all it is," Ellis replied.

He nodded with downturned lips. "All right. If you say so. How's his shoulder doing, by the way?"

"Better," she replied. "His physical therapist says he'll regain all range of motion."

"That's damn good to hear." Abbott slipped on his reading glasses again. "I need to finish updating the status reports. I'll call the briefing in about an hour."

Ellis supposed that was her cue to leave. "Yes, sir." She spun around and headed into the corridor. As she made her way back toward the bullpen, Pelletier emerged from the breakroom.

The slightly plump, boyish-looking thirty-three-year-old had light brown hair and the most beautiful cornflower-blue eyes ever seen on any human. He'd never been married and had worked in Robbery/Homicide in Portland. He and Ellis had been almost inseparable—until Euan McCallister arrived.

The two walked side by side. "Hey, Bryce. How you doing this morning?"

"Good, thanks. You?" he asked.

"Another day."

Pelletier groaned. "I guess so."

They carried on in silence for a few moments. Their friendship had become strained a while back after he'd confessed his feelings for her. By that point, Ellis was already taken with McCallister, and she let down Pelletier, who'd been her closest friend, as easily as she could. It hadn't really gone all that well, but things were mostly better now.

"Is Sarge ready for the daily brief?" he asked.

"He says to give him an hour," Ellis replied as they arrived back at the bullpen. "Catch up with you then?"

EUAN MCCALLISTER HAD his back against the weight bench, his legs straddling either side and arms resting over his chest. His T-shirt was wet with perspiration; he was out of breath and feeling every bit his thirty-eight years.

The physical therapist, an athletic young man, held a ten-pound dumbbell. "Why don't you sit up, and I'll have you do a few more reps with this? I'll go easy on you this time."

"Gee, thanks." McCallister chuckled as he pulled up into a seated position on the bench. He'd been injured during an investigation, which had led, in part, to his leave of absence. Since then, he'd been focused on his physical therapy because it was the only way he could keep his mind off the job—and off her.

"Here you go." The therapist handed him the free weight. "I want you to raise it over your shoulder as high as you can go this time."

McCallister gripped the weight and squeezed shut his eyes, groaning as he raised it. He kept his hair longer on the top, and its soft brown waves fell into his eyes. He blew them away and held the weight over his head. He was no body-builder and, in fact, was probably a little on the wiry side, but he managed the ten pounds, feeling a little embarrassed by the not-so-amazing feat.

He'd been going to PT since he was shot by a drug dealer they eventually brought down. The timing of his injury was used as a way to coincide with Bangor PD's supposed review of his Boston incident. A tragic case of an accidental shooting, for which McCallister would never forgive himself. Nevertheless, he understood and didn't want to jeopardize his job. After all, he'd only been with the department about seven months now. And he knew it was probably the only place left that would keep him after what had happened.

"You're not done yet," the therapist said. "I want three sets of eight."

McCallister's arm trembled as he raised the dumbbell above his head again and again. His shoulder felt like it was on fire, and he winced at the pain. "I think that's enough for today," he said as he put down the weight.

"Fair enough. I'll cut you some slack, but come back next week ready to finish up our time together." The therapist patted him on his good shoulder. "You're improving every day, man. Don't give up. You're just about there."

THE SUMMER EVENING stretched long and warm as Ellis felt the sun still intense against her back. She stood at the door of McCallister's second-floor downtown apartment, which overlooked the Penobscot River. Despite having changed from a pants suit into a soft, flowy sundress, she still had to work hard at reminding herself she was a woman. With her hand balled into a fist, ready to knock, the door opened.

McCallister stood before her, his smile enhancing his square jaw. His short-sleeved button-down shirt was left untucked over casual summer pants. God, she'd almost forgotten how good he looked. "Here." She handed him a bottle of wine. "I brought this for dinner."

"Thank you." He stepped back. "It's good to see you, Becca."

She walked inside, and he wrapped his arm around her waist, drawing her close for a gentle kiss. "It's good to see you too," she said as she pulled away after the long moment. "How was your PT today?"

McCallister closed the door behind her. "Not bad. I'm

getting better. How about I open this bottle, huh?" He walked through the sparsely decorated living space, which had only one or two pieces of art on the walls. A slightly sad-looking fake tree was shoved into a corner, but a nice comfortable sofa pointed toward a giant television on the opposite wall. It was a small place but seemed to suit him well.

"I'd love a glass." Ellis followed him into the kitchen, which appeared recently renovated with white cabinets and quartz countertops.

He poured a glass from the bottle of chardonnay and handed it to her.

"Aren't you having one?" she asked, taking it from his hand.

"Maybe just a little. Gotta watch it with the painkillers. I usually need one after therapy." He poured half a glass and held it up as if to toast. "I'm glad you're here."

"Me too." She gently tapped his glass, eliciting a high-pitched chime. Ellis wasn't much of a wine drinker; she preferred beer. Growing up with a cop for a dad and hanging around all his buddies while they played poker at the house lent itself well to that choice of drink.

She realized he'd gone quiet a moment and figured he waited for news. She wished she had something different, but it would be more of the same. A wait-and-see game neither of them could stomach for much longer. Ellis swirled her glass, keeping her eyes on it for a moment too long.

"No news?" McCallister asked.

She turned up her gaze at him, wearing guilt on her face. "Nothing definite."

McCallister set down his glass. His shoulders dropped,

and he pressed his lips together, letting out a bit of a snort through his nose.

"He said he was going to talk to Serrano," Ellis added. "They said six weeks, and it's been six weeks. I'm sure the rest is just a formality."

"I'm sure you're right." He walked around to meet her on the other side of the breakfast bar and brushed the back of his hand against her rounded cheek. "I'm just glad I have a woman on the inside to keep me informed."

Ellis chuckled. "I've got your back."

"I know you do." His eyes crinkled as he grinned. "And maybe someday, you'll allow me to have yours."

2

Sydney Manning's eyes snapped open as she lay in bed next to her husband. She turned to see that he hadn't been roused by the noise. The faint sound was something like a thud on the downstairs floor. Maybe in the kitchen? Could've been in the living room. All she knew was that she had to investigate.

The mother of two teenaged boys, she was already a light sleeper, and now that she approached menopause, her sleep was often disrupted by night sweats. Her usual solution was to go downstairs into the kitchen and stick her head in the freezer for a minute or two until it passed. But this time, she would check out the noise because something didn't feel right.

Dressed in only a long T-shirt, Sydney crept out of bed, tucking her short auburn hair behind her ears as she moved. She padded in bare feet to the bedroom door, the cool wood floor sending a slight chill up her legs.

She opened it slowly, careful not to make a sound. Her neck craned out into the hallway, glancing left, then right.

Everything was shrouded in darkness except for a faint light coming from the bottom of the staircase. Sydney stepped out into the hall, trepidation gripping her chest.

Taking one discreet step at a time, she made her way down the stairs, pausing every few moments to listen for any other noises. The silence seemed to amplify every creak and groan of the steps, and she began to feel more anxious with each one. As she reached the bottom, sweat formed under her arms. That could've been the menopause, though.

This felt like a mistake—coming down here alone. Surely it was nothing, but something pricked the back of her mind. That sense of imminent danger, which sent her pulse to rise. She glanced up the staircase, remembering that her boys still lay asleep in their beds. If someone was in the house, she wouldn't dare let the intruder pass. Not while she lived.

Maybe this was just Sydney's mind freewheeling against her better judgment as she walked into the unlit living room. This was a safe neighborhood. They had security cameras and sensors on the doors and windows. All the things needed to ensure a sense of security.

Sydney surveyed the home she knew so well, everywhere the nighttime shadows would let her see. The horizontal wood blinds on the front window were closed. Nothing appeared out of place. Nothing appeared to have fallen to the floor. *The kitchen.*

A few feet away, on the other side of the foyer, was the kitchen. A soft green glow emanated from the microwave clock and the oven clock. The screen on the refrigerator came to life as she walked toward it. She had enough light to confirm that no one and nothing was here. This was all in her head.

Sydney stood inside the kitchen when a brush against her leg forced her to jump. Looking down, she spotted Monty, their Jack Russell terrier. "Oh my God." She let out a quiet, but nervous laugh.

The dog tilted his head and perked up his ears, thwapping his tail back and forth.

She squatted low and scratched under his chin. The dog's eyes seemed to stare right through to her soul. "Monty, how did you get out of your kennel? I thought we locked you in before going to bed."

He looked up at her with an expression that suggested he had a secret but wasn't ready to tell.

"Come on then," she said gently as she scooped him up and made her way back to the laundry room. "And here I thought someone was in the house. Let's get you back to bed, little guy."

SYDNEY AWAKENED to a bright sun shining through the slats in the window blinds. She glanced over to see her husband was no longer there, but soon heard the shower running in their adjacent bathroom. He was already up and getting ready for work.

Now, to get her sons up. Making two teenaged boys get out of bed this close to summer vacation was like negotiating a sale. Give and take, compromise, until no one was happy. But school was almost finished for the year. Soon enough, her sons would sleep until noon, play video games until six, eat dinner, go out with friends, and then back to bed at two a.m. Such was this stage of her life.

She climbed out of bed and stepped into the hallway,

listening for signs of life behind her boys' bedroom doors. It sounded like they were at least moving around in there, which was a bonus.

Sydney carried on downstairs to let Monty out of his kennel. Last night had seemed strange, and she still wondered how the dog got out. They were a smart breed, but smart enough to open a kennel door? There was no other explanation, she told herself.

"Let's go, boy." She opened the kennel gate, and Monty scampered toward the back door to be let out. "Go on. Outside you go." She opened the door and closed it again before heading over to make breakfast. As she started cracking eggs into a bowl, her eldest son, Brayden, stumbled into the kitchen.

"Mom, were you or Dad in my room last night?" He rubbed his eyes and stood in a long stretch. The fifteen-year-old was already almost six feet tall and looked like he would blow over in a light wind.

Sydney froze, her hand hovering over the bowl of eggs. She hadn't been in there last night...had she? The strange events from the previous evening came back to her, and it seemed possible that she had gone into his room without realizing it. But no. Maybe not. "No," Sydney replied. "I didn't go in there. Why do you ask?"

Brayden shrugged and opened the refrigerator door. "Some of my stuff was moved around. Like, it was weird. My game controller was on my dresser. I'm sure I left it on my nightstand. Oh well. Doesn't matter." He grabbed the orange juice and took a swig directly from the bottle.

"Brayden!" Sydney called out. "Get a glass, would you, son?"

"Sorry, Mom." He returned the bottle to the fridge. "It's not like I'm sick or anything. Geez."

She shook her head and carried on making breakfast. But something had happened last night. Monty had been out. She remembered that much. But going into her son's room? Seemed an odd thing to do. She'd stopped checking in on them like that a long time ago. She wasn't crazy, was she?

ELLIS ARRIVED at her father's house early this morning. She usually checked in on him in the evenings, after work, but last night she'd had other plans. A brief knock on the door and she inserted her key to open it. "Dad? It's me. You up?"

"Course I'm up," he called out from the kitchen. "You want a cup of coffee?"

She headed into the kitchen and noticed Hank at the small dining table with a newspaper in his hands. Yeah, he still read a newspaper. "Morning. Sure, I'll take some coffee if you have any to spare."

He jerked his thumb over at the coffee pot. "You know where everything is."

Ellis grabbed a mug from the kitchen cabinet and poured it full of steaming black coffee. She preferred flavored creamer, but Hank couldn't stand the stuff. So when she was here, she used milk instead. "How you doing this morning, Dad?"

"Fine. Fine." He glanced at her with a knowing gaze. "How was your night?"

"Good. Euan made me dinner, and we watched a movie."

She studied him a moment, noticing how his age had caught up to him, especially since the stroke.

At sixty-three, Hank was a tall man. Six feet, to be exact. He'd been on the force for twenty-three years and retired about five years ago, just around the time his daughter passed her detective's exam. He carried a little too much weight around the middle, but she tried to cut him some slack. The stroke he'd had a few months ago was a direct result of a case she'd worked. Of course, Hank blamed himself since the case stretched back a couple of decades, and the people involved were the same ones he'd once confronted.

Never mind now, that was all over. Ellis wanted to help him focus on his recovery. But she knew that soon enough, Carter would be out of rehab and back in their lives. She'd done her best to keep him inside after learning what he'd done as a child years ago, but she'd had no legal footing on which to stand. No charges she could bring. Regardless, it was something she had yet to reveal to Hank, knowing how much it would upset him. And setting back his recovery wasn't an option.

Ellis took a sip of her coffee while Hank continued to read the paper. "So, anyway, I thought I'd stop by to see you this morning since I didn't get around to it last night."

He finally set down the paper and laid eyes on her. "Kid, you gotta start worrying more about yourself and less about me. You know that, right?"

Her face masked in resignation. "Do we have to have the same conversation every time I visit you? Can't you just accept that you're my dad and I love you? And I want to spend time with you."

Hank pursed his lips. "Fine." He picked up the paper again. "So, what's happening down at the station?"

Ellis grabbed her cup and joined Hank at the dining table. "A few cases here and there. I guess I should be glad it's been somewhat quiet, considering we're short-handed right now."

Hank looked down at her over his reading glasses. "You want me to talk to Serrano? See if I can nudge him along?"

"No, Dad. I appreciate you wanting to help, but this is about making the department look good. Proactive, you know?"

"By doing something it had no business doing?" Hank pressed. "Euan got a bad deal, you ask me. The man took his punishment back in Boston, where it was warranted. But to punish him here? Makes no goddam sense. Can't figure out why Serrano would make that call."

Ellis shrugged. "It was more of a cover-your-ass situation. Things have settled down a lot, so I'm sure this will be over soon. I do know Euan's anxious to get back to work."

"And his injury?" Hank continued.

"Doing better."

He paused a moment, looking as though he wanted to say more. "Let me ask you this, kid...are you planning on taking the next steps with him?"

"What do you mean?" She knew exactly what he meant.

Hank wore a derisive gaze. "That's how you want to play this? Come on. It's me you're talking to. Your old pops. I'm asking if you feel ready to move ahead with this man. You've been divorced a while now. Don't you think it's time you find some happiness again?"

IT WAS Sydney's day to drive the boys to school, and she arrived in the nick of time. Pulling up to the curb, she peered over her shoulder at her youngest in the back seat. "Don't forget to turn in your math homework today, you hear me? It's your last shot."

He rolled his eyes and opened the rear passenger door. "I won't, Mom."

Sydney turned back to her fifteen-year-old in the front passenger seat. "Have a good day, Brayden."

He grabbed his backpack and opened the door. "Thanks, Mom. You too."

As they stepped out onto the sidewalk, she leaned over. "Love you guys." To no one's surprise, they ignored her.

But just as she was about to pull away from the front of the school, one of her neighbors approached on foot. Sydney rolled down her window. "Hi, Janie. What's going on?"

The reedy, dark-haired woman of about thirty-five wore a tight brow and had crossed her arms firmly against her body as if it was forty degrees outside. The morning had already reached a balmy sixty. She leaned down. "Sydney, there's been some talk this morning."

"Oh, God. About what?" She expected whatever rumor the mill was about to churn out was likely regarding her boys. "What'd my kids do this time?"

"No, it's not them." Janie darted her gaze. "A bunch of us were talking and posting on the community Facebook page."

"About?" Sydney pressed.

"About weird stuff going on in our homes."

Sydney tilted her head a smidge, thinking back to last night. "What weird stuff?"

"Like, I don't know, but everyone thinks someone's

coming into their houses and sneaking around or something. It's super creepy."

Sydney's heart skipped a beat. Was it possible that someone had been in her house last night? The strange events with Monty and Brayden suddenly took on new meaning. She decided to confirm her suspicion with Janie. "Have you experienced it, too?"

Janie nodded. "A couple nights ago, I woke up to a noise. Checked it out but didn't see anything. And then the next morning, I noticed a few things were moved around."

Sydney's anxiety skyrocketed. "Oh my God, Janie. That's terrifying."

The woman's expression turned grim. "I don't feel safe, you know? I mean, should we call the police?"

Sydney hesitated to admit she'd experienced the same thing. It was easy to get this group riled, especially on the community Facebook page. She'd seen it plenty of times before. But this could be something. "I don't know. Like you said, if nothing was stolen or whatever, can they even do anything about it?"

Janie shook her head. "I have no idea. But you haven't felt anything weird or seen anything strange?"

"No. Not yet, at least," she replied. "Look, let's make sure everyone knows to keep their eyes open. We can post on the page that we need to stay vigilant."

"I don't know, Syd." Janie clutched the pendant on her necklace. "Everyone's freaked out. I think we need to tell the police."

ELLIS APPRECIATED her father for a great many things. He'd always been there for her when it came to advice about the job. He'd had her back from the moment she'd entered the force to this very day.

He also had much for which to make amends but had done a pretty good job of it up to now. So much so that, in all honesty, he owed her nothing. Not anymore. And when it came to her relationships, his advice was generally spot on, no matter how much she tried to deny it. He'd offered words of wisdom when she'd considered taking her budding relationship with McCallister a step farther. Now, he wanted to know what was next. Well, she really had no idea.

Nevertheless, Ellis would carry on heeding Hank's advice because a time would come when he could offer no more. When she would only hear an echo of his voice that she could hardly remember, like a distant memory. And she would be alone in this world. But that time was not now.

Now, Ellis entered the stationhouse lobby, glancing up the staircase to the landing at the top. She continued inside and heard an officer at the administration desk on a call.

Her brow drew in with concern. The officer sounded as though he was attempting to calm down the caller. Ellis stopped at the desk.

The officer turned up his palm as he spoke, appearing uncertain about the entire situation. She listened in to his side of the conversation.

"Yes, ma'am. I completely understand your concern; however, if nothing's been taken and you don't know that someone, in fact, came into your home, I'm not sure what I can do for you." He cast Ellis a doubtful gaze. "Yes, ma'am, I understand that several of your neighbors have said the same thing. What about security cameras?" He continued to listen. "I see. No one caught anything suspicious. That is strange. I'll tell you what." The officer grabbed a pen and slip of paper. "Why don't you give me your name and number? I'll take the information to the captain, and he can have a couple of units make a few extra rounds to check out your neighborhood. Would that be helpful? Maybe they'll see something or someone who appears out of place." His face took on a look of relief. "Okay. Great. I've got a pen. I'm ready when you are."

Ellis glanced at the paper as he wrote down the name of the woman. *Janie Federoff*. He jotted down the name of the neighborhood as well. *Woodland Heights*. It wasn't far from the university on the east side of the Fifteen. Nice area.

"I've got it. Someone will be in touch to let you know. Thank you, ma'am. Goodbye." He ended the call and unleashed a heavy sigh.

"What was that all about?" Ellis asked.

"I don't know, Detective, but this woman and a few of her neighbors are certain they've got some sort of peeping Tom lurking around their homes."

"And nothing's been stolen?" she pressed.

"Not that any of them have noticed," he replied. "I've got her details and the neighborhood. I'll take it to Sergeant Moss and see if he thinks it's a good idea to step up patrols in the area."

Ellis glanced over her shoulder toward the hallway that led to Moss and his department. "Listen, why don't you let me walk it over? I'll talk with him and see what he thinks."

"You don't have to do that, Detective. I know how busy you guys are upstairs."

She raised her hands. "Don't think twice about it. Please. I'll take it to him. Sounds unusual for that part of town."

"Well, it does, yes." He reluctantly handed over the paper. "I appreciate the help. Thank you."

"Don't mention it." Ellis nodded and turned on her heel. She stepped into the hall toward the sergeant's office, bypassing the patrolmen's bullpen, where officers chattered on phone calls and among each other. She appreciated the guys down there, especially Officer Triggs. He'd gone above and beyond when it came to her brother, Carter. And he'd helped McCallister and Bevins on that drug dealer case that resulted in McCallister getting shot.

She spotted Triggs at his desk just as she walked by. "Morning."

"Detective, hi. How's it going?" he asked.

"Just fine. Thanks. Hey, uh, we'll catch up soon?"

Triggs bowed his head. "You got it."

Ellis smiled and continued beyond the bullpen, reaching Moss's office. She knocked on his door and waited a moment for him to answer.

"Come in."

She opened the door and stepped inside. "Sergeant Moss."

He looked up from his laptop and grinned. "Detective Ellis, what are you doing down here in the trenches?" Moss was around thirty-three and was the day-shift sergeant. His shoulders were square and his face narrow, offset by a prominent nose. His brown hair was worn short, but not quite a crew cut.

Ellis meandered inside with the slip of paper in her hand. "I wanted to pass along some information. The front desk got a call, and I happened to overhear it." She offered the paper.

Moss read it. "This is in the Woodland Heights area." His brow creased. "That's pretty upscale."

"Yeah, that's what I thought," Ellis replied. "Could be a guy scoping things out to see who owns what."

"Recon for a crew?" Moss asked. "Maybe. Seems a risk to go inside while folks are home."

"You're right about that." Ellis pinched her brow. "You think it's worth stepping up patrols in the area?"

"Probably." He wore a crooked grin. "You interested in doing my job now, Detective? Because you are more than welcome to it."

"Thanks, but I have enough problems of my own." She chuckled. "No, I was just thinking maybe you could keep me posted on this? See if anything else happens."

He stared at the paper a moment longer and returned his attention to her. "Why? What are you thinking?"

"I'm not sure yet." Ellis scratched the side of her head. "But to strike a few homes in a short period of time...homes that have security...well, it kind of raises my hackles a little."

3

Detective Lori Fletcher was just twenty-seven and had made detective a year ago after working four years as a traffic cop. Some called her a prodigy. Others called her ambitious. Mostly, she was just tough as nails and never took shit from anyone.

Part of it was her small size. A woman of barely five three and about one hundred pounds—wet—making it as a cop was harder for her than most. Fierce was what her former male counterparts called her. That was often code for "bitchy." Fletch didn't care, though. And over time, they'd come to accept her. Now that she was a detective, the level of respect for her grew.

And she was the one who had pushed for McCallister's leave of absence. Protecting her unit, her department, was paramount in her eyes. McCallister came along, a veteran homicide detective from Boston, and sucked up all the oxygen in the room as far as she was concerned.

She eventually came around to thinking he was all right, and once Ellis caught feelings for him, Fletch had softened her stance. But the risk he'd put the department in was too great not to act on it.

She had convinced Abbott and Serrano to put McCallister on leave to "recover" from his on-the-job injury. It was an excuse. A coverup for stepping onto the sidelines while the *Boston Globe* reporter published the article about his role in the shooting incident that killed a fifteen-year-old boy.

The department risked backlash, and she couldn't allow that to happen. Worse than that, McCallister had kept this little secret hidden from all of them, even Ellis, up until it all came to a head.

Now, maybe the time had come to re-evaluate the situation. The initial six weeks was up. McCallister had done his time, so to speak. She could test the social media waters to ensure the outrage had quietened. And there was no denying the fact that McCallister had done his best to make amends—to her and to the rest of the team.

She knocked on Abbott's door and waited a moment. His voice trailed, giving authorization for her to enter. "Hi, Sarge. Can I talk to you a minute?"

"Fletch, come on in." In his usual fatherly way, Abbott leaned back in his chair and cocked his head as though waiting for a confession from one of his children. "You look like you have something on your mind." He gestured to the chair across from him. "Take a load off."

"Thanks." Fletch lowered onto the chair that felt oddly too large. With her index finger, she tucked a swath of highlighted brown hair behind her ear. "As you know, I've been monitoring the situation regarding Euan since he was placed on leave."

"I'm aware," Abbott said.

"And it seems that things have settled quite a bit now. It's been several weeks..."

"Yes, it has." Abbott rubbed his index finger and thumb on the marks left by his reading glasses. "And I have discussed this with Lieutenant Serrano as well as the union rep. You see, I hired McCallister already knowing about his past. Something I'm not entirely sure you considered."

"No, sir," she replied with a downward gaze.

"But you weren't wrong," Abbott continued. "The press, social media...it got ugly there for a while, and I, too, see that things have settled."

Just as she was about to speak, he raised his index finger to stop her.

"That said, you should know that while I appreciate your concern for your colleagues, the decision to bring Euan back rests on my shoulders. Mine and Serrano's. That is to say—not yours. Fletch, you are damn good at your job, and I know you have your sights set on bigger and better things."

"Sir, if I could just say—"

"But for now," he interjected, "this team is under my charge, and I will decide what's best for it. Now, if you have a problem with that—"

"I don't, Sarge. Not at all."

"Okay then," he continued. "I appreciate you coming here. I really do. I know you feel responsible, which you shouldn't. I know you want to make things better for the team, which you should. So, I want you to go away this morning knowing that this had to happen, and you aren't the one to be held responsible. You didn't make that reporter write her article."

"Thank you, sir," she replied.

"This will all be over soon, and we can get back to the business of running this team the way it should be run."

Fletch stood up to leave but stopped and turned back. "One more thing, Sarge."

He raised his chin. "Yes?"

"Connor?"

"You let me worry about him, all right?"

ELLIS WAS at her desk and caught sight of Fletch returning to the bullpen. She raised her hand in a slight wave. "Morning."

"Hey, Becca." Fletch set down her things and pulled out her chair.

Ellis understood why Fletch was concerned for the team. She didn't fault her for going to Abbott about the article. McCallister should've come clean much sooner. Fletch was known for her black-and-white stance about almost everything. But Ellis knew there were so many shades of gray it was hard to distinguish between them in looking for the truth.

"I'm sure it's been tough for Sarge," Ellis said as she walked around her desk, approaching Fletch.

She donned a rueful smile. "You knew I was in there talking to him?"

Ellis sat down on the edge of Fletch's desk. "You kind of have it written all over your face."

"Becca, I didn't mean for any of this to change our team dynamics, but I know that it has."

"It wasn't your fault," Ellis continued. "I didn't know until it was virtually too late. None of us did. And I know Euan feels awful about that. But it's his price to pay. Not yours and not mine."

"The sarge says he and Serrano are in discussions about Euan's return, so I guess that's good."

Ellis nodded. "That's what I hear."

"It's what you hear?" Fletch asked, looking down her nose. "Becca, you can be honest with me. You two are official now, right?"

Ellis noticed Pelletier from the corner of her eye. "I'm taking a wait-and-see approach."

"Sure you are." Fletch seemed to notice Ellis had shifted her gaze. "Then there's that whole situation, huh?"

"You mean?" Ellis tossed a nod toward him. "He'll be okay. Bryce is a good friend. Neither of us want to lose that. In the meantime, I appreciate you working to see Euan brought back. We'll just have to wait it out like he's been doing." She pushed off the desk.

"But he's okay?" Fletch asked. "Otherwise, I mean. With his injury and all that."

"Yeah, he's okay." Ellis smiled. "Thanks for asking, and I'll tell him you're thinking about him."

What the team really needed was a sense of normalcy to return, Ellis thought, and they would get there soon enough. It would be nice to share a drink with them all again. It had been too long. And a lot had happened.

THE RAIN HAD SUBSIDED, leaving dark clouds to cast a somber shroud over the suburban neighborhood as night arrived. Streetlamps reflected off the wet asphalt, and the sound of water running into drains filled the air.

A solitary figure on the empty streets, he dressed in black and moved with practiced stealth along the shadowy edges. His target loomed ahead. The white, vinyl-clad home, lined with flowers and trimmed bushes. Its two stories topped off with a pitched roof and black shutters around the windows. A warm amber glow radiated from the coach light that hung over the door of the double garage. The house exuded an air of comfort and love, but it was the secrets within that enticed him to risk everything.

Raindrops trapped on leaves now fell from the trees that lined the street and helped conceal his footfalls. His movements went unnoticed among the drawn curtains and shuttered blinds. The darkened windows and locked doors. He'd gotten into their heads and would not find open windows or lax security. But their efforts wouldn't be enough to stop him.

Crouching low, he made his way toward the side of the house, out of view of the wide-angle security cameras. His gloved hand reached into a pocket inside his hooded jacket, withdrawing a sophisticated device capable of disabling the humble security alarms. This tool, acquired through dubious channels, had been a failsafe thus far.

With deft precision, he accessed the maintenance panel, an inconspicuous metal box designed to grant authorized personnel entry to the inner workings of the electrical and security systems.

In a symphony of calculated movements, his fingers maneuvered around the wires and switches. He bypassed layers of inept design, exploiting vulnerabilities overlooked by lazy engineers. If there was one thing he knew, it was security systems and those passed off as such.

His eyes narrowed under a penlight held between his

lips and fixed on the small wires. With a final clip, the security system's fortress crumbled.

The front window was locked, and now that the sensor was deactivated, he only needed to insert a knife between the sashes and carefully push up to disengage the latch. He'd practiced the technique over and over, ensuring he would leave no trace of damage behind. A waft of cool air from inside the home spilled out as he pushed open the window. Darkness swallowed him as he climbed through and now stood in the living room of number four.

With a steady resolve, he ventured farther in and could almost hear the pleasant sounds of deep sleep. Three children upstairs. The parents, downstairs.

He roamed freely, quietly visiting each child, watching them sleep, their faces innocent and helpless. He imagined how their parents would feel at their demise. Their devastation. Their grief. But he had to leave his mark, so he took items from each of them. They had to understand that he could get to them at his will. Their defenses rendered useless against what he needed.

No disruptions this time as he made his way downstairs to the bedroom door of the mother and father who slept behind it. They'd left it open a crack, just enough to hear their names should a child call out.

Rage boiled in his gut as he stepped inside, his hand on the knife tucked in his belt. The wife was beautiful, even in the dark. Her hair fanned out beside her atop the pillow as though she floated in water. An exposed shoulder that appeared like porcelain.

He took in a breath through his nose, inhaling the scent of their bodies and a lingering hint of floral perfume. The handle of the knife warmed in his hand. It would take only a moment, and it would all be over. They deserved it, but that wasn't why he was here. Not yet.

He stepped out of the room, resting the door on its frame. Treading carefully down the hall once again, he heard a growl. The shape of a dog appeared just feet away. The whites of its teeth in stark contrast to the darkness, baring them at the intruder. One bark from this animal would end everything. The mystery of his presence would be revealed.

He froze, not wanting to make any sudden movement that might provoke. The dog growled again; its eyes homed in on its potential prey.

Ticktock.

He had but moments to decide.

He held out his hand as though offering a treat. "Good boy, come here," he whispered.

The dog sniffed, taking slow steps toward the intruder. But it growled once again.

"Sorry, boy. It's you or me."

THE MORNING HAD ALREADY GOTTEN off to a rough start. Ellis was on her way to meet with Pelletier at a riverside restaurant that had been robbed and vandalized overnight. The thieves apparently took all the booze they could carry in addition to breaking into the safe and getting away with the previous night's cash payments.

She rolled up in her white Chevy Tahoe and parked along the curb. A patrol unit was just ahead, and a few feet behind her was Pelletier's silver Chevy Impala. Ellis stepped down from her SUV and approached the entrance. A window was shattered; the door was covered in spray paint. And the inside was worse.

As she stepped over broken glass on her way in, she spotted Pelletier talking to a broad-shouldered, middle-aged man, who she assumed was the owner. Ellis made her way over. "I'd say good morning to you, sir, but somehow, I don't think it is." She offered her hand. "I'm Detective Ellis."

"Detective," the man replied.

"Thanks for coming down," Pelletier added before turning back to the owner. "What else can you tell me about your staff?"

"I hired a new sous-chef last week," the man said, folding his arms and shaking his head. "He came highly recommended. I can't say this was his doing, but I don't know... seems odd this would happen after he came on board when I've never had any incident like this since I opened ten years ago."

"Do you have security cameras?" Ellis asked.

"Yes, ma'am," the owner replied.

"We should take a look."

"I already did," the owner cut in. "Whoever broke in disabled them."

She looked at Pelletier. "Someone who knew where the system was and how to cut it off."

He nodded. "Right."

Ellis's phone rang; it was the station. "Excuse me for a moment. I need to take this." She stepped away. "Ellis here."

"Detective Ellis, it's Triggs."

"Hi. What's going on?" Her immediate thought was that somehow her brother was out of rehab and already causing trouble. But it couldn't be that. She would've heard if he'd gotten out. Or if Hank got him out.

"Sergeant Moss asked me to let you know that we got a call this morning relating to that neighborhood you both discussed yesterday."

"Right, okay. What happened?" she asked.

"A family called in to say that someone murdered their dog. It was from the same neighborhood—in fact, the same street—as the original call that came in before."

Ellis considered what this could mean. "Are they certain someone killed their dog? Were there obvious injuries? Can you tell me how he died?"

"Here's the thing about that, and the reason Moss asked me to reach out to you." Triggs took a moment. "This family —they think their dog was choked to death. They woke up this morning, one of their young kids, their daughter I believe, found him downstairs."

"Jesus." She turned her gaze to the restaurant's front door.

"The dog was lying by the staircase," he continued. "Look, I know how this sounds. I mean, the dog could've died from natural causes. You just don't know."

"But you and Moss don't think that, do you? Or you wouldn't be talking to me right now."

"Well, I was going to head over to talk to the family. Moss suggested I ask if you wanted to come along and see for yourself what's what," Triggs said.

Ellis looked back at Pelletier, who continued to make the rounds with the owner and a few other witnesses. "I'm at a restaurant where a robbery occurred. I know what's been going on in that neighborhood, and I get those people are nervous. But it seems a little bit of a leap to assume their dog was murdered. Is there a way they can get the animal to their vet to confirm whether it died of natural causes or not?"

"You want me to ask the family to have an autopsy performed on their pet?" Triggs asked.

"Well, now that you say it out loud, it does sound like an unusual request."

"If you're busy, I get it, Detective, you don't need to come along," Triggs added. "I can talk to them and get a sense for the situation. Moss just wanted me to reach out because he said you were curious."

"No, I am. He's right." She checked the time on her phone. "Can you give me an hour?"

"Of course. I'll send you the address and meet you there."

"Great. Thanks. I'll see you soon." Ellis ended the call and returned to Pelletier.

"What happened?" he asked. "Who was that?"

"Officer Triggs." She pocketed her phone. "Something is happening in Woodland Heights. I'm going to go talk to a family whose dog died, they think, under suspicious circumstances."

"A dog?" Pelletier asked, his lips pulled into a smirk.

"I know how it sounds. You think I can take a run out there in an hour and meet you back at the station to file this report?"

"Sure. No problem." He looked back at the damaged restaurant. "Without video, I'm not sure how successful we'll be at finding out whoever did this."

Ellis surveyed the place. "I might have a few ideas."

4

Ellis rolled up to the home of Neil and Patricia Barber in Woodland Heights. Officer Triggs's patrol unit was parked curbside, and she stopped behind him. She watched as he emerged from the vehicle and approached her.

The dark-haired, fresh-faced young officer had an eagerness about him, the kind Ellis hardly remembered from early in her career. Ten years on the job could feel like a lifetime. She climbed down from her SUV and joined him on the sidewalk in front of the home.

She observed the lush green grass that was perfectly edged to the sidewalk and driveway. A row of manicured evergreens and pretty flower boxes lined the home's exterior. Ellis noticed the window on the right. *That's where he went in.* Holly was generally the best type of plant to place under windows. It grew full and tall—and the leaves were sharp with spikes: a solid deterrent to would-be intruders. But the evergreens here were easily scalable with their soft glossy leaves.

"Good morning, Detective. Glad you could be here to lend a hand," Triggs said.

Ellis returned her attention to him. "I'm just along for the ride, so I appreciate the invitation."

The stocky cop placed his hands on either side of his duty belt and started on toward the white two-story home. He glanced over his shoulder at Ellis, who trailed only a step or two. "You should know that the family did take their dog to their vet, and after a brief examination, he was able to determine the dog was choked to death."

"Conclusive?" Ellis pressed.

"Well, the dog's tongue was purple, and he noted bruises on his neck, and X-rays revealed bone fractures."

She groaned. "Sounds pretty definitive. So this prowler or peeping Tom has stepped up his game."

They reached the front porch, and Triggs turned to her. "Including this place, we have four complaints so far, but this is the first time the intruder turned violent. Honestly, we have no way to confirm whether the other complaints are legit. I mean, no one's seen this guy. Nothing's been left behind or even stolen. If this dog hadn't been killed, I doubt we'd even be here right now." He knocked on the door, and it opened to reveal the couple. "Mr. and Mrs. Barber? I'm Officer Triggs, and this is Detective Ellis. We're with Bangor Police."

"Yes, please come in," Patricia Barber replied. The beautiful woman with long black hair looked to be in her early thirties. Slim, form-fitting T-shirt and denim shorts. Her brown eyes appeared red from tears.

Ellis stepped in behind Triggs as they entered the foyer. The dark hardwood floors gleamed. The walls were painted a sage green and decorated with large canvas paintings of mostly wooded landscapes. She glanced to the right and noticed a family room with oversized furnishings and totes filled with children's toys shoved in the corners. The window where she assumed he'd entered was closed. "Did anyone touch that window?"

"No, ma'am," Neil Barber replied. "Why? Do you think that was how he got in? Because I couldn't find any other way."

"That would be my guess." She turned to Triggs. "You have a kit on you?"

"I do."

Ellis nodded. "We'll need to check for prints." She turned her eye to the staircase, where three young children gathered, wearing forlorn faces. A boy of about ten, another boy of about eight, and a girl who appeared maybe five or six. Ellis recalled it was the girl who'd found their dead pet only feet from where they now stood.

"We can talk in the living room," Patricia said before looking to her eldest boy. "Parker, why don't you take your brother and sister to your room while we talk to the police?"

The boy gathered his siblings and shepherded them upstairs.

"Right through here, please." Neil Barber was a well-built man. Neatly styled dark hair. Nice clothes. About the same age as his wife. He gestured to the family room. "My wife told you what our vet said about our dog."

"She did, Mr. Barber, and I'm very sorry for your loss." Triggs took a seat on the couch.

Ellis moved in next to him. "We're also aware that there've been a few calls into the station regarding a possible intruder in your neighborhood."

"That's right." Patricia joined them. "A lot of us have

talked, and we're certain someone's been coming into our houses while we sleep and just creeping around. And it wasn't until poor Hailey...."

"Hailey?" Ellis asked.

"Our dog," Neil cut in. "Look, Detective, you need to find whoever's doing this. Because I'll tell you what, if the police don't, we will. And I'll kill the son of a bitch."

Neil Barber was a large man with arms the size of some people's thighs. No doubt he could easily follow through on his threat. Ellis needed to cool the situation, so she raised a preemptive hand. "Mr. Barber, we understand your anger."

"Do you, Detective?" he snapped back. "My daughter came downstairs this morning and found Hailey with her tongue hanging out of her mouth, lying dead on the floor next to the stairs. Do you have any idea what that did to her? Or the rest of my kids?"

"I can only imagine," she replied. "Have you noticed whether anything was taken?"

The parents glanced at each other when Patricia spoke out. "Yes. A bracelet was taken from our daughter's room. An action figure was taken from our youngest son's room, and Parker noticed his pop figure was taken."

"I'm sorry?" Ellis creased her brow. "Pop figure?"

"It's a small bobblehead of a character, usually from a TV show or movie," Triggs answered.

"Oh, I see." Ellis glanced toward the window again. "Do you mind if I take a closer look at the window? I'd like to see if he left any shoeprints outside or dragged material inside. It could help us identify this person."

"He disabled our security system, Detective," Neil added. "I don't know how, but he did. That window was locked when we went to bed. I know it was. He disabled the sensors and opened it. The son of a bitch climbed right in."

"We have noted that the other calls from your neighbors indicated a few things were rearranged in their homes," Triggs began. "While nothing else has been noted as being stolen, it seems clear that we're dealing with the same suspect."

Patricia wiped away a stray tear. "What do you plan to do about this, Officer? We don't feel safe in our home anymore."

Neil took his wife's hand. "I suggested she and the kids go to her mother's house for a while now that school's finished. I don't want them here until we know who this person is, and that he's been caught."

ELLIS MET TRIGGS BACK at the station to brief Sergeant Moss on the situation. Her gut told her this was no ordinary peeping Tom or prowler. And as she entered Moss's office, where Triggs waited, she prepared to give her thoughts.

Moss regarded her. "Appreciate you taking the time to tag along with Triggs on this. He says you two had an interesting conversation with the Barber family."

"You could say that." Ellis joined Triggs as he sat across from Moss. "You have, what, four families now who've called in reports of an intruder over the past couple of days? And apparently, more who haven't called in? That's too many already."

"Agreed," Moss said. "And this one with the family dog, well, that changes things."

"That's exactly what Triggs and I thought," she continued. "This goes deeper than how it appears. The pet probably confronted the intruder, and fearing he would be caught, he had no choice but to silence the animal. But more importantly, this person seems to have a fair amount of knowledge regarding security systems."

"Could be someone in the industry," Triggs added.

"Absolutely," Ellis agreed. "And the first place you should look is at whoever installed the systems in these homes. You get a lot of businesses going door-to-door, and once one family uses them, it's easier for them to attract more business in the neighborhood. Because it looks like this person was both familiar with the systems and with the homes he entered. Otherwise, I can't imagine how he roamed inside those houses completely undetected."

"Who knows how long ago their systems were installed, though," Moss said. "That community is, what, ten years old?"

Triggs nodded. "About that, but unless or until we get prints, I'm not sure there's a better place to start. I had a kit with me and dusted around the window where we believe he entered. I pulled what appeared to be at least a couple sets, but they could belong to the family. I won't know until they're processed."

Ellis stood from the chair. "I have a feeling this is going to get worse, Sergeant, so I'd like to be kept abreast of any developments, and if I can help, let me know."

"You got it, Detective," Moss replied. "We'll keep you in the loop unless this thing takes a darker turn. Then it might fall in your lap anyway."

"Let's hope it doesn't." She returned a slight nod to her colleagues and made her way into the hall, heading back toward the lobby.

Ellis entered the bullpen upstairs and noticed Pelletier

wasn't at his desk. She'd assumed he would've returned from the restaurant by now. Bevins' desk was next to his, and she caught his attention. "Hey, Connor, have you seen Bryce?"

"Downstairs in Forensics."

"Is it for the restaurant break-in?" she asked.

Bevins shrugged. "I assume so, but I didn't ask."

At twenty-five years old, Connor Bevins was the youngest detective on the force. His good looks and cocky attitude had gotten him pretty far in this world, except for when he joined Bangor PD. The West Point cadet was athletic and not a little arrogant. But he had mellowed over the past few months, thanks, in part, to McCallister's mentoring. Ellis always defended him to the rest of the team, who often tired of his arrogance. However, she had been proven right. Given time, he would settle into the role, and it seemed he had.

"Thanks, I'll run back down and see what he's got." Just as Ellis prepared to head downstairs, he called out to her.

"How's Euan holding up?"

She stopped and turned around. "He's doing all right."

"Maybe I'll give him a call," Bevins said.

"I'm sure he'd appreciate that." Ellis headed back into the corridor, rushing downstairs. She spotted Pelletier in the hall just as he appeared to have left Forensics. "Hey, I was coming to see you. You found some evidence?"

"We collected prints, and I brought them down for scanning. Should know something soon," he replied. "What's going on with that home invasion case?"

"You mean the creepy guy watching families sleep and killing their pets?" Ellis asked. "Triggs has it handled for now. We'll see where it lands. Not really for our department —yet. So, listen, what can I do to help?"

Pelletier thrust his hands into his pockets. "I have a ton

of paperwork to file if you want to jump in on that. Otherwise, we're at the mercy of Forensics."

"Great. I don't mind pushing some paper. Let's go take care of that now." She followed him upstairs, and they returned to the bullpen, where Ellis trailed him to his desk. "Hand over what you have, and I'll get started."

He retrieved his files and offered them to her. "Thanks, Becca. I appreciate the help."

"We're a team, aren't we?" she asked, with a smile.

He returned a half-grin. "Yeah, we are."

EUAN MCCALLISTER HAD DONE his best to own up to his mistakes. His biggest? Killing a kid he thought held a gun in his hand. His second biggest? Keeping that a secret from his team. The situation had died down, and he could begin the process of atoning for his second mistake. But no matter how hard he tried, the first mistake could never be absolved.

Today, however, he was scheduled to have lunch with an old friend from Boston, who also happened to be a former colleague. And as he arrived at the restaurant, he remained in his car, wavering for a moment.

This man was his friend and had been there after the incident. But McCallister hadn't spoken with him since leaving the department. Nevertheless, it was best to know how things were going back in Boston, especially after the civil trial from the dead boy's family.

He inhaled a breath through his nose and stepped out of his Ford SUV, walking toward the riverside restaurant. It was nestled on the banks of the Penobscot, and in fact, McCallister could see the stationhouse in the distance. Maybe he would stop by and say hi to everyone. Maybe he would see what Ellis was up to.

McCallister entered the restaurant, which was busier now, as the days had grown warmer. A wall of floor-to-ceiling windows overlooked the river. Worn, wood floors and distressed paneling brought in a nautical feel. Tables were scattered throughout, and a bar lay off to one side. Soft contemporary music played in the background.

He noticed his friend already sitting at a nearby table next to a window. The sun shone down on his full head of black hair. It didn't look as though the man had aged at all. McCallister arrived and offered his hand. "Charlie Thorne, it's been too long, man."

"Euan McCallister. Yes, it has. Good to see you, bud." Thorne returned the greeting.

McCallister pulled out a chair and took a seat. "I can't believe it's been, what? Almost a year?"

"Just about," Thorne replied.

"So are you in town for a reason or just to see me?" McCallister asked.

Thorne slung his elbow over the back of his chair. A five-o'clock shadow speckled his face, and fine lines formed at his green eyes as he began. "You are one of my favorite people, Euan, but I'm actually here with my family. My wife's parents live in Augusta, so I figured I could make the drive to see my old friend."

"I appreciate you carving out some time to see me," McCallister said, the inflection in his voice sounding a little more Boston than usual.

"I hear they still got you on administrative leave, huh?" Thorne asked.

"Technically, medical leave thanks to this." He patted his

injured shoulder. "But we both know it was more than that." McCallister glanced through the window. "I thought it was done, you know? It was the whole reason I left Boston."

"You ran away, man." Thorne took a sip from the glass of water the server brought over. "You could've stuck it out until things blew over. They eventually did."

"Yeah, well, I guess I wasn't feeling it from the rest of the department." McCallister paused while the waiter returned and proceeded to take their order. After he left, McCallister continued, "I feel like shit over all of it, even still. What was worse, I let down my team...like I'm not being the leader everyone needs anymore." He felt his throat tighten as his emotions climbed to the surface.

"You gotta let it go, brother," Thorne said. "You're not doing yourself any good, or the ones around you. What happened back in Boston was a fucking shit show. We all know that. But it's done. And I know the civil suit brought all of it back into the daylight, and there's nothing you could've done about that. The family was compensated." He scoffed. "No amount of money's gonna fix their broken hearts, but it was all we had to offer."

"Brass says I can come back on duty once my doctor releases me. I'm working on that now."

"I hope they keep to that." He eyed McCallister's injured shoulder. "You look all right to me."

"It's healing up fine," McCallister said. "You've been hit worse than this."

Thorne swatted at the comment. "Long time ago. Listen to me, brother...You're a damn good cop, okay? Yeah, you should've come clean with your new people, but that's in the past now. Just take the hit and be better for it." He glanced away, taking a beat. "Trust me, you don't want to be back in Boston. Nothing's the same there, and it never will be."

McCALLISTER DECIDED to stop by the station and catch up with the team. The lunch with his old friend had helped clear his head, and it reminded him of who he was and why he was a cop. He stepped inside the lobby and aimed his sights on the front desk. A smile arose on his lips at the sight of Officer Yearwood.

"McCallister?" Yearwood said with a youthful grin. "They let you back already?"

"They can't keep me away, man," he replied as he continued his approach. "No, I'm just stopping in to catch up with the crew upstairs. How's things here?"

"All right. Same ol', same ol'." He tossed a nod toward the stairs. "Go on up. No doubt they'll be happy to see you."

"Thanks." He started on. "And hey, I'll be back before you know it."

Yearwood laughed. "Thanks for the warning."

McCallister climbed the steps and reached the landing. Probably should stop in and see the boss first. He continued into the hall until he reached Abbott's office. "Hey, Sarge."

Abbott shifted his attention. "Euan, well, hello. I wasn't expecting to see you. Did we have a meeting on the books?"

"No, sir." He ambled inside with his hands in his pockets. "I was in the area, having lunch with an old friend. Figured I'd stop in and check on everyone."

"It's good to see you, son." Abbott offered his hand.

McCallister accepted the greeting and took a seat. "I wanted to let you know, Sarge, that things are going well. I'm getting better." He rotated his arm as if that served as proof of his fitness. "I'm just waiting on the doctor's signature."

"And as soon as I have that, you're golden." Abbott pulled up closer to his desk. "Fletch says things out there have calmed quite a bit. That's good news."

"That was my understanding too." He sighed. "Maybe I can start being a cop again."

"I agree it's time you moved forward," Abbott replied. "But listen, we need you. We want you on this team. That hasn't changed."

McCallister smiled. "That's good to hear, Sarge. Thank you. Listen, uh, I'd better go say hi to the team, make sure they remember me, yeah?"

"Sounds good. We'll be in touch."

The Woodland Heights neighborhood had planned an emergency gathering. The meeting was to be held at the local community center, where many had already arrived.

The center was an impressive two-story, red-brick building, trimmed with black accents. An Olympic-sized pool was just inside the entrance to the right, the heavy chlorinated smell wafting into the lobby. To the rear was a gym, and down the hall were several rooms used for meetings, events, and classes. Inside one of the rooms, the neighbors had assembled.

The Woodland Heights homeowners' board took their seats at the row of rectangular tables lined up at the front of the room. The president of the board, a middle-aged rotund man by the name of Russell Poe, garnered the attention of the neighbors still engrossed in private conversations in their seats. "Excuse me. We'd like to get started with the meeting." He waited for the chatter to subside. "Thank you. As you know, we are all here today to discuss the recent spate of break-ins our community has experienced as well as security measures to put in place that will help protect our families and properties."

"Those were just break-ins, Russ," Neil Barber shouted. "My dog was killed. You know that, right?"

"I do know that, Neil, and I'm so sorry for your family." Poe's voice was calm, but then he returned his attention to the audience. "I have a plan to help. First of all, we need to form a neighborhood watch."

The crowd groaned.

"I think that's a good first step. And I'm not alone in that idea." Poe eyed the other board members. "We can install lighting around the open spaces. Even consider cameras on the street corners."

"Jesus, Russ, this isn't China," Derek Cannon shouted as he stood from his chair, his sharp features hardening. "I don't want to drive into our neighborhood and see a bunch of cameras following me. That's bullshit."

Barber spun around to face Cannon. "You'd feel differently if it was your house this sicko broke into, Derek. You and Lorna haven't been affected like some of us have."

Cannon raised his hands in defense before returning to his seat. "I'm sorry that happened to your family, Neil."

Vicky Boyles, who was sitting next to Cannon, reached out to him and, in a low tone, continued, "It's okay, Derek. Neil's been through a lot. He doesn't mean to lash out at you."

Cannon rubbed her arm. "Thanks, Vic, I appreciate it. Listen, the four of us should get together soon, okay? We all need each other right now. And if Brian is heading out of town anytime soon, let me know, and I'll swing by to make sure the place is locked up for you, okay?"

"I appreciate it," she whispered as eyes were drawn to them.

The man behind them stood up and shouted, "What we need are the damn cops to help us out."

"Assuming we put all these measures you're talking about in place." Sydney Manning rose from her chair. "How effective are they going to be when you have someone who knows how to hack into our home security systems? And how long is it going to take to get all this done? Does the association have the budget to cover it, or are we going to have to put up the money?"

Murmurs erupted as everyone started asking questions about the proposed security measures, voicing their concerns. Some asked if there were any other ways they could help make their community safer. Others questioned the costs and timing associated with the implementation of the new security protocols.

Poe tamped down his empty coffee mug on the table to return to order. "Let's all settle down, all right? We aren't going to get anywhere talking over each other like this."

The room quietened.

"Thank you," he continued. "I do think the police can and should offer to increase patrols around our neighborhood. That's probably the most effective and cheapest measure we can implement. And we can do that immediately. The board and I will set up a meeting with them and ask for their help."

"The cops aren't taking this seriously," Barber called out again. "Look, I don't have an answer. Maybe you're right, Russ; maybe asking the cops to step things up around here will help. But my concern is for my family." He cast out his gaze over the audience. "Now I'd suggest we all arm ourselves so when this son of a bitch decides to come into our homes, we're ready."

"Well, that's just great, Neil." Vicky Boyles threw her hands in the air. "You want all of us aiming guns at our front doors? That'll go well."

"All right, all right." Poe raised his voice. "Let's stick to the topic at hand, shall we? Now, the board will reach out to the police to discuss the situation. In the meantime, lock your doors. Lock your windows. Use security lights all around your house if you have them. But I can assure you that this will be properly handled by the police." His gaze swept around the room, and his voice hardened. "And we will catch this guy."

ELLIS OWNED a three-bedroom bungalow in the south part of the city. She'd bought it with her ex-husband about one year after their wedding. They'd divorced only four years later, and the idea of moving still swirled in her mind.

Now, as twilight cast shadows through the windows, a knock sounded on her door. She already knew who stood on the other side.

Ellis opened it. "Hi, again. Come in." McCallister walked inside, and she closed the door behind him. "The team seemed happy to see you today. It was good you stopped by."

"Yeah, it was great to see everyone." He kissed her gently on the lips. "I hadn't realized how much I missed them, but you know, don't tell Connor. Wouldn't want the kid to get a bigger head than he already has."

"He's gotten much better since that case you two

worked." She walked into the kitchen. "Care for a beer, or are you on any..."

"I'm off the painkillers. Figured I could handle it from here," he interjected.

She returned with two bottles in her hand, offering him one. "Then you're improving. That's great." Ellis took a swig and headed to the sofa. "I have to apologize. It's been a crazy day, and I didn't have time to go to the store and pick up dinner. Don't suppose you mind if I order in?"

"Not at all." He joined her. "I'm just happy to share dinner with you two nights this week."

An impish grin pulled at her lips. "Careful. We wouldn't want to make a habit of it."

"So, tell me what's going on with this new case," he said, tipping back the bottle of beer.

"I'm not sure what to make of it yet. The intruder is taking small articles from the homes. Moving things around, and then today, or last night...he strangled a family's pet." Ellis curled her legs onto the sofa. "He's getting in by disabling security systems. And these are homes in the Woodland Heights area."

"Wealthy neighborhood," McCallister observed.

"Very. Anyway, the station's logged four complaints, with this most recent one. No one's seen this guy. So far, we don't think he's leaving prints, but we're working on that."

"This isn't your average cat burglar," McCallister said.

"No, it's not." Ellis peered through the front window at the approaching sunset. "Which is why I have a bad feeling about it."

"He might have been testing the waters."

She turned back to him. "Exactly. And now that he's been able to get away with it, he will become emboldened."

"Therein lies the problem. You don't know how far he'll go. And you still have no idea why he's targeting this community," McCallister replied.

She let her gaze roam over his features, marveling at just how similar their thoughts were when it came to the job. "I wish you were there to help. Everyone wants you back."

"Soon." He raised a shoulder. "Just know that I'm here to bounce ideas. I'll help however I can."

Ellis placed her hand on his cheek. "I know you will."

He moved her hand from his cheek and kissed her palm.

She noticed, maybe for the first time, that he appeared genuinely happy to be with her. It wasn't just the prospect of where this night would end up, but rather the prospect of a future. Was that what she wanted? Was she ready for it?

So much of her was wrapped up in her job. Love—real love—was meant for people who worked nine to five in a high-rise building. People who didn't have to worry about whether they would still be alive at the end of their shifts. People who never saw the underbelly of humanity. It was all her ex-husband, Andrew, had wanted, and she couldn't provide it for him. What made her think this time would be any different?

And there was something else she hadn't considered. Deepening this relationship with Euan meant she would be faced with those same prospects—loving someone who put the job first. Could she share him with the force, as he would have to share her? It was too much to think about now as she watched the longing grow in his gaze.

Do you love him?

THE NIGHT WASN'T OVER YET. Ellis had other obligations, though she'd placed those obligations on herself, but McCallister respected that and left her to check in on Hank, as was her routine.

She drove under a clear black sky dotted with bright stars. The city streets had stilled as she made her way to Hank's. On her arrival, Ellis parked behind his old Chevy truck, which didn't look like it had moved in a while. A sign he wasn't getting out of the house much, which was cause for concern.

Ellis shouldered the responsibility of caring for her father and didn't mind it one bit. Because if she didn't, Carter would use him and toss him aside penniless, homeless, without a second thought. She would never allow that to happen.

Hank's front door was unlocked, and all she could do was shake her head. No matter how often she reminded him to lock it, he never did. Even after what had happened months ago before his stroke. She'd begun to think it was more of a forgetful thing rather than him believing he was safe, because they both knew that no one was safe.

She stepped inside and heard the television blaring from the nearby living room. "Dad? Hey, Dad, it's me." Ellis walked in and spotted Hank in his favorite reclining chair. "Dad, you still up?"

"Of course I am." He glanced over his shoulder. "How you doing, kid? You bring me food?"

Ellis smiled and sat down on the couch. "No, I didn't bring you food. Didn't you eat dinner?"

"Yeah, but it's so warm out, an ice cream might've been nice." He turned down the TV and gave her his full attention. "It's good to see you. What's the latest?"

Ellis filled him in regarding the restaurant burglary.

"And Euan?"

She shook her head. "Still on leave. Not for much longer, though. He said he talked to Abbott, and they're working on getting his doctor's release."

"That's good to hear. You all are always short-handed as it is. Maybe I should talk to Serrano about opening up another detective slot."

"Hey, if you have that kind of pull, I'm all for it," Ellis replied. "I even have someone in mind. A kid in Patrol named Triggs. I see that spark in him. But, anyway, I noticed your door was unlocked again. We've talked about that."

"For your information, little miss, I knew you were coming over, so I unlocked it."

She returned a sideways glance. "Did you?"

He chuckled. "All right. You caught me. I'll remember for next time."

"Dad..."

"I know. I know." He held up his hands. "I know it's important. I got that. So what do you think's going to happen with this intruder? That still top of mind?"

She noted his sudden change of topic as he sought to move on from her pointing out his lax memory. A red flag rose in the back of her mind. "It's concerning, yes. Triggs is running the case and keeping me posted, but I believe Moss was planning to step up patrols in the area." She paused a moment. "I think what concerns me most is that the first few times it happened, no one was really certain anything actually happened. Nothing was taken. No noises in the night. He slipped in and out completely undetected."

"How do they even know he was there?" Hank pressed.

"Items were moved around. Some noted that their security systems were off when they were certain they'd been set. That was how it started. But his MO has changed. Now he's taking things. And then last night, he killed a family pet."

"Christ." Hank turned serious. "And what does that say to you about this person?"

She leaned over with her elbows on her knees, staring at her shoes. "I think the dog was unexpected for him, and he knew he'd be caught if he didn't silence it. But the trinkets from the kids' rooms?" Ellis pulled back up again. "To me, it means this guy is thinking about harming someone. And that's what terrifies me."

IT HAD TAKEN years to gather what he needed to execute this plan. And now that he'd begun, he questioned whether he could see it through without getting caught. The dog...that wasn't supposed to happen, and it would change things. It would trigger an increased police presence. Increased vigilance on the part of the community. His goal would become that much harder to accomplish.

But as he stood in front of the pinboard propped on a table in his bedroom, he had no intention of stopping. They had brought this on. And he would see it through to the end.

His temporary accommodation was a run-down first-floor apartment in an older part of town, far away from the luxury community of Woodland Heights. The place was furnished, though the décor left much to be desired. An old brown sofa with cigarette burns in the arms. A laminate kitchen table with wicker chairs. A twenty-seven-inch console TV he was surprised still worked. Hardly mattered, though. He only planned on being here a few weeks, maybe a month. Time wasn't much of an issue for him anymore.

He stared at the names and faces on the pinboard. Each one with sticky notes placed around them, notating their schedules, when they were home, when they left. Everything about their lives—at least, what he knew of them—was on this board. And what he knew was a lot.

The Madsens were next on his list. They would be number five. The couple had a large house, fancy cars, and two older children who didn't live at home.

The plan was simple. Stick to what he knew. And he knew them. All of them.

Wait until late at night when everyone was asleep, then disable the security system and get inside undetected. Fear, anxiety, anguish—this was the price they would pay, and they would never know what it felt like to be safe again.

He went over every detail of his plan, from when he'd need to arrive at the house, to where he should park his car, and how long it would take him to get inside. However, the challenge of a likely increase in their vigilance would mean a slight alteration. He would remain armed with his knife. And if an issue arose again between him and whoever stood in his path, then his choice would be clear.

6

Ellis couldn't escape the images that floated through her mind. A little girl finding her pet dead on the floor. A stranger at a sleeping child's bedside in the black of night. This felt far more ominous than any cases she'd worked before, not only because children could be harmed, but also because of the prospect of unknown future actions. What would this intruder do next? Would he slaughter an entire family? Would he kidnap a child? Would he set fire to a house while a family slept within?

Inside the stark halls of the station's ground floor, Ellis walked ahead with a weight on her shoulders. A sinking feeling pressed down on her, one she hadn't experienced since she was a child, when she knew something would happen to her mother—and was still helpless to stop it.

Sergeant Moss was in his office when she arrived. "Hi, Sergeant, you have a minute?"

Moss stared down his sizable nose at her. "Sure. Come in."

Ellis walked in, arms crossed, gaze down. "I was

wondering how things went last night in Woodland Heights. Any clues turn up? Possible sightings?"

He returned his attention to his laptop and keyed in a few strokes. "I'm looking at the write-ups now." Moss appeared to study the screen. "No, it doesn't appear as though they saw anything unusual." His expression wore disappointment as he looked at her again. "I'm sorry. I know that's not what you hoped to hear. But neither did I."

"No, sir. It's not." She took a few steps closer to his desk. "Could I get the reports you have? The people who've called in believing he was inside their homes?"

"Of course." Moss ran the report. "You met with one of the families—the Barbers. What are your thoughts?"

Ellis unfolded her arms and rested her palms on the back of the chair. "I know you have your people keeping eyes out, but I think I need to take a look at these homes. Meet the victims. All of them." She chewed on her lip as she considered her plan. "Sergeant, these people are afraid, and I don't blame them. I don't know what to make of what's happening, but it warrants a harder look. Do you object to me talking with these families?"

"No. Not at all," he replied. "Look, it's not good. I get it. This isn't just some guy breaking into houses in search of valuables, or spooking people like a peeping Tom. But no one has any idea what this person looks like. They can't point to anything of value having been stolen...and the whole dead-dog thing is still a question mark." Moss raised his shoulders. "There's not much more I can do besides catch him in the act."

"I can't argue your point," she added. "But maybe by sitting down with these people, I might find a reason why they're in his line of sight. And I'll do some homework first.

Take a look at the area in terms of recent crimes. See if anything like this has happened in other parts of town."

"I have done some of that legwork already, Detective, and I wasn't able to find a connection to other communities with similar break-ins." Moss appeared to consider an idea. "Listen, do you want Triggs to come along?"

"No, I got it this time. These people are already scared. I'd like to keep the conversations low-key. Not a lot of guns hanging around."

"Okay." He nodded. "Let me know what you find out."

Ellis turned around and headed back into the hall. She had just a few minutes to prepare for the morning's briefing, so she gathered the report Moss had printed as well as the file on the family she'd already met. She was going to have to convince Abbott that this was worth their time.

The team soon arrived in the briefing room upstairs. A podium and whiteboard stood at the front of the room with a monitor mounted behind them. The rectangular tables were lined up three rows deep. This was where cases were assigned, updates given, help requested. It was the meat of their jobs.

Abbott was the last to arrive. Ellis sat at the front table, with Pelletier next to her. A spot formerly reserved for McCallister. Bevins and Fletch sat behind them, and Lewis wrote a last-minute update to her investigation on the board.

Abbott called them all to order. "Good morning, everyone." He slipped on his reading glasses to peer at the papers laid before him on the podium. "Let's jump right in with the restaurant robbery." He eyed Pelletier. "Where is Forensics at on the evidence you collected?"

While Pelletier offered his update, Ellis kept her attention on him. He spoke with a firm voice and dogged determination. She believed she hadn't given him the credit he deserved at times. And while, on their last case, he'd crossed a line, Ellis knew he'd done so in order to get to the truth. Something she'd been guilty of at times, and she had no right to condemn him for it, rightly or wrongly. Nevertheless, it had been a risk that could've cost him his badge. But to listen to him now served as a reminder of who he was, and what he was capable of accomplishing.

"Isn't that right, Becca?" Pelletier asked.

"Sorry?" She shook out of her trance. "What was that?"

"I said that the robbery appeared to be an inside job and that we're running prints on all the staff."

"That's right, yes," she replied. "The owner has concerns about his sous-chef, who he recently hired."

"So that's where we're at right now," Pelletier said. "I hope to have more from Forensics in the next twenty-four to thirty-six hours."

"All right." He eyed Ellis. "Becca, you wanted to present a case?"

"Yes, sir." She gathered her materials and approached the podium. "This is something that's come into Patrol. I've met with Sergeant Moss and Officer Triggs, and I have been out to speak with one of the families affected."

Ellis presented the case as it currently stood, pointing to a map of the neighborhood and the homes that had already been targeted. "This house here, this is the family Triggs and I spoke to—the Barbers. Their six-year-old daughter found their dog dead next to the staircase."

Fletch raised her index finger. "And the family is certain the pet was killed?"

"They took it to their vet, and he agreed the animal had been strangled." Ellis listened to the murmurs among her colleagues. "Yeah, that's pretty much what I thought. So I met with Moss again this morning to confirm whether his units had any sightings overnight. Unfortunately, they didn't."

"What's your plan, Becca, if this is assigned to CID?" Lewis, the former Chicago detective who'd worked mostly cybercrimes relating to money laundering and finances, had an eye for detail. And when it came to investigations, details were everything.

"I'd like to talk with each of the families," Ellis began. "Take a look at the homes, find out if this intruder has taken anything else and check for any commonalities among them."

"But you said Triggs already did that?" Bevins asked.

Ellis had grown accustomed to Connor Bevins and his desire to stand above the rest of them in the eyes of top brass. Though it seemed he'd matured somewhat, he still had a ways to go to reach the level of maturity necessary to have the right kind of perspective for this job.

"Like I said, we met with only one of the families. The one whose pet was killed. I'd like to get a sense of what this person is looking for with each house. Is he targeting those with kids only? Do the neighbors belong to a social group this guy might be part of? There are several things that still need to be explored. And the thing is..." She swallowed hard. "I have a bad feeling he's looking to escalate this."

"You think he might take a human life next?" Pelletier asked.

Ellis deepened her gaze. "I think the longer he's successful at getting in and out of these homes unnoticed, the more daring he'll become. The more risks he'll take. I think this could be a game to him. And he wants to see just how far he can take it."

―――――――――

ABBOTT AGREED to let Ellis pursue the investigation that was officially still in Sergeant Moss's unit. The CID didn't handle incidents like these, but Ellis had made a strong case. She returned to her desk and noticed Bevins approaching.

The dark-haired detective stood before her with his hands at his sides. "Hey, uh, you heard from Euan lately?"

"I have," she replied.

He nodded with downturned lips. "Cool. I texted him the other day. Asked how he was holding up. Says he's bored as hell."

"That's what he tells me," Ellis replied. "Hey, you doing all right?"

"Me?" Bevins aimed his thumb at his chest. "Of course. Yeah, I'm fine. Just feels a little strange without him here, you know? Guess I sort of got used to having him boss me around."

"Yeah, I get that." She donned a thin-lipped grin. "So Abbott's got you prepping to testify at that trial, huh?"

"It's in a couple of weeks, so I've been meeting with the state prosecutors on what to expect." Bevins shrugged. "I honestly have no idea what will happen. I've never had to testify at a trial before."

"The only advice I can offer is to keep to the facts," she began. "Don't let the public defender rattle you in any way. Just remember that you did your job."

"Yeah, I will. Thanks, Becca. So, hey, you need any help

with this situation you got going, be sure to let me know, okay? I'm not Euan, but I can throw in my two cents."

Ellis chuckled. "I'll remember that. Thanks, Connor." She gathered her things. "I suppose I should head out and try to make some progress. I'll catch up with you later."

She headed onward to the stairs and descended into the lobby. A quick stop to see Moss to let him know she'd made appointments to meet with the families who'd been targeted — and that she was handling this on her own for now.

She spotted Triggs at his desk and veered off to see him. "Hey."

"Detective Ellis, how you doing?" he asked, his usual bright-eyed stare engaging her.

"Doing all right. I thought I'd give you a heads-up. I was just on my way to see Moss. I got the okay to interview the victims we know about."

"You don't want me to come along?" he asked.

"I appreciate the offer." Ellis noticed the light behind his eyes dim just a little with disappointment. "But I'm doing my best to keep this low-key. I intend to get in and out without bringing attention to the problem, like to the press or social media."

"Yeah, of course. Keep me updated."

"Sure thing." Ellis walked to Moss's office, feeling guilty at not including Triggs when it was still technically his case. She'd noticed his interest in investigating when he helped out with McCallister's case. He'd make a good fit, and she wondered if he might one day want to take the detective's exam.

Finally, she arrived at Moss's office again. "Sergeant?" She waited until he noticed her standing in the doorway.

"I'm heading out to meet with the families. I'll let you know how it goes."

"Appreciate that, Ellis. You sure you don't want Triggs as backup? I think the kid looks up to you."

Ellis grinned. "That's nice to hear, but I want to do this my way and see what happens."

He nodded. "Understood."

She walked back into the lobby, pushing through the glass door out into a beautiful summer day. A few white puffy clouds floated above in the gentle breeze. The warmth of the sun shone down on her face.

Ellis unlocked her SUV and climbed inside, pressing the ignition. The interior had already heated, and she turned on the air conditioner before heading onward to Woodland Heights.

The drive took about twenty-five minutes, and the landscape changed from buildings and shops to homes and schools, the wide roads lined with trees chock-full of leaves, shading the ground from the summer sun.

Ellis stopped at the home of Janie and Mark Federoff. They lived on the next block over from the Barber house. This family had made the first call when they suspected someone had been inside their home. It was time to learn more about them.

She climbed down from her Tahoe and smoothed the seatbelt wrinkles from her silky beige blouse. A stone path from the sidewalk led to a small porch wrapped with white columns and gray siding. It was decorated with two white Adirondack chairs and throw pillows. In the far corner stood a big-leafed tree and a flowerpot brimming with pink and white pansies.

Ellis knocked on the storm door and rang the bell. She

waited only a moment before hearing the lock disengage. A woman answered. Looked to be mid-thirties. Thin, with dark hair. Pretty. And absolutely frightened. Ellis displayed her badge. "Good afternoon. I'm Detective Rebecca Ellis. Mrs. Federoff?"

"Yes, ma'am. Come in. Call me Janie. My husband, Mark, is here too. He's just in the back."

"Of course." Ellis continued inside, taking note of the quaint, yet updated home. Fresh light grays. Airy, open interior. Light wood floors. "You have a lovely home, Mrs. Federoff."

"Thank you. And please, it's just Janie." She glanced over her shoulder with a smile. "We like it here. Well, up until now. Right through here is the kitchen. Can I get you a cup of coffee? Glass of iced tea?"

"No, thank you. I'm all right." Ellis noticed a breakfast table tucked into an alcove of a bay window. The kitchen was white. Almost too white. A pop of yellow in the form of cannisters appeared along the back wall of cabinets near the gas stove.

"Then why don't you have a seat at the table? I'll go check on my husband." Janie slipped away.

Ellis retrieved her files and notes. It appeared, at first glance, that the family was well off. The upscale area was obvious, but also the furnishings, the interior of the home. All these things suggested they didn't worry much about money. Could've made them a target. But then why didn't the intruder steal from them? As she mused, she caught sight of the couple's return.

"Hello, Detective Ellis. I'm Mark Federoff." The husband, a thirty-something man with a shaved head and slim build, offered his hand. "I can't tell you how happy I am that you're here." He glanced back at his wife. "We weren't sure the police were taking us seriously."

"I promise you, we are." Ellis returned the handshake. "Thank you for sitting down with me. I'd just like to ask you a few questions."

The husband and wife took a seat, and Mark replied, "Whatever we can do to help you find this sick person."

Ellis prepared her notes. "Why don't I start by asking when you first realized someone had been in your home?"

Janie glanced at her husband with some uncertainty. "I'd like to answer that if I could."

He gestured for her to continue.

She set her attention on Ellis. "I heard something. I thought maybe I was just dreaming, but I opened my eyes for a moment, and I was freezing, which was strange considering I was under a blanket. But in that moment, I'm sure I saw something moving in our bedroom."

"And you believed it was the intruder...did you happen to take note of any identifiable features?" Ellis asked. "Height, build?"

"No." Janie looked down in disappointment. "Like I said, it was only a second, and I closed my eyes again, I guess."

Ellis noticed Mark anxiously rubbing his hand on his bald head, his eyes shifting as though attempting to rein in a rising anger. She turned back to Janie. "And then what happened?"

"I'm sure the next morning I noticed things had been moved around," Janie added.

"But all of this, you thought it was a dream?" Ellis continued.

"Yes, ma'am. God, I thought I was going crazy or something. It wasn't until we started talking to some of the neighbors." She hesitated a moment. "I drop off my kids at school, and one of the ladies who lives down the street, she mentioned that she felt like someone had been in her home, but couldn't be sure. And I thought, oh my God. It's the same thing. It did happen."

"Where are your children now?" Ellis asked.

"They finished school this week, and because of all this, they're with my mom in Portland," she replied.

Ellis tilted her head. "You sent them away?"

"Yes." Janie took her husband's hand. "I know how this must sound to you, Detective, but I've never felt anything like that moment. It was nightmarish, which was exactly what I thought it was—a nightmare." A tear streamed down her cheek. "I don't know why he didn't take anything or hurt any of us, but I'm so grateful."

Ellis took in her surroundings, pondering, *why these people?* Why any of them? Triggs was still working on nailing down whoever had installed the security systems in these homes, but she felt there was something else. Something darker, more sinister in how this intruder conducted himself. He wanted them to be afraid—he wanted to terrorize them.

She laced her fingers and rested her hands on the table. "Mr. and Mrs. Federoff, how well do you know your neighbors?"

7

All the victims had said the same thing. All had feared the same prowler, that much was clear. But this person's identity was a complete mystery. He was a shadow to some. A whisper to others. A breeze from a window left open. They all felt him. No one could define him. Who had this ability to present themselves so imperceptibly and leave no other mark?

Items had been taken from some of the families, but not the Federoffs. The Federoffs could think of no one—no neighbor, certainly, who would do this. So Ellis had no choice but to find the motive on her own.

She moved through the home of Michael and Debi Madsen with an eye on every detail. They were last on her list. They had been number five.

The Madsens were unsure whether anything from their home had gone missing. How was Ellis to know if they didn't? The difference here? The Madsens had no children at home. Their children were grown and had their own lives elsewhere. And they had a small Yorkshire terrier, who had been unharmed.

The two-story home was the least updated of all of them. This couple had lived here for years, and it seemed once their kids were gone, they had no use for modernizing. Only in their early fifties, they behaved much older. Maybe they'd lived a life that drained them of whatever energy they had, and little remained to enjoy their impending golden years.

As Ellis continued through the first floor, she walked into a small bedroom that appeared to serve as both a guest room and an office. A wrought-iron daybed was pressed against the wall just inside the door. Along the opposite wall was a small writing desk and chair. No dresser for clothes. It was then Ellis noticed a wire running along the joint between the ceiling and the wall. She followed it down to where it dropped to a closet with sliding doors. She opened one door and, with a flashlight, peered inside to see the wire. "Security?" A panel on the wall of the closet suggested it was the heart of the security system. So if someone had bypassed it, they would've already been inside. Meaning the exterior cameras would have captured the intruder's entry, but on that night, they hadn't armed their system. Convenient.

Ellis returned to the living room, where the couple sat beside each other on the couch. "Mr. and Mrs. Madsen, I noticed your security system goes into a closet in the back bedroom."

"Yes, it does," Mr. Madsen replied. "We had the system retrofitted after our kids moved out. They insisted it wasn't safe for us to be here alone."

"And was it armed on the night you believe the intruder entered your home?" she asked.

"Uh, no, it wasn't," he replied. "Honestly, we don't use it much anymore. My mistake to think we were safe here."

"I'm wondering, then," Ellis continued, "would your cameras have been on if the system wasn't armed?"

"Yes, of course, but I have looked at the files, and there was a noticeable time period where they appeared to have been off. It was on the night the intruder came."

"So they aren't tied to your security system?"

"No, ma'am. I simply get alerted when there's motion," Mr. Madsen added. "It was as though the cameras malfunctioned and cut out during that time."

It was then that Ellis considered the idea this intruder had the means to scramble signals to the cameras. Sophisticated devices, jamming devices that emitted radio waves would do the trick. And the notion that this person worked for a security company strengthened.

Ellis noticed the bookcase on the living room wall. She walked over to it while the couple looked on. "I've been told that your neighbors experienced items being moved around, and a few smaller things being taken." She turned around toward them. "You aren't sure whether anything was taken?"

"No," the wife said. "I wish I had more for you, Detective."

Ellis turned back toward the bookcase, noticing a light layer of dust that surrounded the edge of the dark oak shelf. One of the books appeared to have been pulled out of place, disturbing that layer of dust. She aimed her finger at it. "Have either of you read this book recently?"

Mr. Madsen got up from the sofa and walked toward her, deepening his gaze. "I actually don't recognize that book, Detective. I don't believe that's mine." He glanced back to his wife. "Hon?"

"It's not mine," she replied, her tone certain.

Ellis stepped back a moment and observed the rest of the shelves. Nothing else appeared to have been touched. "I need to take a look at this." She reached into her pocket and pulled on a pair of latex gloves. And with careful hands, she picked up the book and noted the title. "You say this isn't your book, sir?"

Mr. Madsen looked at it closely. "I can say with utmost certainty that is not my book, Detective."

Ellis turned to view the cover. "*The Lies They Told*." The author was unknown to her, and she looked at Mrs. Madsen. "Ma'am, this isn't yours either?"

The wife joined them and examined the book. "No. It doesn't look like the kind of book I read. I mostly read romances."

Based on the cover, Ellis realized this was no tale of romance. "Do you mind if I take this in as evidence? I don't want to get ahead of myself, but if neither of you recognize this book and it appears to have been recently placed here, then it could have been by the intruder."

"But why?" Mr. Madsen asked. "Why some cheap dime-store mystery novel?"

Ellis placed the book in an evidence bag. "I wish I had an answer for you, sir."

The title wasn't lost on her, and now she wondered what lies the Madsens had told to make them a target. It was the first time the intruder had left what she was certain was a specific message. But what did it mean?

THE WAITRESS CARRIED two plates of food and set one down in front of Ellis. The other, in front of McCallister. Ellis nodded her appreciation. And when the woman fell out of earshot, she continued, "It was absolutely a message meant for the Madsens. None of the other victims have been left—as far as we are aware—with something so pointed."

McCallister placed his napkin on his lap. "But you turned it over for prints?"

"I did," Ellis replied. "That'll take a day or two, and if it turns up clean, I want to take a deeper dive into it and search for more meaning. I didn't examine it closely enough for any other clues he may have left. I had to be sure to clear it for prints first. I do know that the prints on the Barbers' windowsill that Triggs pulled came up as belonging to the family. So that's another dead end." She plunked a French fry into her mouth.

"If this guy is as smart as I think he is," Ellis continued. "Disabling security systems, cameras, getting in and out of homes without notice. I mean, his only wrong move was the family dog. I have to believe he's not dumb enough to leave prints. Not on that book. Not anywhere, so I need to find more."

"I think that's what you need to say to Abbott," McCallister said. "He has to know your gut feeling about this."

"He's aware." Ellis dabbed her lips with the napkin. "And he's given me time to work the case, but if I don't get something soon, he'll toss it back into Moss's court."

McCallister took a bite of his cheeseburger, and after swallowing it down, he sighed. "I wish I could help you with this."

"Soon. Any day now, right?" she asked. "You know, Connor asked how you were doing. Said he texted you."

"He did. It was nice of him."

"Connor looks up to you now. You made an impression on him. I wasn't sure that was possible, given his personality."

"The way it stands, we have a lot more in common than we thought." McCallister glanced away for a moment as his expression turned contrite. "You know I met with an old co-worker yesterday for lunch?"

"Before you stopped into the station?" she added.

"Yep. I asked him how things were going. What the latest was on the civil case." McCallister took a drink from his glass of water. "He says it's all over. The family was, of course, awarded a settlement. But he says there's too many other things going on in the city, and no one seems focused on that anymore."

"But the reporter..." Ellis began.

"She was looking to stir the pot. To get clicks on her article. Which she did. And I'm here because of it." He raised his hands. "Look, I don't blame the reporter. I blame myself."

"I know you do." Ellis reached for his hand. "But maybe the best way to get past it is to keep doing your job."

THE LIGHT FIXTURE in his bedroom ceiling cast shadows over the pinboard and made it difficult to see the details he'd written on number six. His map was marked with red Sharpie and colored pins to indicate location and timing.

Patrols in the area had indeed increased, as he'd noticed when he made use of the daylight earlier by driving around the neighborhood. So he devised new paths to stay out of their purview. The cops weren't going to stop him. No one was. Not until he was finished.

He stood in front of his table, dressed in black, leaving his hooded jacket for last, as the summer heat proved too much. Long legs, broad shoulders, thick arms. Most men in their late forties had nothing on him.

But for all his effort to keep his health, he remained an empty shell inside. His tired brown eyes, heavy with lines, stared at the board until finally a tear shed down his cheek. A hard wipe at it with the back of his hand and he wondered —if it appeared they might take him tonight—what could he do to inflict maximum damage? What could he do to make his mark so that they would remember him for the rest of their lives? However, if he was lucky enough to survive, the last one on his list would know exactly what that damage would be.

He clenched his fist and rammed it at the board, busting a hole in the cork. The drywall split behind it, revealing the gray masonry block structure. "Fuck!" Shaking off the pain in his hand, he snatched his tools and carried them to the dining table.

His fleece jacket lay over a chair, and he pulled it on, raising the hood over his head. Now his face was cast in shadow as he threw his tools into a bag and made his way to the front door.

The evening air was calm as he stepped outside. The night was clear and warm. He thought back to his life before this and how this had always been his favorite time of year.

Never mind that now. He carried on to his gold Toyota sedan and tossed his bag into the passenger seat. Keying the ignition, he reversed out of the parking lot and headed toward where the rich people lived.

As he drove, he replayed the plan in his mind. Each step had to be executed with precision, or this could end tonight, and no one would know why he'd done it.

He parked in the designated location. Taking to foot, with only his essential tools in his jacket, he carried on through the footpath at the back of the street between the homes and the elementary school.

Soon, however, he arrived at the rear entry gate and scaled the pedestrian access until he dropped over the other side.

He sensed the fear that dangled over the homes inside the charming Woodland Heights neighborhood. Unbeknownst to them, he now stood in the shadows, waiting to make his move.

The uptick in police patrolling the streets did little to deter him as he adapted to their schedule, accessing the community through the footpath. And now, through the window, he peered into the Dobsons' living room. The unlit house suggested everyone had gone to bed.

He shot around at the sound of a car and dropped below the wall of greenery fronting the window.

Headlights shone as the car slowly drove along the street. He peered between the thick branches and noticed the patrol car approaching. "Right on time," he whispered. But as the police cruiser passed, his eyes narrowed, focusing on the target—the side door to the garage around the corner. He would remain out of sight to passersby on the road.

Silently, he moved through the well-manicured garden, his steps soundless atop the dew-covered grass. The moonlight gleamed on his gloved hands as he pulled out a set of lockpicking tools, his fingers working skillfully to disengage the lock on the side garage door.

The minutes stretched for too long as he worked with minimal light. Sweat trickled down his forehead, diluting the anticipation of what awaited him. Finally, with a satisfying click, the lock gave way.

Carefully, he pushed the side door open, cringing at the faint creak that escaped into the night. But this door led only to the garage and likely disturbed no one. The second door, the one that led into the home, would be easily unlocked, and he already knew where the security maintenance panel was located. It would take mere moments to shut it down.

The garage held no cars, only cardboard boxes and plastic totes that were placed on standing shelves. The panel was on the front wall on the far right. He examined the system and recognized the maker. It held no challenge for him. Within moments, he'd disengaged the alarm.

He stepped toward the door that led inside the home. An easy pick, and no deadbolt. Sometimes he marveled at the complacency of others. Who truly believed this was a safe place? He did not. He knew better.

Stepping over the threshold, he entered the house, blending seamlessly into the darkness within. His steps were light as he moved through the hallway. Shadows enveloped him, providing the perfect camouflage. Inside the Dobson residence, where a family remained unsuspecting of the danger that lurked, the sound of a ticking clock ruptured the silence.

He hovered in front of the door to the master bedroom and listened, waiting for assurances that the couple slept. Just as he turned into the hall again, a noise, like a shuffle of feet, thumped through the quiet. He froze mid-motion, every nerve jangling with alarm. He knew a child had awakened, and that child was only steps away, likely preparing to call out a warning.

Panic surged through his veins as he realized that once more his plan had been compromised. He had but milliseconds to decide. Take action or leave. This child wasn't the family dog and would not so easily be taken down in utter silence. And the idea of it...

A tiny voice, laced with fear, emitted a sound. "Who are you?"

Ellis sat alone on her couch. Her eyes were focused on the television and whatever was being broadcast, but her mind was fixed on the intruder. She'd handed over the book as evidence, and it was simply a waiting game now. What did it mean, and why them?

With her laptop next to her, Ellis opened it and reviewed the files once again. She noticed that the neighborhood had held a meeting last night to discuss the break-ins. "I should've been there." But it appeared as though they hadn't invited law enforcement at all. Perhaps thinking it was too soon, all things considered. However, if she had been there, she might've gained insight into the people who were being targeted. What was it about this community in particular that drew this person to them?

The first thing that came to mind was to carry out a search for similar investigations. Had this happened before, and if so, where and when? And was there a pattern she could follow?

Ellis had taken notes on the makes and models of the

security systems installed in the homes she'd visited. The information had been passed on to Triggs, who worked to home in on a company who might have serviced that area.

A knock on the front door startled her. She noted the time; it was almost ten o'clock. Her first thought was that it was Piper. Her best friend had recently broken up with a man—again—and maybe she needed to talk.

Ellis reached the door and peered through the fish-eye lens. She pulled back, startled, and stood still for a moment.

"It's me, Becca," said a muffled voice on the other side. "Can I come in, please? I know it's late..."

"Jesus," she whispered before unlocking the door and opening it. "Andrew, what are you doing here?"

Andrew. Her ex-husband whom she hadn't seen since the divorce, since he'd left for Connecticut for some job. She looked at him now under the muted amber light of her porch. His brown eyes held a sort of supplication. But for what? What did he want? Why was he here?

He looked thinner than she remembered. Not a particularly tall man, he stood around five feet ten, wore a white Oxford rolled up at the sleeves and black dress pants. No jacket. No tie.

"I'm sorry for just stopping by." Perspiration on his lip and forehead made him appear as though he'd run from someplace. "Can I come in, Becca?"

She peered beyond him, noting what looked to be his car parked along the front curb. For a moment, Ellis pondered whether he was in trouble—or danger. "Yeah. Come in, I guess." Her senses heightened, she let him in and closed the door, making a point to secure it behind him.

Ellis felt his gaze roam over her and folded her arms

across her body in a defensive move against the unwanted intrusion.

"You look great, Becca," he said.

"Thank you." She spun around and headed into the kitchen, scenarios running through her mind as to the reason for his arrival. "Can I get you something to drink?"

"Uh, sure. I'll take a beer." He trailed her, rubbing his hands on his pants as though they were clammy.

Ellis walked in bare feet and retrieved a couple of bottles of beer from the fridge. On her return, she handed him one. "Here." A long swig followed, with her keeping one eye on him.

"I imagine you're surprised to see me." Andrew tossed back his drink.

"You could say that. Come and sit down." She motioned toward the sofa and walked over to take a seat. Her laptop was on the edge of the cushion, so she closed it and set it on the side table.

Andrew sat down on the love seat next to the sofa. "How's Hank? Carter?"

Frustration climbed up her spine at the sound of his voice. The divorce had been mostly amicable. But somehow, his presence here set off a charge inside her. Was it anger? Pain? "They're fine," she replied. "Andrew, please tell me why you're here. We haven't spoken or seen each other in almost two years."

"I know, and I should've at least called, but I wasn't sure you'd answer. I wasn't sure you wanted to hear from me at all."

That part might have been true, but Ellis kept silent, hoping for a suitable answer—and soon.

Andrew wiped his brow with the back of his hand. His

knee bounced, and he kept his eyes aimed at the coffee table. "I—uh—I need to ask a favor."

"I'm listening," she pressed.

"I need help, Becca." He licked his lips and cleared his throat. "I'm in trouble."

Now, as they locked eyes, relief washed over her. Okay, yes, Andrew was in trouble, but this was a far better reason for his arrival than what she had anticipated. Trouble—she could deal with. Anything else—anything personal—was something she could not. "What are we talking about here?" she asked, as her cop instincts kicked in.

"Let me rephrase, actually." Andrew rubbed his palms together. "It's not me who's in trouble. It's my fiancée."

This was news to Ellis. "Your fiancée?"

"Yes, I was going to tell you, but then all this stuff happened, and now, well, now I'm asking for your help." He sighed. "She needs help, Becca, and I didn't know who else to turn to."

"Okay," she said, realizing he'd lured her into his world under false pretenses. And now he wanted her to help his soon-to-be wife. Why was she surprised?

"I know how all this must sound, Becca," he began.

"I don't think you do," she shot back. "Look, why don't you tell me what kind of trouble she's in, and I'll tell you if I can help."

He nodded and was silent for a moment longer. "This is a lot harder than I thought it was going to be. But Becca, please know that I'm only here because I know the kind of detective you are. How good you are at your job. I saw it firsthand."

"Andrew, please."

"Yeah, sorry." He looked down a moment and drew in a

breath. "So, uh, Myra—that's her name—we work together at an investment firm."

"Like the job you had here?" Ellis asked.

"That's right. And it's how we met," he continued before allowing his words to tumble out in a rush. "They're saying she committed fraud, Becca. The kind of fraud that would see her put behind bars for the next decade. Maybe longer."

8

His trembling hands clenched the steering wheel in an attempt to still them. Rage balled in his gut, and the veins in his neck bulged as a roar clawed up his throat. With his car doors and windows shut, he unleashed that roar at deafening heights.

Yanking on the wheel, he pushed and pulled, striking the back of his seat, yelling until he grew hoarse. "You had to. You had to!" He finally stopped and peered through the windshield with wide, blank eyes that spilled tears. His cheeks red, his hair disheveled, his left hand throbbing. "You had no choice."

As he stared at his swollen knuckles, images of the boy's terrified face and the pajamas he'd soiled wormed through his head. The weightlessness of him as his unconscious body went limp in his arms and he set down the boy on the cold floor. "He'll live."

And now, he glanced at the passenger seat. The tools in the bag that lay wide open. His face deadpanned as he peered into it. Thrusting a hand inside, he shuffled the various implements necessary to enter the houses. But something was missing. "Where the hell is it, goddam it!" Racking his brain, he couldn't recall what had happened. Had he left it in the house? Dropped it somewhere along the way as he ran back to his car? "Son of a bitch."

Failure breathed down his neck. Shame at what he'd done to the child suffocated him. And now he'd left something behind. Getting inside that bedroom had been his only purpose. To instill in John and Heather Dobson the fear that he could get to them anywhere at any time. It was all to lay the groundwork, but now he'd just lost the upper hand.

The time had come to push forward his timeline before they figured out his blueprint and discovered who would be next. Still impassioned, with anger burning in his chest, he turned the engine and drove back to his shitty apartment, which reeked of dog piss and mold. Along the way, he spied a bar that was still open—and a familiar vehicle.

He killed the headlights and rolled to a stop at the far end of the parking lot, away from the few other vehicles that remained. With his eyes fixed on the door, he waited. Two minutes. Three minutes. Five minutes. Finally, the door opened, and a man spilled out. Stumbling over his feet, he reached into his pocket and retrieved a set of car keys.

Thick waisted. Clean shaven. Average build. Drunk off his ass.

"Here we go." The light inside the Toyota illuminated as he opened the driver's side door to step out. Closing it quickly, he pulled up his hooded jacket and walked toward the man as he staggered and swayed to his truck. "Hey."

The swaying man wore a smile. "Dude, what are you doing here?"

He grabbed the man by the shoulder, yanking him close. "You fucking asshole." He plunged his knife into his side.

The man doubled over, but before he could let out a sound, he was pulled up again—the knife thrusting deeper in his gut. Only inches lay between them as he stuck him over and over, noticing the look of shock on the drunk man's face. Blood splattered on his cheeks and clothes. Finally, he released him, letting the man collapse to the ground only a foot away from his vehicle.

He peered back at the door to the bar before marching to his car and climbing into the driver's seat. He pulled off his hood and gasped for air. His breaths were heavy and shaky while a surge of adrenaline brought on a euphoric sensation, releasing him of the rage and guilt he'd felt. Blood dotted his face and lips as the familiar metallic taste spilled into his mouth. The knot in his stomach loosened as he keyed the ignition and drove out of the parking lot, keeping an eye in the rearview for witnesses.

Son of a bitch had it coming.

ELLIS BLINKED to clear her vision as she awoke to the vibration of her phone. Taking note of the caller ID, she answered the line. "Sarge, what's going on?"

"A call came into Dispatch," Abbott said, sounding as though he'd been roused from sleep too. "Someone was stabbed to death at the Lighthouse bar off Broadway and Judson. I need you to head down there ASAP."

"Yes, sir." She scrambled out of bed.

"And one more thing—"

"Okay."

"He hit the home of John and Heather Dobson. Their young son was injured. He's been taken to the hospital."

"Oh no." She placed her hand on her forehead as she stood at the edge of her bed. "I should go there and talk to them."

"They're with their son while he's receiving treatment," Abbott replied. "I called Connor. He'll meet you at the bar. Moss has an officer with the family now. You can interview them after this." He sighed. "Christ, if these crimes are connected..."

"I'm on my way." She ended the call and snatched a pair of jeans and a T-shirt hanging in her closet. Her gun was secured in a box on the shelf above. She pulled it down and entered the code. The lid opened, and she retrieved her sidearm.

A quick pitstop in the bathroom to run a brush through her hair and freshen her breath, and then she'd be out the door.

Her head still fuzzy from the abrupt awakening, she splashed cold water on her face. Upon looking into the mirror, her thoughts turned to Andrew. He'd dropped a bombshell, but what had actually happened tonight? No way could she allow herself to be distracted by him or his problems. Could she even do anything to help his fiancée? Maybe. Maybe not. But it wasn't her top priority.

Stepping outside into the damp predawn morning, Ellis jumped into her SUV and headed out. She pressed her Bluetooth and made the call to Bevins.

"Yeah, where are you?" he answered.

"On my way." Ellis kept her eyes fixed on the darkened road ahead. "ETA about fifteen. You there?"

"Almost. Yearwood was the responding officer."

"Good," she replied. "He knows what to do. I'll see you soon." Ellis ended the call and carried on down the Fifteen, which turned into Broadway. She wondered if Moss had called in Triggs.

Without another thought, she called him, and he answered. "Are you with the Dobsons?" she asked. "At the hospital?"

"Yeah. You heard?"

"I did. And about the stabbing. I'm on my way there now. Listen, keep a pulse on that family, you got it? I'm grateful their kid is okay, but if he saw our guy—"

"Exactly. I'll stay on it," Triggs replied. "And I'll be in touch soon."

As she drove ahead, flashing red and blue lights appeared in the distance, beacons in the darkness. Moments later, Ellis pulled into the parking lot and spotted Bevins already heading over to Yearwood. An ambulance waited near the entrance.

She parked several feet away, killed the engine and hopped out, jogging toward the front of the building. The body still lay on the cool damp ground where blood pooled around it. "What the hell happened?"

Yearwood and Bevins appeared to notice her arrival.

"Do we know who this guy is yet?" she pressed.

"Taylor Burnell," Yearwood said. "According to the owner, Burnell left around one this morning. His final customer took off at quarter till two and noticed Burnell on the ground. He was already gone."

She turned to Bevins. "Anyone find a murder weapon yet?"

"The guy was repeatedly stabbed, but no knife has

surfaced yet," Bevins replied. "No one's touched the body either."

Yearwood hooked his thumbs over his duty belt. "Figured CID should take a look before we load him up in the truck."

"That was the right call," Ellis replied. "Let's document everything here and get him in the ambo."

"Yes, ma'am." Yearwood moved on to speak with the other officers.

"What do you think?" Bevins looked out over the parking lot.

"I have no idea." She kept her eyes fixed on the body. "No one else saw anything?"

"Not from what we know right now," he replied. "And I already asked about security. There isn't any."

"Damn it." Ellis turned away a moment. "Okay." She squatted low to examine the body, shining her flashlight on him. "I don't see any bruises on his face."

Bevins joined her. "So probably not a bar fight gone wrong?"

"Doesn't look like it. The guy could've pissed off someone inside, and that person took it out on him here."

"The owner says it was his usuals here, and he didn't pick up on any issues between anyone," Bevins continued. "So who would've done this?"

Ellis returned upright again and peered out at the ambulance. "Another family was hit tonight. The intruder hurt their son. They're at the hospital now."

"Jesus." Connor turned down his gaze. "Coincidence?"

She scoffed. "That's the million-dollar question, isn't it?"

Dawn had emerged by the time Ellis and Bevins arrived at the stationhouse. The sun's rays spilled inside the first-floor lobby as she pushed open the glass door.

"I need a cup of coffee. I'll see you upstairs." Bevins headed up to CID.

As he reached the staircase, Ellis turned and noticed Triggs marching toward her. "Has the boy been released yet?"

"Yes. He'll be fine," Triggs replied. "Can't say as much for the parents."

"How old?" Ellis asked.

"Eight. The father made the 911 call while the mother ran outside to flag down one of Moss's patrolmen. The son of a bitch got inside, but he didn't take anything. Not that they were aware of. I tried to keep my distance at the hospital, like you suggested."

"Good." Ellis rubbed her forehead. "We need to know if that boy saw him."

"Yes, ma'am," Triggs agreed. "I figured you'd want to interview them this morning. But I have to say that the timing is suspect between what happened at the Dobsons' and the murder at the bar."

She tilted her head. "How so?"

"Heather Dobson flagged down the patrolman maybe thirty minutes or so before that call came in at the bar. I was looking into it with Dispatch earlier." Triggs stood at attention as he voiced his suspicions. "Detective, what if it was the same guy?"

Ellis pondered the idea, and in her exhausted state, she struggled to make sense of it. "But why?"

"I have no idea because we can't ask a dead man," Triggs replied. "But look at where that bar is at. It's not far from the

Woodland Heights area. And then think about the time of night. It can't be a coincidence. Shit doesn't happen around here like that, you know?"

"The thought had crossed our minds last night," Ellis added. "So let's say it's him. Say he stopped at that bar after fleeing the Dobson home. Why did he murder a random person?"

"We don't know for sure he was random." Triggs raised his index finger. "And after what the intruder did to the boy, the dog, we know he's capable of violence."

"And now he's graduated to murder." As Ellis considered his theory, it became clear that Triggs was a detective at heart. Methodical. Logical. He could slip right into CID. "Okay, so what does that say about the intruder?"

Triggs knitted his brow. "I have no idea."

"It says he's reached his tipping point. That he's snapped for whatever reason, and now he's completely unhinged." She glanced upstairs and noticed Abbott on the landing, looking down at her. "Where are you at on the security companies?"

"I've narrowed it down to three who've worked in that area over the past five years. All three had been hired by several in the community, including our victims. I still need to confirm which of the victims used which company. I should have that soon."

"The sooner, the better. Let's go see Moss. I need to know everything about what happened with the Dobson family. And find out when we can talk to their son." She followed Triggs as they started toward the bullpen.

A few officers milled around—grabbing coffee and conversing with each other—including Graham Yearwood. He raised his hand as they walked by.

"Detective Ellis."

She veered toward him. "Morning, or is it still night? I'm not sure." She offered her hand. "Thanks for all your hard work."

"We didn't find the weapon," he replied.

"I didn't expect you to." She thumbed back to Triggs. "We're headed in to see Moss. If you think of anything or hear anything more about last night, give me a shout, okay?"

"Will do. Thanks, Detective."

"Thank you." She turned around and rejoined Triggs in the hall. A moment later, they arrived in Moss's office.

Triggs stood at ease. "Good morning, sir."

"Triggs, Detective," he replied, "sounds like we have some catching up to do."

"I know you're aware of the murder at the Lighthouse bar last night," Ellis began as she walked inside and sat down.

"I am," Moss replied.

"And now we have a potential witness with the Dobson boy."

"Let's not get too hopped up about that. The kid's eight. He's terrified. The parents are too." Moss leaned back in his chair. "We need to tread lightly."

"We can't afford to lose time on this, Sergeant," Ellis continued. "That boy could be our best shot at ID-ing this guy. He hurt the child. I understand the parents' reluctance. But the longer we wait, the less he'll remember."

"I hear what you're saying. I do." Moss's gaze wavered between Ellis and Triggs. "You mentioned before you thought he would escalate this thing."

"And I think he proved that last night," Ellis said. "We're now dealing with a man who's feeling like he's hit the end of his rope. I don't know why. I don't know exactly what's triggered it. Maybe hurting the boy set off something in him that he can't control. And maybe it is too far-fetched to consider we're dealing with the same guy in both incidents, but if we are, that boy could hold the answers for us."

ABBOTT HAD INSISTED that Ellis work on this case alone. After all, it was still in Moss's court, because all they were dealing with was an intruder who had yet to take anything of enough value to consider felony charges. But now the game was changed; a child had been hurt. And someone had been murdered, even if it was still possible the two incidents were unrelated. Ellis noticed the look on Abbott's face when he gazed down from the landing. He knew it too.

She worked her way upstairs again and huddled with Bevins to ensure they were on the same page about last night's brutal murder of Taylor Burnell. "Okay, so are we ready to brief the sarge?"

"Ready when you are."

The bullpen was quiet on this early Saturday morning, and it was just her and Bevins. They walked onward into the hall and stopped at Abbott's desk.

"Hey, Sarge," Ellis began. "You have some time for us?"

"You're the only reason I'm here." He removed his reading glasses and folded his hands on his desk. "You two have had quite the night."

"Yes, sir," Bevins replied. "Wasn't as fruitful as we'd hoped."

Ellis sat down. "I just met with Moss and Triggs. And with this recent murder, we think there could be a connection to the intruder investigation. I'm hoping to speak to the

Dobson family soon to see if they'll allow me to talk to their son. He's been injured by the man, and we hope he could offer a description."

He leaned back in his chair. "All right. Give it to me straight, then."

She continued to brief him on the events of the previous evening. The stabbing death of a drunk man and the incident with the Dobson family. "Sir, Patrol is in agreement that things have escalated, and CID needs to take over this investigation."

Abbott regarded his detectives. "What's your plan of action?"

"Connor is going to keep on top of the Burnell murder while I look for a connection to the intruder case. I hope to have more details after speaking with the boy. I might be able to get something from him that our sketch artist can work with."

"I plan on heading out to see the ME later today and go from there," Bevins added.

"Sounds good." Abbott slipped on his reading glasses and turned to his computer screen. "I want regular updates."

Ellis nodded. "Yes, sir."

THERE WAS something about this case that pricked the back of Ellis's mind and was only enhanced by the idea that this murder may or may not be connected. Why these people? Why this neighborhood? Triggs currently worked on answers to the question of the security company. It was a possibility that still needed to be ruled out, even more so now.

And as she drove onward to Woodland Heights, she called McCallister.

He answered. "Becca, hi."

"Hi, listen, I wanted to run something by you," she said. "Is this a bad time?"

"Not at all. I literally have nothing else to do right now. How can I help?"

She went on to detail the new murder investigation as well as what had happened with yet another family inside Woodland Heights. "This time, the family's child was attacked, and I'm praying he can offer us a description. I'm on my way to see them now."

"Okay. And what else?"

Ellis exited the highway toward the neighborhood. "My plan is to search their house to see if the intruder got sloppy when the boy caught him off guard. Maybe he left something behind."

"He hasn't yet," McCallister added. "But this time was different."

"I agree." She turned right onto the residential street. "So, barring any new details this family can provide, it's another game of wait and see."

"Right," he replied. "I suppose a question you could ask is whether the family, the parents, have any reason to suspect a certain person."

"A common enemy?" Ellis pressed.

"Someone who knows these people. You have to admit, his ability to maneuver inside these homes undetected suggests he's been in them before," McCallister said.

"It's something I've considered, but on asking that question of other families, they have no idea."

"We both know these home invasions aren't random," he

continued. "There could be several ways the intruder is connected to these people."

She slowed down and peered through the driver's side window at the addresses on the houses along the side of the road. "Understood. I'll keep exploring. Listen, I just arrived. Thanks for your help, Euan. I appreciate it."

"I only wish I was there with you now," he replied.

Ellis smiled. "Me too. I'll keep you posted." She ended the call and climbed down from her Tahoe. The home before her was one of the nicer ones in the community. Manicured lawn with abundant hydrangeas along the front. A small porch with farmhouse-style columns. A three-car garage with two luxury cars parked in front of it.

Ellis walked along the brick-paved path to the front porch and stepped up to the door. She rang the bell and heard it echo inside. The couple had agreed to meet at noon, and Ellis noticed it was ten past twelve. She was ten minutes late.

The door opened to reveal a man and woman. He was at least six feet tall. She was probably five eight. Both appeared exhausted and afraid.

"Hello, I'm Detective Rebecca Ellis. I'm so sorry I'm late." She offered her hand to the husband.

He accepted the greeting. "I'm John Dobson; this is my wife, Heather. Thank you for coming out, Detective. Please come inside."

They stepped away from the door as Ellis entered, Heather Dobson closing it behind her. The feeling of déjà vu was insurmountable. How many times was she going to do this before finding the person responsible?

"Thank you." Ellis took in the beauty of the home. These people had money. More than their neighbors, by the look of things. "I'd like to ask you some questions, as you know, about what you or your son recall from last night. How is he doing?"

"Resting for now. Come and take a seat, please." Mrs. Dobson walked into a formal living room, where two sofas faced each other with a coffee table in the middle. The back wall had a floor-to-ceiling marble fireplace with a stone hearth. A large front window overlooked the colorful hydrangeas.

"Thank you," Ellis said, taking a seat. "Your home is beautiful." She waited a moment for them to settle in before continuing, "As you know, I've spoken to your neighbors who've also gone through this. And I know everyone is on edge, fearing for the safety of their families—"

"Pardon the interruption, Detective," John began. "But we've asked the police to help, and all they've done is send more police cars to drive around our neighborhood. My boy..." He choked back his emotions. "He could've been killed. This person came for us. Came for my family. None of us knows what he wants or why he's doing this."

"Which is why I'm here, sir," Ellis cut in. "I'm here to find that out. And stepping up patrols in the area is how we start. By making our presence known."

"Clearly, it hasn't worked," Heather shot back. "So what are you going to do now? Wait for one of our children to disappear? To be murdered?"

Ellis understood the brewing anger, and she had to give them something because they were all at the end of their ropes. "If it's all right with you, I'd like to speak to your son."

"No." The husband gestured firmly with his hands. "Absolutely not. He's been through enough. I won't put him through anything more."

Ellis couldn't argue with that, but she could do her best to persuade them. "John, Heather, I'm so very sorry about what happened to your son. And I'm so grateful he'll be okay —in time. But he could be the only person who can tell us what this man looks like." She held up her hand. "I completely understand that you don't want to make this worse for him, but what if he can make it better for another family? Your neighbors?"

The couple traded glances before John spoke up. "He said he saw a tall guy in a dark jacket. His face was covered by a hood."

"That's a good start," Ellis replied. "What if I could get a sketch artist to meet with your son? They know the questions to ask and how to put it on paper. Would you object to coming into the station with your son and doing that? John, this is the first real lead we have. If you want this to end, and I know you do, please—please let your son give us whatever he can remember. Anything will help."

9

The guilt that Connor Bevins felt over McCallister's leave of absence overwhelmed him at times. He'd confided in McCallister, telling him about the horrible accident that killed his friend. And how his father had orchestrated the cover-up. It was all done to save his future, according to his dad.

Bevins knew his dad had been right. It had saved his future in that he wasn't sitting behind bars right now. He also wasn't working at the Pentagon or as an aide to some member of Congress. But over time, he'd found himself happy here, for the most part. And now that someone else knew, his defense mechanism—that false bravado—could be scaled back. He could begin to reveal his true self and hope he wasn't the asshole everyone thought he was.

Things had been different without McCallister around, and he was certain it had everything to do with Ellis. She held the team together. They all coalesced around her—mostly, but not entirely, because of her father, Hank.

But now with McCallister on leave, Pelletier turning

inward because of Ellis's rejection—yeah, everyone knew about that—the team felt fractured. And it made Bevins question whether it was fair that McCallister was left hanging in the wind while his secret remained hidden. The two incidents weren't the same, but they weren't all that different either.

He'd invited McCallister out for a beer and was due to meet him in twenty minutes. Maybe it was also so he could run through this new investigation into the murder of Taylor Burnell. He was still learning, and he trusted McCallister's advice.

Bevins grabbed his car keys from the bowl on his side table and headed out the door. Jogging down the steps from his top-floor apartment near the riverwalk, Bevins pressed the remote to unlock his car. Under the bright afternoon sun, the black Mustang gleamed—and he thought again how he loved that vehicle almost more than life itself. He slipped onto the black leather driver's seat and pressed the ignition, smiling as he felt the V8 engine rumble.

The Waterfront bar, also known as the local cop joint, was where they were set to meet. Bevins was familiar with the place, as the team was known to gather there on occasion, though not so much lately. On entering, he spotted McCallister sitting in a corner booth, gazing out across the water.

He made his way over, hands in his pockets, feeling guiltier as he drew near.

McCallister pulled his attention from the outside view and raised his eyes to meet Bevins'.

"Hey, it's good to see you, man." He offered his hand but remained seated. "Take a load off. I just ordered a couple beers."

"I'm on duty, but thanks for thinking of me." Bevins returned the handshake and climbed into the booth across from him.

It appeared to dawn on McCallister. "That's right. You and Becca are working on that stabbing. This will be your first time running lead, right?"

"Yep," he replied. "Hey, I'm sorry I didn't reach out sooner."

"Don't be. We're good. And I'm glad Abbott is giving you this shot. You've earned it."

The server arrived with two bottles of beer. "Here you go, gentlemen. Can I get you anything else?"

"Maybe a Coke for this guy. Thanks," McCallister said, pulling both bottles toward him.

Bevins couldn't shake the guilt that weighed on him. He watched McCallister take a long drink of beer. "Listen, uh, I feel like you got a raw deal with all this, being on leave and shit," he began, his eyes downcast. "After what I told you...I feel like you're the only one who's paying the price, you know? You should be back with the rest of the team."

McCallister leaned to the side, raising his good arm over the back of the booth. His sights focused on Bevins. So much so that Bevins began to feel as though a shoe was going to drop, but instead, McCallister went another way.

"I appreciate the sentiment, Connor, but it's not that simple. It doesn't matter what you did or how it was handled. This is my problem. I messed up, and I should've come clean a long time ago. You all were right to be pissed. I only hope that in time, things will get back to business as usual."

Bevins nodded, his expression serious. "The experience you bring to this department is invaluable, Euan. You should know that first and foremost. Look, I know I'm not the easiest guy to get along with, but you're one of the few who has managed to see past the front."

"You can thank Becca for that," he replied. "She's advocated for you since I came on board. And look." McCallister picked at the label on his beer bottle. "The fact you trusted me with your situation just goes to show me that she was right."

BEVINS TOOK his leave not long after they sat down. He'd picked McCallister's brain on how best to proceed with this new murder investigation. McCallister was happy to help. It made him feel part of the team again. Something he sorely missed. Now, he bided his time, drinking a glass of water and grabbing a bite to eat before heading over to see Ellis.

He was curious as to how the interview had gone with this intruder's latest victims. The case was intriguing, but he feared elbowing in on her investigation. It was easy for him to become overzealous and end up taking over.

McCallister reached for his wallet and paid the tab. Through the window, he noticed the sun dangling above the river as the long summer day waned. He slid out of the booth and headed into the parking lot, thinking about how much he appreciated Bevins reaching out like he did. He hoped the young detective was sincere. Time would tell.

The short drive south to Ellis's home left him little time to ponder the uncertainty in their relationship. He was never great at reading women, but he felt the distance between them—he sensed that she was holding something back.

He arrived just as the sun fell below the trees in her

backyard. And when she opened the door, standing before him in linen shorts and a white T-shirt that fit her frame perfectly, he was reminded that, to him, everything about her was perfect. It was the only time in his life he could recall feeling that way. He'd begun to question whether he was capable of such feelings. A man in his thirties who'd never been married, never been in a relationship that lasted longer than two years; well, some women might question what was wrong with him.

"Hi, come in." Ellis tucked a swath of her smooth blond hair behind her ear, accentuating her smile. "I, uh, thought I'd take a stab at making dinner. I hope that's okay. It felt a little therapeutic, if I'm honest, especially after today."

McCallister stepped inside. "Things went that well with the interview, huh?"

"The stabbing death of some poor man. The interviews..." She carried on into her galley-style kitchen and opened the fridge. "I feel for these people, I really do. Their frustration and fear. And I can't do anything about it. I don't know where this person will strike next. What he'll do." She grabbed a couple of beers and handed one to McCallister. "They're the very definition of sitting ducks. But I have my fingers crossed about this boy who was hurt...I'm hoping he'll be able to give us a face."

Ellis stepped in front of her stove, where a pot boiled. "I'm making pasta and grilled chicken. Hope that'll do. I don't cook much, and I have, like, two recipes. This is one of them."

"It sounds perfect." With the beer in his hand, McCallister leaned over the kitchen island. "So, no new information?"

"I managed to convince the parents to bring the kid to

our sketch artist. They said they'd drop by in the morning," she continued. "Won't be as busy at the station on a Sunday. Which I'm hoping could help them feel more relaxed. Anyway, we'll see how that goes." Ellis stirred the pot of pasta. "I really feel like we're at a point where the dam is about to break."

He could hear the frustration in her voice but felt helpless to do anything about it. If only he was on duty again, maybe he'd have an answer. Instead, he offered her an embrace as he wrapped his arms around her waist while she stood with her back to him at the stove. "There has to be a missing piece. Something that will reveal a reason as to why these people are being targeted."

She turned around, laying her arms on his shoulders. "I'm doing my best to find out what that is."

***

In the darkness of her bedroom, Vicky Boyles slept, but was only drifting half in and half out of consciousness. She had insisted her husband take that business trip because he couldn't risk his anticipated promotion. Now, she was left alone while a prowler roamed free in their neighborhood. But she was used to being alone. Brian traveled a lot, and they had no kids together. She was the second wife, and his kids were grown.

Derek Cannon came through on his offer to give the house a once-over earlier tonight. Making sure the place was secure. She could've done it herself and was usually very independent. But maybe just this once. It was nice having him help her like that.

And Brian had insisted their neighbor across the street keep eyes out too. He was being overprotective, as usual.

No one wanted her to be in Woodland Heights alone, and her friends had suggested she stay with them until Brian returned. But she was a forty-five-year-old woman, and she wouldn't be run out of her home by the possibility of some nutjob breaking in. She was prepared. She'd taken self-defense classes. Brian kept a hunting rifle locked in his closet. She wasn't afraid.

But then a feeling of dread descended on her, and she snapped open her eyes. "Stop freaking yourself out." She looked at the time on her bedside table. "Jesus. It's one a.m." And as she closed her eyes again, a creak sounded on the wood floor of their single-level home. Her bedroom was at the back of the house. The sound came from the hall.

He's here.

Swiftly and silently, she clambered off the bed and padded toward her bedroom door, pressing her ear against it. No more noises emerged, but she felt compelled to look.

Don't be stupid. It's nothing.

She opened the door, craning her neck, but all she saw were shadows playing tricks on her. No movement. No sound. Vicky stepped into the hall, a lone figure in the dark, dressed in light summer pajamas, her blond hair wrapped in a bun on top of her head. She glanced around, expecting to spot the prowler jumping out from behind another door, or hiding in a murky corner. But all remained still. She breathed a sigh of relief.

And then, in answer to her newfound confidence, she heard another sound—the faintest whisper of footsteps heading away from her. *He's getting away.*

She followed the sound through the darkness,

approaching the living room. Her throat tightened with fear, and her mouth dried. *Stop. Go back. Let him leave.* Brian's rifle would've come in handy right now.

He stood in the foyer—a broad figure dressed in black, moving toward the door.

She was only steps away. "The cops are coming." Her words echoed in the still house.

He kept his back to her. Could she stop him? He was a sizable man, and she was unarmed, but this was the man who had terrorized her friends and neighbors. If she could just get to the door and call out for the police. They wouldn't be far away.

"Get out of my house."

It seemed as though he pondered his next move before he slowly turned around.

She stood firm, refusing to back down an inch, even as fear coursed through every vein in her body. His face lay in shadow, like that of a specter, but his eyes...

"I swear to God." But what could she do? Investigating a sound when this man roamed free, and to do so without protection. *Stupid.* Time seemed to stand still as she faced him off in a battle of wills.

There was total stillness between them—until he made his move.

He charged at her, his body a blur of motion cutting through the dark. Vicky clawed at him, her body her only means of defense. Her clenched fists swung, and she connected with his jaw, but he was not deterred. She kicked at him, screaming in hope the cops driving by would hear.

She fought him off with everything she remembered from her self-defense class. He snatched her arm and pulled it hard. With her free hand, she clamped down on the hand that gripped her, but only succeeded in tearing off his rubber glove.

He moved in close and clutched at her neck, spinning her around until he had the advantage. She worked to pry his fingers away, but he was too strong. In that moment, she knew she'd lost, and that this man was far more dangerous, far more deadly than any of them knew.

He threw her down, her head striking the edge of the table along the way. Stars floated in her eyes, a sharp pain pierced her temple, and warm blood spilled down her face. She landed hard on the floor. Her eyes looked up at his shadowed face hovering over her. He was the last person she saw.

ELLIS RUSHED ONTO THE SCENE. Patrol cars flashed their lights. Officers milled about the grounds. And the first person on her team to arrive was Fletch. She walked ahead toward her colleague, donning a knowing look. "You drew the short straw, huh?"

"I volunteered," Fletch said. "Figured it was time to move past all this crap I let get between us. You know I'd do anything to protect you, Becca. At least, I hope you know."

"I do, and it's over now." The home's front door was wide open, and inside, all the lights were on. Ellis shook her head at the scene. "It finally happened. He killed one of them."

Fletch nodded. "Just like you thought."

"I wish I'd been wrong. Do we know who she is?" Ellis pressed.

Fletch reached for her notebook that had the name scribbled in it. "Vicky Boyles. Her husband, Brian, is on a business trip. He has been notified and is on his way back."

Ellis led the way inside the home and noticed the woman's body covered in a blue blanket. "Jesus, can't they get her out of here yet?" She looked at one of the officers. "Someone call the coroner, for God's sake."

"Yes, ma'am." The officer hurried away.

Ellis and Fletch moved on to the living room. She leaned over and, in a whisper, continued, "This house is four doors down from the Dobson home I went to yesterday. This is number seven."

"Seven?" Fletch replied. "You think that means something?"

"I don't know. Maybe."

"Keeping in mind the proximity, no doubt these neighbors are talking to each other. Someone could be listening," Fletch added. "Maybe someone on this street."

"At this point, it's time we consider that the suspect is one of them—" Ellis began before she was caught off guard by a short, stout man rushing up to her.

Fletch drew her weapon. "Stand back!"

"You know who did this!" the man shouted as an officer hurried to grab him from behind. He struggled and yelled in rage and frustration. "Let me go, goddam it! I fucking live here!"

"Let him go," Ellis ordered before turning to Fletch. "It's okay. Put away your gun." She didn't recognize the man but felt confident he was telling the truth about living in the area. "What's your name, sir?"

The man, who appeared about forty, wore anger in his gaze. "Grant Harden. My family and I live across the street. I knew this shit would happen again after what happened with the Dobsons' boy. Vicky is—*was*—our friend and neighbor. You all don't know what the hell you're doing, do you?"

"Mr. Harden, I'm Detective Rebecca Ellis. I'm so sorry for your loss."

"Fuck you and your apologies, Detective," he spat. "You all knew this was coming, didn't you? And you did nothing. Now she's dead. Brian's my best friend. What the hell am I supposed to tell him, huh?"

Ellis lowered her gaze a moment. "Sir, could I ask you some questions?"

"Questions?" he scoffed. "What the hell do I know? I was asleep in my bed next to my wife. Our kids were asleep in their rooms. That son of a bitch could've just as easily come into *my* home and harmed *my* family." He took a step forward. "You already know who did this."

Fletch clutched her weapon with one hand and thrust her other hand out in front of her. "Sir, I'm going to need you to take a step back."

"It's okay," Ellis said before turning to him. "We're here to do everything we can to find the person responsible for this, Mr. Harden. We will get to the bottom of it." She took a breath while the man appeared to calm himself. "You mentioned you live across the street?"

"Yeah, that's right."

"You didn't see or hear anything?" Ellis pressed.

"No. Like I said, I was sleeping." He appeared to swallow his emotions. "I knew Brian was going away for business. I told him I'd look after Vicky. That she'd be fine. What the hell do I say to him now?"

"This isn't your fault, Mr. Harden," Ellis said. "This person knows what he's doing. Sneaking around. She must've heard him and come to confront him."

"It appears she did her best to defend herself," Fletch added.

"Yeah, that's just like Vicky. A fighter." Tears spilled down his cheeks. "I can't believe she's gone."

Ellis looked at the officer. "Would you mind helping Mr. Harden get back to his house?" She eyed him again. "Thank you for your time, sir. You should go be with your family now." Ellis nodded to Fletch and led her a few feet away. "Listen, this guy, whoever he is, we know he gets into these homes by disabling their security systems. But I'm wondering..."

Fletch tilted her head. "About?"

Ellis glanced through the front door. "Mr. Harden's home. The other adjacent neighbors." She set her hands on her hips. "I'm wondering if they have any video of this house. Maybe they captured this guy breaking in over here."

Fletch raised her brow. "If he's disabling his victims' security systems, he wouldn't think to disable, say, the house across the street?"

"Right." Ellis looked at the body again. "I don't know if any of them had cameras set on the street, but someone somewhere in this neighborhood had to have captured a vehicle traveling or a figure lurking." She turned back to Fletch. "We'll get Harden's statement, and then we need to hit up every one of these homes. We're out of time."

10

It was time to brief Sergeant Abbott on what had transpired. This case had just taken a hard left turn, and CID was going to have to run the show from here on out. Ellis and Fletch rushed back to the station and asked Abbott to come in. It was four in the morning, and Ellis knew he would be in a cranky mood, especially after being called in early only a day ago.

But it seemed misery loved company; he requested the rest of the team come in as well. It was Sunday, and the sun wasn't up yet, but they all knew this was the job sometimes. And to Ellis, his actions indicated that Abbott was ready to tackle this head-on.

As they gathered, only one person was missing, and that was McCallister. Ellis felt his absence. She was pretty certain they all did.

Abbott walked into the bullpen, wearing a polo shirt and khaki pants. He never wore anything to work but a suit, and it was odd seeing him dressed so casually. Ellis noticed the look on his face: distressed, almost as if he hadn't expected any of this, even though she had all but assured him this was going to happen.

"All right. Now that we're all here, I'll turn this over to Ellis and Fletch," Abbott said. "They can get everyone up to speed, and we'll come up with a plan of action."

"Thanks, Sarge." Ellis briefed the team on what had transpired overnight in Woodland Heights, along with a rundown of what she knew about the case as a whole since the beginning. The murder of Vicky Boyles, a woman who appeared to have been defending herself in her own home, was the end result. And the Burnell murder? Well, it remained to be seen whether it was connected.

"Right now, while the scene is still being processed, I thought it best we partner up and knock on doors," Ellis said. "I want to know if any of the neighbors have cameras pointed at the streets, at their neighbors', scanning the areas behind their homes. Anywhere this guy might've been spotted lurking around. He's smart enough to have evaded the increased patrols and disable the security systems of the homes he's entered, but he just left us an opening, and we need to jump on it. And when we get the sketch from the Dobson boy, that could be one more essential tool for us."

"The neighbors must already be aware of what happened," Bevins said. "And from what you've mentioned, they're already on edge."

"That's right," Ellis replied. "Which is why I think now's the time to show them we're serious about ending this thing. We have to assuage their fears and keep them from going rogue. If we're proactive, we stand a better shot at their cooperation. But I'm going to need your help."

Pelletier nodded. "Then let's get out there and see what this son of a bitch left behind."

DAYLIGHT EMERGED, and the team prepared to leave. Ellis headed into Abbott's office for a final sit-down. "Sarge?"

He raised his eyes to meet hers. "Yeah?"

"We have roughly a five-block perimeter to cover, and the quicker we can cover it, the quicker we'll learn if the intruder has shown up on any surveillance."

"Get to the point, Becca. I know you have one."

"Yes, sir. It's just that I think we could use Gabby and Euan on this. That'll give us three teams, and we'll cover much more ground."

"Why not ask Moss for additional help?" he pressed.

"No offense, but this should be handled by CID now. I've got Triggs running on another lead, so he's tied up. But the longer it takes us to put together a coordinated effort, the better shot this guy has at getting away."

"I'll give you all the resources we have to canvass the neighborhood today. But I can't afford for my entire department to work on one investigation. Connor has the Burnell murder. Bryce has the felony theft. And Euan's a no-go for now. You already know this. Get what you need today, so the rest of the team can keep working their own cases."

ELLIS AND FLETCH joined Pelletier in his car, while Bevins and Lewis teamed up in his. The entire Woodland Heights community consisted of five blocks and about seventy-five homes. It was a lot of ground to cover, but their focus would be on the homes already hit and adjacent neighbors.

They divided up the area, splitting into two teams. She

could've used McCallister for the even three, but that was a battle Abbott wasn't willing to have. The union rep hadn't signed off on the doctor's release yet. The process for his return seemed longer than his actual leave at this point.

Ellis, Pelletier, and Fletch parked across from the Boyle home, while Bevins and Lewis hit the next street over. They started with the Hardens, who Ellis had gone toe-to-toe with only hours earlier.

The door opened, and Mr. Harden stood inside. "For God's sake, what the hell are you doing here?"

"Good morning, sir," Ellis began. "My team and I are canvassing the area in search of surveillance footage from you or your neighbors that might've captured the intruder."

Harden peered back over his shoulder. "Look, I got my kids in here. They don't need to see the cops coming round."

"We just want to know," Pelletier interrupted, "if you think you might have captured any images of this man."

"I don't know." He sighed. "I don't think so because I would've received an alert. I'll take a look and get back to you. How's that?"

It wasn't the answer Ellis hoped for, but the relationship with this man was already contentious, so it was best to let it slide. "Fair enough, Mr. Harden. Please take a look, and we'll stop back by again after we've finished speaking to your neighbors."

"Fine." He closed the door.

Fletch jerked back a little. "Let's hope the rest of these people aren't like this guy."

As they pressed on, they found that some residents were still in shock and didn't want to answer any questions, while others were more forthcoming.

One woman, in particular, caught Ellis's attention. "My

husband and I were up late watching TV when we heard a loud noise outside," she said, her voice shaking. "Like something metal dropping on the street. A clanging sound."

"Did you go outside and have a look?" Ellis asked.

"No, we didn't," she replied. "Honestly, we were scared out of our minds. You have to understand, we're not exactly young and fit anymore. But my husband called the police, and they told us to stay inside until they arrived."

"About what time was that?" Ellis asked.

The woman looked up in thought as she stood at her door. "Oh, the *Late Show* was on, so I guess about midnight, twelve thirty, maybe a little later. I was already dozing off."

Ellis scribbled down notes on her notepad. "Thank you for your time. We'll be in touch if we need anything else."

As they walked back to the car, Pelletier spoke up. "I didn't notice anything on the street. Did you?"

Ellis shrugged. "No. But if it was him on this street, we still might get lucky with a camera picking him up. Let's keep moving."

They continued to knock on doors and gather information, but it was slow going. Residents were mostly too scared or too traumatized to provide any useful information. And not everyone had cameras on their homes.

As the afternoon hit its peak, they caught up to Bevins and Lewis and offered to help them with the final few houses.

As they approached the next house, Ellis knocked on the door, and a middle-aged man answered, his face lined with worry. "Bangor Police," Ellis said, holding up her badge. "We're investigating the break-ins that have happened in your area. Can I ask your name, sir?"

"Russell Poe. I'm on the homeowners' board, and I'm

well aware of this situation." He regarded the detectives. "How many cops does it take to find this guy?"

"We're canvassing the area because of last night's murder of Vicky Boyles," Bevins said. "Sir, we're here to ask whether you think you might've captured this person over the past few days on any surveillance cameras you have around your home."

"Are you kidding me?" Poe shook his head. "I've been checking it every day. If I'd seen this asshole, you'd know by now."

But as he spoke, Ellis noticed the look on his face, as though he held back something. "Sir? Is there anything more you'd like to say?"

Poe licked his lips and swallowed hard. "Well, there was something that happened earlier in the week. I was up late, couldn't sleep with all this craziness going on, and I heard a car pull up. I didn't think much of it until I heard the door slam shut. I peeked out my window and saw a guy walking down the street. It was too dark to make out any details, but he was moving quickly. He fell out of view soon after."

"You didn't think to call us?" Lewis asked.

"No, I didn't. I guess..." He sighed heavily. "I guess I didn't really think it could be *the* guy. I mean, at that point, we'd had only a couple situations come up, and no one could be certain anyone had actually been in their home."

"But you don't have any of this on video?" Fletch asked.

"I don't. I'm sorry," Poe replied.

"Thank you for your help," Ellis said, jotting down more notes. "If you remember anything else, please don't hesitate to contact us."

They headed back toward their vehicles.

"I don't know, Becca," Bevins started. "I can't believe this intruder is so good that no one's cameras have captured him."

"Well, I'm almost certain whoever Mr. Poe heard in a car wasn't our guy anyway. Not a chance he's driving into this community, parking in front of his victims' homes and then driving off." Ellis's phone buzzed in her pocket, and she noticed the caller ID. "It's Triggs." She answered. "Hey, tell me you have some news. I'm going to put you on speaker. I've got the whole team here."

"Hey, everyone," Triggs began. "SafeHome Security. They installed the systems of four of the victims."

"Okay," Ellis replied. "What did you find out about them?"

Papers shuffled in the background as Triggs continued, "They've got a clean record as far as the business goes. Nothing out of the ordinary. No complaints. But I did find out something interesting. The owner of the company is an ex-con."

Ellis and Fletch exchanged looks. "What was he in for?" she asked.

"Assault," Triggs replied. "He did time for beating up a guy pretty badly. But that was years ago, and he's been running his business without any incidents since then. I don't think he's our guy, but it's worth checking out the staff."

"Agreed. We're still talking to the neighbors. You mind reaching out to SafeHome and digging a little deeper on that?" Ellis asked. "It's a great lead, and we could use your help on it."

"Yeah, I'll dig a little more and let you know," he added.

"Thanks, Triggs. Talk soon." Ellis ended the call. "Okay, we have one house left." She pointed behind her. "Let's see if we have better luck with them."

They arrived at their last hope, and Ellis knocked on the door.

An older man—his build still burly, but his hair in gray sprigs—answered and let his eyes roam over the detectives before he spoke. "I heard you all were talking to the neighbors. They say you're looking for video of this prick."

"Yes, sir. Do you use security cameras on your home?" Ellis asked.

"I do. Come on in. I'll let you take a look." He stepped aside. "I don't know what you'll find. I'm two streets down from where that woman was murdered. I don't know many folks on that street. But I've seen the posts on the community Facebook page."

"Well, I appreciate you giving us a chance to take a look," Ellis replied as she entered.

The man led the detectives to his office. "It's on my laptop, which I keep in here."

"You work from home, sir?" Lewis asked, seeming to take note of the several computers in the office.

"I do, as a matter of fact. I'm a financial consultant. Been home since the virus and haven't been asked to go back into work yet. Can't say it bothers me much." He took a seat behind his desk and opened his laptop. A moment later, he retrieved the files. "This is the system I use."

"Who installed it?" Ellis asked.

"I did. I'm kind of handy that way," he replied. "Anyway, the files get deleted after about a week. Otherwise, I wouldn't have room to store them all. So, you got the past week to see if this person happened to be walking along my street."

"That'll do."

Ellis and Fletch moved around to view the screen. As they watched the footage together, it became clear that nothing suspicious had occurred. The man's camera only covered a small portion of the road, but it was enough to determine that no one had used this street as a thoroughfare during the time in question; they only saw residents pulling into their own driveways.

Ellis couldn't help but feel a sense of frustration. They had canvassed the entire neighborhood, yet they still had no real leads on the killer. It was as if they were chasing a ghost. "Just when I thought we were getting somewhere," she muttered under her breath. And then she spotted something in the street. "Hang on. Can you zoom in on that thing in the road?"

"Sure." The man did as requested. "What is it?"

Ellis leaned in. "When was this?"

The man looked at the timestamp. "Two nights ago."

"The Dobsons." Ellis looked at Fletch. "He had to have barely gotten out of that house after what he did to their son. He could've been disoriented, afraid of being seen by the cops. He could've dropped something."

"Whatever that is," Bevins added. "It's not there now. I didn't see anything when we walked up."

"Maybe it's been pushed into the gutter?" Ellis said. "Let's go take a look."

They walked outside, and the team fanned out in the man's front yard and driveway. Ellis carried on toward the street, and the homeowner trailed several steps behind.

She stopped at the curb and looked left, then right. Then she squatted low and peered along the gutter for several feet. "I see it." Ellis returned upright and jogged down a ways. "Right here."

Fletch joined her, leaning in for a closer look. "A small box of tools?"

"These are tools used to pick locks. We need to bag this and send it to Forensics."

The homeowner watched them. "Do you think it could be related to the murder?"

"Given what we know, it'd better be, or we have a whole new set of problems," Ellis replied, her eyes still on the plastic box. "It's definitely worth testing for prints."

She pulled out a baggie from her pocket and carefully placed the box inside. "We'll log this as evidence and send it over to the lab for analysis. Thank you for your help, sir. We'll be in touch if we need anything else."

11

The hazy afternoon sunlight diffused through the window of the second-floor bullpen, where Ellis stood at the map on the wall only feet from her desk. The team had divvied up the CCTV footage obtained during their questioning of the residents of Woodland Heights. Ellis had requested copies from them, hoping that one of them would have picked up their suspect roaming the streets or scoping out one of their neighbors.

The case board was next to the map, and Ellis vacillated her gaze between the two. Had their suspect been in search of something in these homes? Did he know the occupants? Why those particular people? "What the hell are you looking for?" Ellis finally blurted out, as if speaking directly to the suspect himself.

Frustration built as she raked her fingers through her hair. The intruder had to have a motive for breaking into those homes. He couldn't just be doing it for the thrill of it. But what could his motive be? Money? Revenge? Something else entirely?

Her ringing cell phone interrupted her thoughts, and she answered the call. "Triggs," she said, turning back to the map. "Hey, what's going on?"

"I have news," he said. "SafeHome's owner, the ex-con I told you about? I missed something. He was charged with breaking and entering. He did time for it about a decade ago."

"Was it felony theft, or are we talking trespassing only?" Ellis contained her rising enthusiasm until she could be sure it was warranted.

"Theft," Triggs replied. "Though it wasn't in connection with SafeHome. At the time, he was working for a different home security company," he added. "You want me to bring him in and talk to him about what's been going on?"

"So we know his company did work in Woodland Heights. And at that time, of course, we're aware they didn't report any criminal activity. Now here we are, years later, and whoever's getting into these homes seems to know their systems well." Ellis paused to consider whether to raise the red flag. "We have to be careful how we play this. Find out whether this owner or any of his staff has gone back out to the Woodland Heights area in recent weeks. And then, depending on what he has to say, we can get specifics as to his whereabouts on the nights the homes were entered."

"On it. I'll let you know what I find. Oh, by the way, how'd you end up out there today?" Triggs asked.

"Nothing so far on any surveillance footage, but the team's working on that now," she replied. "But we did find a set of locksmith's tools."

"Oh, wow. That's something."

"It's something, yes," Ellis continued. "I've handed it over to Forensics, so we'll see if they can pull prints. That could be our smoking gun because, unlike the book he left at the Madsens', this was unintentional, and he could've gotten sloppy."

"Fingers crossed," Triggs added. "I'll let you know what transpires with the SafeHome guy."

Just as he was about to end the call, Ellis stopped him. "Hey, Triggs?"

"Yeah?"

"You're doing a hell of a good job. Thank you."

"Anytime, Detective."

Ellis ended the call and caught sight of McCallister approaching. "What are you doing here?" She glanced at the team, who appeared just as surprised.

He shrugged a shoulder and offered a warm smile. "Abbott said he needed all hands on deck and asked me to come in. He got a verbal from the union rep and expects the sign-off first thing tomorrow morning."

Before she could say anything more, Bevins rushed over with an outstretched hand. "Hey, man. Good to see you. What's up? Why you here?"

"Thought I'd try to help out with this Woodland Heights case." He took Bevins' hand. "Good to see you, and good to be back."

"Welcome back, Euan," Lewis called out from her desk. "'Bout time you started pulling your weight again."

"I'll try not to slack off, Gabby." He laughed. "And thanks."

It wasn't long before Fletch and Pelletier offered their greetings, too, but Ellis noticed Pelletier still seemed to hold back a little, like a part of him wasn't quite ready to accept McCallister back into his good graces.

"Okay, so if you're here to help," Ellis began, "let me give you the rundown." She walked toward the map and got him up to speed as to where the investigation had landed so far. "And the Dobsons brought in their son earlier this morning to sit down with the forensic artist. We should have a sketch soon."

"A description would kick this into gear for sure." McCallister folded his arms and appeared to examine what she'd put together.

Pelletier marched toward them. "Hey, I think I have something here."

Ellis spun around as he approached. "What is it?"

He set his laptop down on her desk. "Take a look at this." He pressed play and aimed the screen at her. "Right here. Top of the screen, right corner."

The rest of the team huddled near as Ellis zoomed in on the footage.

"Tell me that isn't someone walking by over there," Pelletier added.

Ellis narrowed her gaze as they all leaned a little closer. "That's definitely someone. What time was this?"

"According to the file," Pelletier began, "it's two thirty in the morning on the fifth."

Ellis walked around to her desk and opened the file. "A call came in on that day." As she read on, the implications became apparent. "That was the day the Barber family called. The day their dog was killed. And this location?"

Pelletier noted the name on the file. "This is from 3907 Brunswick Street."

She regarded the others. "Who talked to the people at this house today?"

"We did," Bevins said. "Me and Gabby. I remember them. What do you want to do? Should we go back and see them?"

"I don't think they'll have more to tell us, but...this could be our guy," Ellis said. "The timing works. And Triggs has a potential lead on the owner of the security company that installed a few of the systems in that area."

"Then we better find out what that guy looks like and see if he comes close to matching whoever's on that video," Lewis replied.

Ellis eyed her phone as another call came in. "When it rains, it pours."

"What is it now?" McCallister asked.

"It's Seavers." She answered the line. "Hey, you have something already on that evidence?"

"You might want to come take a look at this, Detective," he replied.

Ellis nodded. "I'm on my way." She looked back at the team. "I have to run down there. Fletch, you want to come along?"

"Let's go."

With Fletch at her side, Ellis headed downstairs, and the two women made their way toward the rear of the first floor.

Seavers, who ran the lab, met them just inside its doors. Known for his crew cut and biting wit, the stocky thirty-something had been instrumental in helping out on her other cases. He had proven himself an ally to the entire CID.

Now, he smiled at them. "I kind of like you being at my beck and call instead of the other way around."

"If you have something real, I'll jump. You just tell me how high," Ellis said. "What do you have?"

Seavers turned on his heel. "Follow me, Detectives. By the way, Fletch, nice to see you. You're not down here often."

"I try not to be," she replied. "Good to see you too."

They followed Seavers to a small room with a large table

in its center. On the table lay plastic evidence bags. One with the box of tools and the other with the hardback book Ellis had taken from the Madsen home.

Seavers motioned for them to approach. "I was able to lift a partial print off this box and the tools inside. It wasn't much, but it was enough to run it through the system. Nothing's come back on it, but I'll push it through the other databases and see what turns up."

"Okay." Ellis peered at the table. "So why the rush down here?"

"That book you handed over?" Seavers opened a file that lay next to it. "It was clean. Not a single print. However, I wanted to be sure I didn't miss anything, so I started flipping through the pages."

"And?"

With gloved hands, he opened the book and pressed it down as he reached the page. "This is inside chapter three."

Ellis examined the pages. "There's writing on here." She leaned closer. "It's a little faded, but it looks like..."

"I scanned in that page," Seavers said as he grabbed his laptop. "Come look at this. I can zoom it in." He went to work enlarging the image.

Ellis and Fletch stared at the screen, and it was Ellis who called out, "Number five."

"What the hell does that mean?" Fletch asked.

Seavers eyed them. "I was kind of hoping you two might know. The curious thing is what's written on this page. Check out the first paragraph."

"'They all knew the kind of man he was, the lies he told,'" Ellis read on. "'Yet not one of them had the courage to stand up and say something that might've put an end to his wretched behavior.'" Ellis thought about the passage for a moment. "First of all, the Madsen house was the fifth home to have been hit, and he left this book." She looked at Fletch. "So, are they the liars?"

"Or were the Madsens too afraid to speak up?" Fletch asked. "And speak up about what, if so?"

Ellis peered at the book. "So, if they are number five, that makes the Dobsons number six. And now we have Vicky Boyles—"

"She's number seven," Fletch cut in. "Will there be a number eight?"

———

A PATTERN EXISTED. A reason why this killer was going after a select few in Woodland Heights. And after comparing what Pelletier had found on the video with what Triggs had on the owner of SafeHome Security, it was easy to eliminate him as a suspect. The two looked nothing alike. So now, Ellis requested a warrant for the security company's employee records. The owner's appearance might not have matched what was found on the security footage, but that didn't mean it wouldn't match one of his employees.

Ellis prepared to head over to Hank's house, and as she reached the stationhouse lobby, she noticed Officer Mark Cohen hurrying toward her. A smile tugged at her lips. "You have it?"

Cohen was the forensic sketch artist. A younger man, just about thirty, average height and build. His only remarkable feature was a lengthy scar on the right side of his head where his hair hadn't regrown. A reminder of his tour in Afghanistan. "I have it," he confirmed, and held up his iPad. "Care to take a look?"

She joined him as the two stood in the middle of the lobby, the dusky sky casting it in shadow. "How was the boy?"

"Scared. The parents too, but this is what I got." Cohen opened the file and displayed the image. "It's as detailed as I could get. The kid didn't remember much before he was knocked out."

Ellis took hold of the iPad and studied the screen. The hooded figure looked like the Unabomber without the sunglasses. "Hair?"

"He didn't note any. It was likely concealed under his hood," Cohen replied. "But you can see the facial structure. Rounded features. He appears older, but again, it was dark, and the boy was terrified. He said the man was big. Broad shoulders. Tall."

"From the perspective of an eight-year-old, everyone looks tall." She sighed. "I'll run this through the FBI's facial program and hope for the best. Thanks for putting it together. I have some video to compare it to, as well. So, this is still something."

"Let me know if you need anything else." Cohen tipped his head. "Goodnight, Detective."

"Goodnight." Ellis made her way outside and hopped into her SUV, soon arriving at Hank's house after stopping to grab dinner for the two of them. McCallister had offered to accompany her, but this was something she wanted to do alone. And maybe part of it was making sure he didn't get too close, especially in light of Andrew's arrival. The feeling that those two worlds had suddenly collided put her on a path to isolation. It was how she reacted to situations like this.

McCallister was still in the dark about Andrew's inconvenient ask. She'd hardly had time to make any progress on his request either. Would she tell her father? And could he help? Maybe.

"Hey, Dad. Only me." Ellis walked inside. "I brought your favorite."

"A burger and fries?" he called out.

"Okay, maybe your second favorite." She moved into the living room to find him in his recliner. "I brought you a grilled chicken sandwich and a small fry."

"Second favorite, my ass." Hank reached out for the bag and quickly eyed its contents. "Thanks, kid."

Ellis settled onto the sofa and retrieved her burger and fries. "I was too late, Dad."

He took a bite of his sandwich and, with a full mouth, continued, "For what?"

"This case I've been working. I had a bad feeling this guy would up his game, and he did. He hurt a child, strangled a family pet, and now he killed a woman in her home last night. And there's a distinct possibility he might have murdered a man at a local bar. We're working to see if there's a connection." She took a sip from her soft drink. "We still have no idea who he is, and very few leads. I'm afraid he'll do it again."

Hank set down his sandwich and pivoted in his chair to face her. "What makes you think he'll strike again?"

"Because you taught me everything I know. And he's escalating this thing. I just don't know why he's targeting these people. The woman he killed last night, both she and her husband worked full-time. They had no children at home. Different than the other victims. The only thing I know is that he's numbered them."

"How do you mean?" Hank asked.

"In one of the homes, he left a book, marking it as number five, which was written beside a passage that suggested the people had been liars or knew something and kept it quiet. I don't understand his motive, and I don't know how to stop him."

They ate in silence for a moment. Ellis considered telling Hank about Andrew's situation. It was as though the more she tried to ignore it, the heavier it weighed on her. Hank had liked her ex-husband. Thought he was a good man who didn't realize what he'd gotten himself into when he married Ellis. Was there a chance Hank could offer one of his pearls of wisdom to help her see this through?

"There's something else I wanted to talk about, Dad."

He wiped his mouth with a napkin. "I'm all ears."

"Andrew showed up at my house the other night."

"Showed up?" Hank choked down a fry. "Out of the blue?"

"Yes." Ellis set down her food. "He's getting remarried. And the woman he's marrying is in some kind of legal trouble."

"Some kind?" Hank pressed. "Andrew wouldn't show up unannounced if he didn't need something from you. So what's he want you to do?"

"His fiancée is being investigated for securities fraud. She works with him at another commercial investment firm." Ellis sipped on her drink again. "I guess the IRS came in for audits and found major discrepancies. Long story short, New Haven PD is helping out the feds, and Andrew asked if there was anything I could do."

"What the hell does he think you can do about that from here?" Hank asked.

"You got me." She laughed. "But I told him I'd talk to the

detective. Find out more and see if there was anything I could do."

He nodded. "I see. So you let your guilt get the better of you, huh? Becca, you can't do anything to help him with this. Frankly, I'm not sure you should try. You're opening a can of worms here, and I think you know that."

"Yeah, well, I already told him I would. He's waiting for me to see what can be done."

"For Pete's sake." Hank shook his head. "Look, I get why you agreed, all right? I know you. I know the weight you carry. But this? This is out of your hands. Andrew must know that. Now, I suggest you make it clear to him that this is well outside your jurisdiction."

"You don't think a call to the detective might help?"

Hank scoffed. "Help with what, exactly? Look, you want to keep your word. Fine. I get it. Call the detective. I doubt he'll even say boo to you, but what the hell do I know? Then you can wish Andrew the best of luck and let him move on. This isn't your problem, kid. Let me tell you, you got enough on your plate."

Hank took a sip from his fountain drink. "So here's what you should do regarding the case you do have control over. Maybe this whole thing isn't about the victims, but the location."

Ellis swallowed. "What do you mean?"

"Well, Woodland Heights is known for its exclusivity, you could say. Maybe this killer is targeting the community itself, not necessarily the people who live there. Maybe he wants to make a statement."

Ellis considered this for a moment. "But what statement?"

"That, kiddo, is the question." Hank leaned back into his

recliner, deep in thought. "Maybe he's trying to prove something. Prove that he can get away with it. Prove that he's smarter than us. That the rich are vulnerable too."

"It's possible." Ellis nodded. "But it still doesn't give me any leads on who he could be. We've been going through security footage, interviewing neighbors, but all I have is a locksmith's tools with the prints of someone we can't ID. And then I have a book with a cryptic message and a number." She let out a sigh. "I don't know, Dad. There's a lot going on that I can't begin to explain."

Hank plunked a fry into his mouth. "Might be wise to see who's new to the area. Who's moved out recently. And if they did, why?"

"That's a good angle."

"And that's why I'm here," Hank said, raising his index finger. "Something else to consider. Given that book you talked about, I gotta think this is someone with a connection to this community. He knows the area, the people. Maybe he grew up there. Maybe he lived there once and had to leave for whatever reason. Maybe he knows their secrets. Every neighborhood has secrets. And if you want to stop him before he kills again, I suggest you find out what it is those neighbors are hiding."

12

The first step in unearthing whatever secrets lay hidden in Woodland Heights was to find out who had something to lose if their secrets were revealed—and what they might be prepared to do to keep their secret under wraps. Who in the idyllic neighborhood could've brought this intruder to haunt them? Was it one person? A group of people? Why had the intruder's attacks spread so far among the community to culminate in the murder of Vicky Boyles yesterday morning? And who exactly was Taylor Burnell, and why had he been stabbed to death as he staggered out from the bar?

While the medical examiner's office processed the body of Vicky Boyles, Ellis decided to speak with Dr. Rivera and hopefully learn more about how she died. Located in Augusta, the ME's office was just over an hour from Bangor. She would take Fletch with her on the drive to go see him.

Ellis arrived at her colleague's home not long after the sun came up. Fletch's two-bedroom townhouse was the last one in a row. It had a red-brick exterior, a door painted white, and a small concrete porch that had been decorated with flowerpots. She hadn't thought of Fletch as the flowerpot kind, which made her realize she didn't know all that much about her, even though they'd worked under the same roof for the past five years.

Fletch was almost as closed off as Ellis. Part of that was due to her dogged determination to climb the ladder and possibly move on to a bigger department in a better position. Bangor PD was a stepping stone for most, which was why the department mostly had younger detectives. This was the place to cut teeth, not make a name for yourself. But Ellis hoped Fletch would stay and run the place someday.

Fletch stepped through her front door and walked out to the driveway, where Ellis waited in her Tahoe. She climbed into the passenger seat. "Morning. Thanks for the lift."

"Sure thing. Thanks for coming along."

"Have you talked to Rivera yet?" Fletch asked, buckling her seatbelt.

"I did. He'll see us in his office—he's coming in this morning to meet us," she added. "Said he didn't want to leave it to his subordinates. But I think it's because I mentioned you'd be there."

Fletch scoffed. "Sure. okay. The guy's in his fifties and probably married."

"Doesn't stop a man from admiring a woman, last I checked." Ellis gave her a side-eye grin before returning her gaze to the road ahead. "So, listen, I know things have been weird since Euan was placed on leave, and I never got the chance to really talk to you about that. And now that he's back..."

"I did what I thought was right for the department, Becca," Fletch cut in.

"I know you did. I don't question your motives," she replied. "I understand that the situation escalated with the press and social media. It was the best solution to keep it from boiling over. I appreciate what you did, even if I never said so."

Fletch raised her brow. "Really?"

"Really. I mean, look, Euan suffered an injury. It was best to play that off as the reason."

"It was," she agreed.

"It doesn't matter now." Ellis nodded. "Things have cooled down, and I just want the team to return to normal."

"So do I, Becca." Fletch turned quiet for a moment. "You know, when he was shot, I saw the look in your eyes. It was then that I realized how much you care for him."

"My reaction wouldn't have been any different had it been any one of you guys," Ellis replied.

"Come on, Becca. This is me you're talking to. I didn't know your ex-husband well, but from what I understand, that relationship wasn't great."

"Hence the divorce." Ellis smiled but stayed mum on Andrew's return.

"Exactly. But with Euan..." She glanced through the windshield. "I guess I was afraid you'd defend him at the cost of your own exposure. That was my greatest fear. I thought, the way things were going with the press and such, that they'd dig up your past. I couldn't let that happen. I had to shut it down."

Guilt weighed down on Ellis's shoulders now. Her past was hers to bear. No one else's. And to hear Fletch speak of protecting her, well, Ellis realized just how selfish she'd become. "I'm sorry you felt the need to do that, Fletch. It's not something that should've come into consideration."

"Yeah, well." Fletch shrugged, her tough exterior appearing to harden once again. "Like you said, it's over now, and things can get back to the status quo."

They fell silent for the rest of the drive, with only the radio keeping them company until they arrived at the ME's office in Augusta. The old-style architecture was reminiscent of the late sixties with its off-white masonry block exterior and rectangular shape. The parking lot was nearly empty this early in the morning.

The detectives made their way to the entrance, where Ellis pressed an intercom button on the side of the door; the extra layer of security was due to it being outside normal business hours. "Bangor PD. Detectives Ellis and Fletcher here to see Dr. Rivera."

A moment later, the lock clicked, and Ellis opened the door. She led the way inside, and the two reached the front desk, where Ellis displayed her badge. "Good morning. We have an appointment with Dr. Rivera."

"You can go through," the man replied.

"Thanks." Ellis waved Fletch to follow as the two entered through the double doors into the wide, stark hallway. Toward the end was Rivera's office. Ellis had been here plenty lately, but still the smell of chemicals and death was never really something she got used to. She rapped a knuckle on the door.

"Come in," the doctor called out.

Ellis and Fletch stepped inside, "Dr. Rivera," Ellis began, "thanks for meeting us." She gestured to Fletch. "I think you've met Detective Lori Fletcher."

"It's been a minute." Fletch offered her hand. "Appreciate the help on this, Doc."

"Of course." He accepted the greeting. "Anytime I can help Bangor PD, I'm all in."

Ellis picked up on the smile he offered Fletch and considered that she might have been right about Rivera. "So, we'd like to take a look at Vicky Boyles. The victim brought in yesterday."

"Absolutely. Follow me." Rivera led the way out into the hall again, where they reached a door not far from his office, labeled Autopsy Room 1. "She's in here, Detectives."

They followed him into the autopsy room. The woman's body was already on the table on the right side of the room. A sheet pulled up to her face.

Ellis noticed the jar on the nearby counter. She knew enough about this process to realize that jar contained the contents of the woman's stomach. As she approached the table, the sink, which was a few feet away, had trails of blood flowing into it.

"I thought it best to get started right away," Rivera said, following her gaze. "This time of year, the warmer weather doesn't help with the decomp."

Ellis pressed her hand under her nose as though that might stop the putrid odor from filling her senses. It didn't. "I understand."

Dr. Rivera approached the table and pulled back the sheet, revealing the woman's bloated face and the large contusion on her head.

"My God," Fletch muttered under her breath.

Ellis darted a glance to her as she stepped closer to the table. The top of the Y-incision was exposed just below the woman's neck. Spider veins on her cheeks had spread, and her lips were purple. She'd struck her head, and the gouge was obvious. But it was the bruising on her neck that most interested Ellis. "Strangulation."

"The injuries are consistent with a brief struggle," Rivera began. "And then manual strangulation, yes. But she most certainly died from the trauma to her skull. It resulted in terminal blood loss."

Ellis walked around the body, examining the victim's hands. "Defensive wounds."

"Yes," Rivera confirmed. "I've scraped under the nails and am hopeful I'll find DNA. And given the close contact, we stand a chance at finding DNA through hair and skin transfer."

"That would be helpful," Ellis said. "And as always…"

"Time is of the essence," he cut in. "I appreciate that."

"Noted, Dr. Rivera." Ellis continued to view the body. As she did, she noticed something odd about Boyles' neck. She leaned in closer and studied the bruising more carefully. "Doc, take a look at this," Ellis said, pointing to the bruise marks. "This looks like an imprint from a ring. It's too perfect to be anything else. Could this have been made by a wedding ring?"

Rivera homed in on the area. "I'd say that's a fair guess. I'll, of course, take photos and examine it more closely."

Fletch stepped in with some hesitation. "This could help us ID the suspect."

"I'm not sure," Ellis replied. "But it does offer telling information about Vicky Boyles's killer." She turned to Fletch. "He's married."

THE SECRETS within the Woodland Heights community begged to be exhumed. While Ellis hadn't gleaned as much information from Rivera as she'd hoped, the crucial detail of learning that the suspect wore what looked like a wedding ring offered new insight. But still they had no way to identify him.

When Ellis and Fletch returned to the station, they made their way upstairs to the bullpen. Ellis noticed Pelletier was at his desk. "Morning. Still busy with the restaurant case?"

"Just more legwork," he began. "Figured I needed to make up for lost time."

"Yeah, sorry about that. I owe you." Ellis continued to her desk. "We were in Augusta, meeting with Rivera."

"And how'd that go?" Pelletier asked.

"Becca noticed the suspect was wearing a ring when he choked his victim," Fletch chimed in. "It left an imprint on her skin."

"Good catch," Pelletier replied.

"I'm not sure where that will take us, but it's something," Ellis said. "I also have the sketch from the Dobson boy. Cohen caught up with me as I was leaving last night." She opened her laptop and retrieved the file. "It's not much, but we can run it through the database and see if we get a hit."

Fletch and Pelletier hovered near to glance at the image. "Have you compared it to the video yet?" Fletch asked.

"No." She peered over her shoulder at Pelletier. "You mind taking a look for us? Fletch and I were about to take a deep dive into the people who live in Woodland Heights. Find out how they are connected besides living in the same neighborhood. When they moved, where they came from."

"I'm on it," Pelletier said.

"I appreciate it." Ellis returned her attention to Fletch. "Backgrounds first. Home purchases. Employment. All that."

"You got it," Fletch replied.

Ellis surveyed the bullpen. "Anyone know where Euan is? I thought he'd be here already."

In that moment, Bevins rounded the corner and entered, holding a cup of coffee. "I think he's still with HR and Admin, filling out paperwork."

"Of course." Ellis glanced at McCallister's empty desk. "That'll take a while."

Together, Ellis and Fletch began combing through public records and social media profiles, trying to piece together the lives of the victims. Ellis took notes on each of them, jotting down any inconsistencies or red flags that could potentially be useful in their investigation.

As far as they knew, the intruder first arrived at the Johnson family home. Ellis had learned that they'd purchased their home five years earlier from an older couple, who'd owned it since it was built.

Then she looked into the Mannings. Another couple with two teenaged sons. The wife was a stay-at-home mother. The husband worked in finance. They'd moved into the community six years ago after his transfer to a firm in the area.

Nothing in either of these families' histories suggested anything furtive. But this was just the beginning. Complaints issued to the homeowners' association would be next on her list. Who were the people filing the complaints? Had it been any of the victims? Was this a revenge tactic?

As she continued, Ellis found the community Facebook page for Woodland Heights. "Hey, Fletch, you have a second to take a look at this?"

Fletch walked around her desk and joined Ellis.

"Pull up a chair," Ellis said, waiting for her to sit. "I don't know how far you've gotten, but I've tracked down this page."

Fletch examined it. "Okay. I hear people can get pretty nasty in these groups."

"Well, let's take a look at what these neighbors have discussed. Obviously, the intruder, but let's go back farther." Ellis stopped. "Shit. I can't."

Fletch squinted at the message on the screen. "It's a private group."

"Of course it is." Ellis let out a frustrated sigh. "That was all feeling a little too easy."

Fletch leaned back in her chair, appearing to mull over how best to bypass this hiccup. "We'll just contact the page admin, who's probably a board member, and ask them to grant us access."

"It's worth a shot," Ellis agreed as she quickly composed a message to the group administrator, detailing their involvement in the investigation.

As they waited for a response, Ellis and Fletch continued to scour through public records and online information, trying to find any connections between the victims. Another thirty minutes had passed before Ellis's phone buzzed with a notification. "We're in," she said.

They huddled around the computer screen, scrolling through the posts on the page.

"As I thought, several about the intruder. They're obviously terrified," Ellis said. "But let's look back before this started. I want to see if there's anything that could point to some friction among the residents."

Fletch nodded as they scrolled.

Most of the posts were mundane, discussing community events, agendas for meetings and lost pets. But then they came across a post from a year ago. It was from a resident complaining about a neighbor's loud parties on the weekends that disturbed their peace and quiet.

Ellis took note of the date and the names of the residents involved. She continued scrolling and found another post from a few months earlier, this time from a different resident. They were complaining about a neighbor who always parked their car in a way that blocked their driveway.

"So, we have some conflicts among the residents," Fletch said. "But they're pretty standard. Nothing that screams motive for murder."

Ellis nodded. "Agreed. Let me take a look at something else. We'll check our records to see if anyone's filed a police complaint in the neighborhood over the past few years."

"Yeah, and maybe someone was driven out of the community?" Fletch suggested.

"Anything's possible right now." She was retrieving the records when Fletch stopped her.

"Wait!" Fletch held out her phone. "Oh my God. Look at this."

Ellis took hold of the device and viewed the screen. "What? Wait, this has to be in our files somewhere." She returned to her computer. "Why didn't we know about this?"

"I have no idea," Fletch said.

"Well, this is a secret, a huge one." Ellis continued to pull up the file. "I got it." She opened the case, trying to tamp down on the adrenaline rising in her. "This was filed three years ago. Why don't I remember it?"

Fletch reviewed the report. "Because Finley handled it. Look at the badge number and signature."

"Of course," Ellis said. "And then he eventually left like everyone else."

"And Euan was his replacement."

Ellis read on, summarizing for her colleague. "The victim's family lived in Woodland Heights at the time, but the girl's body was found in Augusta." She turned to Fletch. "The case was transferred because she wasn't found here in Bangor. All that was left of the investigation was the original missing persons report."

"Okay, so what happened to the family?" Fletch continued. "The parents?"

"There's nothing more here," Ellis said. "We'll have to see what Augusta PD has on file."

"This could be what we're looking for," Fletch said. "But we need to remember that the community hasn't seen any trouble since. A couple of nuisance complaints and that's it."

"And we have to wonder how it would've involved anyone in the community to begin with. That's the real question." Ellis leaned back and crossed her arms. "There's a lot we don't know about this, so we'd better find out. And fast. What concerns me most is that if this is in any way connected to the victim in Augusta, then maybe her killer has decided to return to Woodland Heights."

ELLIS MADE this trip to Augusta alone. She was set to meet with the detective who had worked the nearly three-year-old investigation.

She walked inside and noticed the Augusta police station looked about the same as it had the last time she was here—the day she murdered her stepfather. Ellis recalled the cop who had taken care of her that day. How she'd brought her in and called Hank. Ellis had been left alone to deal with the ramifications of what she'd done. Seeing her mother dead on the living room floor. Her stepfather, dead from a gunshot wound, in a pool of blood not far from her. And all Ellis could think to do at that time was call the police. Not Hank. Their relationship had been different in those days. But everything had changed after that.

To be here again felt surreal and brought back memories she'd tried hard to keep locked away. Part of the reason she was a good cop was her ability to close herself off, or at least parts of herself. The downside was that, seeing as how those parts hadn't seen the light of day in years, she couldn't help but wonder what might happen when they did.

Ellis spotted a man leaning on the counter of the front desk, scrolling through his phone. Dressed in khaki cargo shorts and a navy polo, he looked like he'd just walked off the ninth hole, but there was little doubt in her mind that he was the man she needed to see.

"Detective Naylor?" Ellis asked on her approach. When he turned his attention to her, she offered her hand. "I'm Detective Rebecca Ellis, Bangor PD. We spoke on the phone."

"Ah, yes. That's me. Rob Naylor." He put away his phone and shook her hand. "Thanks for coming all this way. You'll forgive my appearance."

"Not at all. It seems I've taken you away from what apparently might have been a nice afternoon of golf."

"Very observant, Detective." Naylor appeared to be in his early forties. Moderately fit with only a slight paunch. A thick head of black hair, and soulful brown eyes. "Why don't we talk in my office?"

"Sure." Ellis trailed him as he started away and noticed he wasn't much taller than she was, maybe five feet ten at best. "I really appreciate your willingness to set aside some time for me, Detective."

"Not at all." Naylor opened his office door. "Come in and take a seat." He gestured, then walked in behind her. "This case you're working sounds intriguing."

"It's driving me nuts, if I'm being honest." Ellis filled him in on the state of the investigation, including the recent murder. "And then my colleague and I happened across a Facebook page and started looking into the interactions between the neighbors and the community."

"Yeah, I hear those community groups are for the old ladies always looking out the window to see who's driving too fast on their street." Naylor chuckled.

"That was pretty much the extent of it," Ellis added. "But then we looked for police complaints. Noise, trash, whatever..." She took a beat. "That was when we saw the missing persons report for Jenna Brooks."

Naylor drew in a deep breath and returned a grimace. "Yeah, that was mine. I found her in the woods near some popular hiking trails."

"How did she die?" Ellis asked.

"It was a brutal murder." Naylor rubbed his face with his palms, as if recoiling from the memory. "She was stabbed multiple times, and her throat was slashed. We never found the murder weapon or her killer."

Ellis had read that the victim was young, a teenager, which made it even harder to hear the vicious nature of her death. "Did you have any suspects?"

"We had a few leads, but none of them panned out. Jenna was only sixteen. She was a good kid. Didn't get into trouble. Her parents were devastated. They moved away not long after the case went cold."

Ellis had seen that plenty of times before. Some parents simply didn't have it in them to stay in the home where their child had once lived. "It has got me thinking that there could be a connection to what's happening in Woodland Heights now."

Naylor shrugged. "It's hard to say. Jenna's case was a while ago, and we never ID-ed a suspect. But it is possible some aspects of the two investigations are tied together."

Ellis regarded him. "I'd like to take a look at everything you have on Jenna Brooks, Detective."

13

Augusta Police Detective Naylor hadn't been as forthcoming as Ellis had hoped on first meeting him. Cold cases were a touchy subject that often plagued a detective's career. She suspected this had been the case with Naylor, which made her job that much harder. He feared she would find something that he'd missed. She could only hope.

With reluctance, he handed over copies of everything related to the Jenna Brooks investigation.

Now, she drove back to Bangor as the sun hung lower in the sky. A call came in, and she pressed the button to answer. "Connor, hi. What's going on?"

"Is this a bad time?" he asked.

"Not at all. I'm heading back from Augusta."

"Listen, I'm out here at the Lighthouse bar, taking a second look at the grounds. You busy? I wouldn't mind another set of eyes."

"Not at all. I can be there in about forty minutes."

"I'll wait. See you soon."

The discussion had already occurred that this murder was somehow connected to the Woodland Heights intruder. Combined with her own theories about the Jenna Brooks case, this investigation had gotten a whole lot hairier.

She continued onward into the city and soon arrived at the bar, noticing Bevins out front. The place had been closed since the murder, and he was there alone. Mistake number one. Chain of custody regarding evidence was often brought into question in situations when a single cop happened upon something relevant.

Ellis parked near the front where Bevins' shiny black Mustang stood out. The bar was an older establishment in need of updates, as was the area in which it was located. She stepped out of the Tahoe and caught up to him as he walked toward her.

"Thanks for coming," he said.

"Of course." Ellis surveyed the parking lot. "You know you shouldn't be out here alone, Connor. It's a breach of protocol."

"It was spur of the moment," he replied. "I just needed to take another look."

"Why? What were you hoping to find?" she pressed.

"Evidence," he stated. "The knife. Something left behind." He set his hands on his hips. "The guy who was killed—Taylor Burnell—he worked for a remodeler. Just a regular guy who came here after work on most nights, according to his wife. Didn't hurt anyone. Didn't have enemies. Why would he have been a target for anyone, let alone the intruder?"

"I don't know," Ellis said as she looked down at the bloodstain on the asphalt where the victim's truck had been parked. "And we can't be sure they're connected."

"Come on, Becca. These incidents happened within, what, an hour of each other? Less than an hour?"

She shrugged, knowing he had a point. "I'll help you look around. Where do you want to start?"

Bevins looked on. "We know the man was killed near his vehicle. The killer never went inside."

"Where's the vehicle?" Ellis asked.

"Seavers has it, but so far, he hasn't recovered foreign prints or DNA."

Ellis nodded. "So the killer overpowers the man, gets close enough to stab him eight times, and then leaves him."

"Right. Are we talking a big guy, then—or at least strong?" Bevins asked.

Ellis considered the video and the artist's sketch. The intruder appeared to be a sizable man, which would track with this suspect's ability to wage such a brutal attack on Burnell. "A drunk man would have a diminished ability to fight back, that's for sure. We don't know how drunk the victim was at the time. The ME should've run a blood alcohol test right away. It's Rivera, so I'm sure he did. That'll tell you whether the victim was intoxicated—"

"Making it easier for him to be overpowered," Bevins added.

"Exactly."

A car sped along the street, catching Ellis's eye. "Was this place on his way home from work?"

Bevins appeared to consider the question. "Yeah, it is, actually."

"Where did he live?"

He pointed south. "Out that way a few miles, in an apartment complex."

"Okay. Talk to his neighbors." She returned her gaze to

him. "Find out what cars they drive, and see if you get a match to any of the tire tracks found here."

"You think it was one of his neighbors?" Bevins asked.

She returned his gaze. "Won't know until you start asking some questions."

ELLIS ARRIVED home and slipped into shorts and a T-shirt before grabbing a bottle of beer from the fridge. She spread out the Jenna Brooks files on her kitchen table and sat down with her laptop. The sun had almost set, but at the height of summer, it wasn't ready to relinquish its authority just yet. The rays sent shimmers of light into her living room, leaving a golden hue inside.

She began to review the details of the investigation into the murder of Jenna Brooks. Ellis's mind raced with possibilities as she delved deeper into the case. The more she read, the more she felt like Jenna's murder was connected to the recent break-ins and murder in Woodland Heights. But a connection wasn't obvious—not yet. The victims were different. The targets were families, not children. And only one person had been murdered, and given the state of the crime scene, it appeared like a struggle had taken place. Maybe he'd never intended to kill Vicky Boyles. He hadn't killed the Dobson boy, which suggested some manner of conscience—or deliberation.

As she continued to read through the files, a knock interrupted her thoughts. She got up from her dining chair and walked to the front door. Upon opening it, she found herself face-to-face with McCallister.

"Hey, stranger," McCallister said, suddenly appearing as

though he wasn't supposed to be there. "Uh, we were getting together tonight, weren't we?"

Ellis hesitated for a moment. "Yes. Yes, we were. I'm so sorry. I completely lost track of time." She glanced at her phone. "I had no idea it was already seven." She stepped aside. "Come in—please."

McCallister walked in and glanced at her dining table. "Wow. You've been busy. What is all this?" He picked up one of the files and flipped through the papers.

She set her hands on her hips. "It's a cold case from Augusta PD. The murder of a sixteen-year-old girl named Jenna Brooks. I think there might be a connection to what's going on in Woodland Heights."

McCallister's eyes widened as he set down the file. "What makes you think that?"

Ellis pulled out a photo of the girl and her parents. "They lived in Woodland Heights when she was abducted from the neighborhood three years ago. Whoever took her drove out to some woods in Augusta and slashed her throat. So, yeah, I think this could be something."

McCallister nodded, taking a seat at the table. "Three years ago, and we're only hearing about this now?"

She pulled out a chair. "That's the thing. Your predecessor worked on this case when it was a missing persons. I don't recall much, if anything, about it. After the body was found in Augusta, he transferred the files to Detective Naylor."

"And not one neighbor mentioned this?" McCallister asked.

"No. Then again, why would they think a prowler would be connected to a former neighbor whose daughter was killed in Augusta three years ago?"

"Fair point." He nodded.

She fanned out the files on the table. "I have to look into the family. Jenna's family. According to our own reports, they made the missing persons request. From there, days later, she was found in Augusta. So if we can find out more about this family's time in Woodland Heights, who knew this girl or this family—maybe something will open up for us."

"What I'm hearing is that you think the killer has come back to terrorize the same neighborhood?" McCallister asked.

"Hard to think of another reason," she replied. "I can pull records on who lived there during that time. Who lives in the Brooks home now. Maybe they were a victim."

McCallister nodded. "Sounds like you'll want to speak to the Brooks family as well."

She eyed the files and turned her gaze to him. "So now that you're back on the clock, you want to help me with this or not?" Her phone buzzed with an incoming text message. Ellis noticed the caller ID and grabbed it off the table. She glanced at McCallister, who didn't seem to pick up on the fact that it was Andrew.

> Please. Can you meet tonight? I'm running out of time.

"Everything okay?" McCallister asked.

"Of course." She pocketed her phone. "But it looks like I need to run out for a while. Raincheck?"

THE DECISION TO keep this from McCallister felt like a betrayal. Nothing was going to happen with Andrew, that was an absolute certainty. But Ellis had kept this whole issue from him, nonetheless. However, tugging at that thread might unravel feelings she wasn't prepared to address. At least, not now when she was after a killer.

Ellis wore a loose black T-shirt and dark jeans. Her hair was pulled back in a short ponytail. A few blond strands floated around her cheeks. She entered the bar where she'd spent many an occasion with her team. Sometimes to celebrate, sometimes to console one another. Andrew knew the Waterfront was where the cops hung out. He wanted to be seen there with her. Manipulation was a strong word, but it sure seemed to be exactly what was happening right now.

She made her way to a booth at the back along the window overlooking the Penobscot River. "This isn't the best time for me, Andrew."

"I know. I'm sorry." He rose from the chair and opened his arms as if for an embrace. "Thank you for coming."

When he went in for a hug, Ellis took a small step back and minimized the contact. "I don't have anything for you, if that's what you were hoping." She sat across from him.

"I realize that. I also realize I've dumped a pile of shit right into your lap. But I have to know if you can help us, Becca," Andrew said. "Myra didn't steal from anyone. She's innocent."

"What are you drinking?" Ellis asked.

"Vodka tonic. You want one?" He raised his hand to garner the server's attention. When he arrived, Andrew began, "She'll have a vodka—"

"Cranberry, please," Ellis cut in. "Vodka cranberry."

"Of course. I'll be right back with that." The server took his leave.

She donned a tight-lipped grin. "I'm not a fan of tonic."

"I should've remembered." He sipped on his drink with apparent apprehension.

"Look, Andrew, I'm not sure what it is you think I can do for you. I've hardly had a chance to ask around—"

"I love her, Becca. Please. She needs your help." Andrew looked at his drink, tracing the rim of the glass with his index finger. "I realize now that you were right to call it quits. As much as it hurt—and it did. We are two very different people, and it took me a long time to see that."

Ellis expected Andrew to move on, and he had. So had she. Nevertheless, his words stung. To hear him say he loved another woman ripped open a wound she didn't realize hadn't fully healed.

She'd become an expert at locking away aspects of her life. Refusing to deal with them while they simmered in her subconscious. But now, those old feelings rose to the surface, yet she knew they weren't real. They were remnants of a past she hadn't let go of yet.

Despite all this, Ellis saw Andrew's pain. He did love Myra, and it was clear that he feared for her.

The server set down her drink.

"Thank you." Ellis examined the sweet libation while she pondered the predicament in which she found herself. "Give me tomorrow. I'll call the detective. He doesn't have to tell me a thing, but I'll ask. Maybe he can direct me to the agent he's working with."

"Thank you, Becca. I mean it." He looked up at her, his face wearing regret. "You know, I thought when we were married, all I wanted was a family. But I realize now that I was asking you to change who you were. And I'm so sorry. You deserved—you deserve—better than that."

She took a long sip of her drink before continuing, "Just answer this one question for me, Andrew, okay?"

"Of course. Anything."

"Say I go into this thing, talk with the detective, see the evidence, assuming he lets me. I do all this and find out something you might not want to know. Do you still want me to tell you?"

Andrew set down his glass. "What the hell kind of question is that?"

"The kind that demands an honest answer."

A NEW MORNING brought with it a new perspective as Ellis arrived at the station. She made her way to Abbott's office for a quick rundown of where things stood. "Sarge?"

Abbott removed his reading glasses; his eyes crinkled as he grinned at her. "Good morning. Come on in. Catch me up."

Ellis walked inside and took a seat. She briefed him on the visit to the ME's office and the Augusta cold case. "Given what we know now about Detective Naylor and the cold case, this is a good opportunity to learn more about Jenna Brooks. She lived in Woodland Heights with her family, sir. If we can find out who knew her or her family, it could point to the idea that this neighborhood is once again being targeted."

Abbott leaned back in his chair, his hands steepled in front of him. "It's worth exploring. What's your plan?"

"I'd like to start with interviewing Jenna's family and the neighbors who knew them," Ellis said.

Abbott nodded. "Agreed. I want Fletch in on this with you."

"Yes, sir," Ellis replied. "We can also cross-reference the police complaints in Woodland Heights with Jenna's case to see if any of the same names show up in both cases."

"All right then. Get started on those interviews and keep me updated on any progress."

Ellis left Abbott's office with a renewed sense of purpose. She still didn't know how the pieces fit together—the lock-pick tools, the wedding-band imprint on the murder victim, the seemingly unrelated stabbing to death of a man outside a bar—but she had a connection to a killing that had likely rocked that community, and maybe this current chain of events was its reverberating aftereffect.

She stopped by to see Fletch at her desk. "You want to join me a minute? I have some new details on the Woodland Heights prowler."

"Absolutely." Fletch rose from her chair and followed Ellis to the whiteboard mounted on the far wall.

"I followed up on that lead we found regarding Jenna Brooks. I drove to Augusta to meet with Detective Rob Naylor, who worked on the case."

"And?" Fletch asked, peering at the board.

"I want to pull the names of the residents who lived there at the time the girl was murdered. It was only three years ago, so who knows whether anyone moved in or out during that time."

Fletch cocked her head. "And the point in that?"

"I have a theory." Ellis focused on the board again. "I think whoever killed Jenna Brooks has come back to taunt the Woodland Heights community for unknown reasons.

And now that a woman is dead because of his actions, I'm thinking he feels set free. Ready to take another life. Ready to take out his aggression on the people in Woodland Heights."

"It's a theory," Fletch replied.

Ellis picked up on the tone in her voice. "You don't agree?"

"The question is why?" Fletch pressed. "Why risk coming back? And what have those people done to warrant his actions?"

Ellis crossed her arms. "Maybe that will become clearer once I've had a chance to speak to the Brooks family. I can read files all day long, but talking to the parents will tell us what they think happened and why."

Fletch nodded, appearing to see the sense of this. "I'll look into property records of who lived there during that time—and if anyone moved out, I'll get their names too."

Ellis grabbed her phone. "Sounds like a plan. I'll start with the Brooks family."

The trick now was to reach out without offering them hope that she would be able to find their daughter's killer. The cold case was still cold, but a chance existed that it was now connected to this current case.

According to Naylor's file, the parents lived in New Jersey. The last known phone number might or might not be accurate, but all Ellis could do was make the call and find out. The line rang several times before someone finally answered. "Hello, is this Mr. Joel Brooks?"

"Yes," the man answered. "Who's this?"

"I'm Detective Rebecca Ellis, Bangor Police. I'd like to talk to you about the cold case involving your daughter, Jenna."

"You mean about how my daughter was murdered?" he shot back. "Have you found something new?"

"Uh, no, sir." Ellis closed her eyes a moment, regretting offering even an ounce of hope. "I'm calling to learn more about the community you lived in—Woodland Heights. I'd like to talk with you about some of your neighbors."

"What? That's a peculiar request," he replied.

"I'm aware, sir, but you see, someone else, a woman, has been murdered in your old neighborhood. And I'm thinking that could mean the person who took your daughter has come back. If so, I'd like to understand why that might be."

Brooks let out an audible sigh on the other end of the call. "I live in New Jersey now, Detective. I don't see how I can help you. I moved away from that place after Jenna died. I'm sure you can understand why."

"Yes, sir, of course," she replied. "Can I ask—did you have any reason at all to suspect someone from your neighborhood? Someone from her school?"

"You're asking the same questions that Detective Naylor asked me. And I can give you the same answer—no."

Ellis had the file in front of her, and she looked at the crime scene photos. The girl's clothing was scattered around her body, which was facedown on the forest floor. And as she looked at the images while speaking with the girl's father, she realized that maybe what she should be asking was along an entirely different line. "Mr. Brooks, I understand that bringing this up forces you to relive that painful time—"

"But?" he interjected.

"But I wanted to ask you something else. Now, I get it if you don't want to meet in person. I understand. But the day your daughter went missing, who did you talk to?"

"The police," he replied.

"That's not quite what I mean," she added. "What I mean to say is, who in your circle of friends, your neighbors, did you go to and ask if they'd seen your daughter? Because I assume she'd been missing, and then, when you realized she was gone, you started making calls."

"That sounds about right," he said, his voice softening. "I suppose I contacted my neighbor at the time. Jake Gladstone. He and his wife have a daughter who was friends with Jenna."

"Okay, and according to the initial police report your address was 1129 Essex Street."

"That's correct. And it was my neighbor, Jake, at 1127, who I called first."

Ellis quickly typed in the address to cross-reference the police reports that had come in recently. That address didn't appear on her screen.

"Detective Ellis, are you searching for the person who murdered my daughter, or the person who murdered the woman in Woodland Heights?"

Ellis took in a breath. "I think they might be one and the same."

14

Pushback from Joel Brooks was to be expected. The man had lost his daughter, and no one had found her killer. His cooperation was something Ellis assumed would be a stretch. But knowing that Jake Gladstone had been the first person Brooks contacted after Jenna's disappearance, and that he still lived in Woodland Heights, gave her something she could work with. Something that might lead to proof her theory was right.

Fletch held the file in her hand, glancing down as she walked toward Ellis's desk. "I've cross-referenced the Brooks case with the current investigation." She stopped and looked up at her. "Any luck contacting the family?"

Ellis leaned back in her chair, tossing a pen onto her desk. "I just got off the phone with Joel Brooks—the father. Needless to say, he wasn't feeling very cooperative. But he did mention that his next-door neighbor at the time, Gladstone, was the guy he contacted before the police about his daughter. He still lives there, but it doesn't appear that his family has been victimized by the intruder."

Fletch turned down her lips and nodded. "Okay, that's something. Sounds like we'll want to push forward with speaking to the families directly associated with the Brooks case."

"My thoughts exactly." Ellis got up from her desk and grabbed her things. "You ready to head there now?"

Fletch gestured outward. "Lead the way."

Ellis jogged down the steps to the first-floor lobby. Peering through the glass door, she noticed a clouded sky and glanced back over her shoulder at Fletch. "Looks like rain."

"And here I am without my umbrella," Fletch quipped.

Ellis pushed outside and walked into the parking lot. Dark gray clouds hung low, and a moderate breeze brushed against her skin. She pressed the remote to unlock her Tahoe and climbed into the driver's seat. After Fletch entered, she fired up the engine and headed out toward the highway, north to Woodland Heights.

"Do we know if Mr. Gladstone is at home?" Fletch asked.

"Probably not, but the wife doesn't work outside the home. I'd like to speak to her first anyway. That way, we stand a better chance at building a complete picture." Her phone rang, and she checked the ID. "I need to take this." Ellis answered the call. "Detective Alcott, thank you for calling me back."

"It's not every day you get a call from a detective whose ex-husband is involved with the target of my investigation," he replied. "How can I help you today?"

Ellis noticed the curious look on Fletch's face. "Like you said, I was contacted by Andrew Cofield. He's asked me to look into things for him."

"Look into what, exactly, Detective Ellis?" Alcott asked.

"Your investigation." She pressed her lips together, knowing this wasn't the place to be having this conversation. Fletch would ask questions. "Forgive me, I realize how this sounds. I suppose I'm looking to help out a friend. What can you tell me about your case against Myra Cook? Do the feds have something concrete?"

"She's a suspect in an ongoing fraud investigation. That's what I can tell you," he shot back. "You want to know more about it? Why don't you come down to see me? I'll tell you what I know. But I won't jeopardize this case, you understand what I'm saying?"

"Yes, sir, I do." The time it would take for her to go to New Haven and dig into this was time Ellis didn't have. But she'd given Andrew her word. She glanced again at Fletch, whose face still wore confusion. "Listen, I can't get down there, but if you have time, could we set up a call?"

Alcott sighed loudly through the line. "All right. I'll give you my time. I'll tell you what I can, but I'll ask that you do me a solid and keep it to yourself. I'm only agreeing to this on the off chance you and I might cross paths again and I can remind you of the favor. How's Friday, nine a.m.?"

"That would be fine, Detective. Thank you."

"Speak to you then. Goodbye."

Ellis heard the line click on the other end and glanced at Fletch. "So, I should probably explain all that."

"Might be a good idea," she replied.

"Andrew—my ex-husband—has found himself in a situation. Well, not him, but his fiancée," she began.

"So, he's here? What does he think you can do about it?" Fletch asked.

"He showed up out of the blue the other night. Asked for my help. As far as what I can do? That's a damn good question." Ellis made the turn into the Woodland Heights neighborhood. "First, let's talk to Mrs. Gladstone and see what she can recall about Jenna Brooks."

They arrived at the front door of the Gladstone home. Ellis knocked, and the wife opened it. "Mrs. Gladstone. Detectives Ellis and Fletcher."

"Oh. What can I do for you?" The middle-aged woman smoothed down her short brown hair dusted with gray roots, as though their arrival had caught her off guard.

Ellis returned her badge to her pocket. "We'd like to ask you some additional questions, if you don't mind. Questions about Jenna Brooks." She noticed Mrs. Gladstone's expression shift.

"Okay. Of course," she said as she stepped aside. "Come in."

"Thank you," Ellis replied. "Is your husband available to speak?"

"He's at work." She closed the door behind them. "I'll answer your questions as best I can." Mrs. Gladstone ushered them into the relaxed and inviting living room. "Please, sit down."

Fletch joined Ellis as they sat on the edge of the light beige sofa.

Ellis reached for her notepad. "The Brooks family lived next door to you, right?"

"Yes, ma'am. They did." Mrs. Gladstone aimed to her right. "Just over there." She took her seat in a chair across from them. "Jake and Joel were good friends. Of course, all that changed after Jenna was taken. Our oldest daughter, who's just gone off to college, was friends with Jenna at the time. It was a terribly difficult situation."

"Did your husband and Mr. Brooks stay in contact after they moved away?" Ellis asked.

"No, ma'am." Mrs. Gladstone glanced away for a moment. "Joel and Maggie didn't stay in touch with anyone after they left. I don't blame them."

"Is there anything you can tell us about what happened to Jenna?" Ellis pressed. "We know Mr. Brooks reached out to your husband, thinking your daughter might've known where Jenna had gone."

"Yes, but unfortunately our daughter hadn't heard from Jenna that day." Her eyes reddened. "Excuse me. It's still fresh in mind—those days. And now with this situation here." She hesitated a moment. "Is that why you're here? Is that same killer looking for someone else to take?"

"We don't know anything right now, Mrs. Gladstone." Ellis raised a preemptive hand. "I'm sorry, I don't mean to upset you."

She wiped away a tear. "Well, it's a little too late for that. We've already lost one person here."

"Did you know Vicky Boyles?" Fletch asked.

Mrs. Gladstone cleared the emotion from her throat. "No, not directly. We were all at the homeowners' meeting last week, though."

"Going back to Jenna's disappearance," Ellis cut in. "What can you tell me about those days?"

"Well, the police talked to all of us, of course, when it happened," she replied. "Jake stuck close to Joel and Maggie. Tried to comfort them. So did I, but what can anyone do in that situation? Honestly, I was just so glad it wasn't my daughter. And believe me, I know how that sounds."

"Not at all, ma'am," Ellis said. "But going back to that

time, do you remember anyone who was associated with the Brooks family who seemed suspicious in some manner?"

"Gosh." The woman sighed. "I do remember Joel getting into a fight with the neighbor behind him. The Johnsons. That was right after Jenna went missing, but before they found her body in Augusta."

The Johnsons were the first home believed to have been hit. Ellis glanced knowingly at Fletch. "A fight? Was anyone seriously injured?"

"I don't think so. Punches were thrown. I think that was about it. Tensions were very high, as you might imagine."

"Of course. Do you remember what the fight was about?" Ellis pressed.

"No. You'd have to speak with Mr. Johnson. I couldn't tell you. But Joel wasn't quick to anger. He was a calm man, very rational."

"Are you friends with the family who live in the Brooks' home now?" Fletch asked.

"No, not really. They have young children. They're younger than Jake and me, so we just don't have that much in common."

Ellis returned her notepad to her bag. "Thank you for taking the time, Mrs. Gladstone. We really appreciate it." She rose from the couch. "Please know that we are working hard to find whoever's terrorizing your neighborhood."

Mrs. Gladstone led them to the front door. "Detective Ellis, I have to think that you're here asking about Jenna Brooks because you truly believe there is some sort of connection to what's happening now. And if so, what could that connection possibly be?"

Ellis eyed Fletch before returning her attention to the woman. "I can't say with any certainty that this situation is in any way related, but it does prick the hairs on the back of my neck. As far as what that connection could be?" She shook her head. "I don't know, but we will find out."

When they returned to Ellis's SUV, she pressed the ignition and then looked over at Fletch. "Why do you think Johnson and Brooks fought?"

Fletch closed the passenger door. "Given the timing, I'm wondering if Joel Brooks thought Johnson had something to do with Jenna's disappearance and the fight was a result of that."

Ellis nodded. "Pretty much what I thought. It'd be a good idea to talk to the Johnsons again and ask them about it."

"Are we getting sidetracked here?" Fletch asked.

Ellis pulled out onto the main road. "How do you mean?"

"This Brooks investigation. I get that the possibility exists this could be the same killer, but figuring out whether these people had neighborly disputes or arguments. Where does that get us in helping to find this guy?"

"Valid question," Ellis replied. "It's just too coincidental —all of this. The murder of Jenna Brooks. The recent break-ins. The killing of Vicky Boyles. This place. Look at it, Fletch. It's like the damn *Stepford Wives*, right? Everything is perfect. Their yards, their houses, their lifestyles."

Fletch peered out at the homes while Ellis drove on. "It does have that vibe. But more than a few of the families who lived here back then don't live here now," Fletch said. "Where's the connection?"

THREE NIGHTS AGO, Taylor Burnell had been stabbed eight times and left for dead outside the Lighthouse bar at about one a.m. Now, Bevins got the call this morning from the ME, notifying him that Burnell's blood alcohol content had been twice the legal limit. Meaning if Burnell had gotten behind the wheel of his small Ford Ranger, he likely would've killed himself or someone else.

Bevins parked his Mustang in front of the apartment building where Burnell had lived with his wife, Shauna. It was an older complex, clad in dark green siding with black trim. Tall trees dotted the grounds, which backed up to the forest.

The wife had already identified her husband's body and had been questioned by Bevins the morning after it happened. He'd gone back out yesterday with the hope that Ellis could help him find more details. Because, so far, he'd run up against a wall as far as any leads were concerned.

On the upside, he had matched three sets of tire tracks found in the parking lot of the bar to their corresponding vehicles. Now, to learn whether Burnell's neighbors, or anyone else he knew, drove any of the three. A longshot to be sure, but Ellis was usually right about this kind of stuff. And he looked up to her, trusted her judgment.

Bevins climbed the steps to the apartment unit above the Burnells' home, figuring it was best to start there. He knocked on the door, holding little hope the occupant would be home, unless maybe he was unemployed.

The door opened, and a man who looked to be in his mid-twenties stood behind it. No shirt, sports shorts, and unruly hair as though he'd just awakened.

"Uh, good morning. Are you Anthony Larkin?"

"Yeah, I'm Tony."

Bevins displayed his badge. "I'm Detective Bevins, and

I'd like to talk to you about your downstairs neighbor, Taylor Burnell. Do you have a minute?"

Appearing skeptical, Larkin glanced out beyond Bevins as though expecting another person to be hiding behind him. "Yeah, sure. Come in."

Bevins trailed him inside, noting the state of the apartment. The trash hadn't been taken out in days. The smell of pizza and stale beer lingered. A black futon was pressed against the back wall, its cushions aimed at a large flat-screen television that sat atop a glass table. The odor of several pairs of sneakers dotted about the floor capped off the experience. "Are you aware of what happened to Mr. Burnell?"

"Course I am. Everyone knows." Larkin dropped onto the futon, his legs spread and leaning his elbows on his thighs. "What's this about?"

"I'm here to learn more about him." Bevins walked to the middle of the small living space. "Were you friends with Taylor?"

Larkin shrugged. "Not particularly. We grabbed a beer every now and again with a few other dudes around here. Just hanging out at the pool, but that was about it."

Bevins surveyed the room. "Can I ask, sir, were you at the Lighthouse bar with Taylor on the night he was killed?"

"No, sir. I was home. I'm on unemployment right now. I don't have money to go out drinking. And if I did, it wouldn't be with Taylor. His wife gets bitchy when he goes out."

"Well, she won't get that chance again," Bevins said sharply. "Can anyone vouch for your whereabouts?"

Larkin jumped to his feet. "I'm sorry, am I a suspect or something?"

Bevins laid his hand on the butt of his sidearm. "I'm just asking you questions, sir."

The man took in a breath. "Sure. Yeah. You know, you should talk to the dude downstairs, next door to Taylor's place. He'll be able to answer questions better than me. Probably saw Taylor more."

"I'll make a note of that," Bevins replied. "I'll just ask you one more thing; can you tell me what kind of car you drive?"

"A Nissan Altima," he said. "Why?"

Shit. "No reason. Thank you for your time, sir. If you think of anything else—"

"Yeah, yeah. I'll be sure to call you," Larkin replied.

Bevins nodded and showed himself to the door, stepping outside once again. "That was a bust," he said in a hushed tone. Jogging down the steps, he prepared to check out the unit on the first floor across from the Burnells'. As he reached the bottom and headed down the path, he glanced down at his phone.

A moment later, he rammed into someone on the path and looked up. "I'm sorry, sir. I wasn't paying attention." Bevins looked at the size of the man. Broad chested with beefy arms and long legs, he looked to be about six feet tall. Dark hair and eyes. Serious. "You all right?"

"Fine. No problem, man. Don't worry about it."

Bevins peered over his shoulder as the man walked on without another word. "Thank you, sir. Have a good day."

ELLIS AND FLETCH had returned to the station to continue their hunt for leads. Ellis walked to the case board, studying her notes and the map of the Woodland Heights neighborhood. Pins had been inserted at the location of each house that had called in reports of the intruder, including the murder victim. She jotted down the number five on the Madsens' home and added numbers to the other two, pondering Fletch's question about a number eight.

Lewis headed over to her. "How's things going over here?"

"Gabby, hi," Ellis replied. "Still trying to piece it together."

"For what it's worth...I think you might be onto something with this cold case."

Ellis turned to her. "Yeah?"

"You ruled out similar crimes in other parts of town, other cities. Any word on that search warrant for the security company's staff records?"

"Triggs executed it and obtained the files," she replied. "So there's still some hope there. Nothing on the artist's sketch, though."

"Sorry to hear that. I feel like there's not much for me to offer, but you know I'm here if you need anything else."

"I appreciate that, Gabby." Her phone rang, and she noticed the caller ID. "It's Detective Naylor. Excuse me a moment." She answered the call. "This is Ellis."

"Detective Ellis, I wanted to reach out to you. When I got in this morning, I recalled something else about the Jenna Brooks investigation I thought you'd be interested in."

"I'm all ears, Detective."

"Look, back when this happened, Joel Brooks and his wife, they were obviously distressed."

"Of course," Ellis added.

"And Brooks went on about how Jenna had been taken

right from their community, and no one seemed to give a damn."

Ellis glanced at Lewis with a raised brow. "Did you find that to be true?"

"No, but Brooks was off the rails. He insisted that someone had to have seen something. I assure you, we vetted everyone even remotely related to the incident. Talked to the girl's school. All of it. And we didn't find any evidence to suggest anyone in the community had anything to do with her murder."

"Okay, so what exactly are you trying to say?" Ellis urged him to continue.

"I'm just warning you that when you speak to Brooks, be aware he holds a grudge in that community, which I'm certain was the reason he and his wife ultimately left. Be careful how far down that rabbit hole you go. I'm saying this from experience. I think we wasted a good deal of time on that scenario, and it didn't pan out."

"Thank you, Detective. I feel as though your call came at exactly the right time. We'll pursue the evidence we have and wait for Forensics. Thanks again."

"Anytime."

Ellis set down her phone.

"What did Naylor have to say?" Fletch asked, approaching her colleagues.

She set her eyes on the board again. "He's trying to keep us from wasting time."

Lewis moved in next to her and studied the board. "Sounds like something a man who doesn't want to be proven wrong might suggest."

15

In the Forensics lab, Seavers continued to work toward uncovering the identity of the person whose prints appeared on the locksmith's tools. So far, the partial he'd pulled hadn't revealed enough, and there was nothing linked to the database. But new techniques could be employed to create a full print in hopes of identifying the individual.

Seavers engaged the reconstruction algorithm, which would form the phase image and convert it to grayscale. It didn't take long for the algorithm to render a fingerprint image as a result, though it wasn't complete yet. Another algorithm was entered for it to draw a complete reconstruction.

As the system continued to run the commands, Seavers stared at his computer, noting the reconstruction and the points he would use to identify the potential suspect. Now, all he had to do was hope the print matched something in the database. If he had that, he'd be able to give Ellis an answer.

When the system finished, Seavers leaned back in his chair and rubbed his eyes. The reconstruction was complete, and he had a full fingerprint to work with. He entered it into the database and waited.

And when he got a hit, he almost surprised himself. Seavers noted the name on the screen. William Pierce. "The guy's clean." No record of criminal activity appeared. The prints were in the system because he had been given some kind of security clearance at some point.

Seavers printed out the information and gathered his things, eager to bring the news to Ellis and the rest of the team. He called up to CID. "Ellis, it's me. I got a match on that print. I'm heading your way now."

The forensics officer arrived at the bullpen upstairs. He noticed Ellis and Fletch near the whiteboard on the back wall. "Detectives?" He hurried with short strides toward them. "I got a match for the prints on the toolbox." He held up the papers in his hand.

"Who is it?" Ellis asked.

"William Pierce. The guy works for SafeHome Security."

Fletch shot a look at Ellis. "That's the company Triggs was looking into, right?"

"Yeah, and the one I had a search warrant issued for its staff," Ellis replied, keeping her eyes fixed on Seavers. "Do you have an address? We'll leave right now and check him out."

Seavers set down the papers on her desk. "Home and work address is in the file."

"And you're sure about this?" Ellis pressed.

"I had to reconstruct a full print, but the identification points match. The system says it's at ninety-four percent."

Ellis nodded. "That's close enough for me. We'll get on this now. Thank you."

By mid-afternoon, Ellis and Fletch were pulling into the parking lot at SafeHome Security Systems near the industrial park on the southern edge of the suburbs. The modern building had an off-white exterior and long, rectangular windows stacked three high. Sharp, square concrete lines in the façade and a black-painted set of doors under a covered entrance.

William Pierce was the man they hoped to find.

"This guy could be here, or he could be out on an install," Ellis said as she peered at the building's entrance. "And when we go in there, I don't want to mention the murder. We're going to call this a string of break-ins."

"Got it." Fletch opened her door and stepped down.

Ellis joined her as the two entered the building. Inside, she noticed the high ceiling with recessed lighting, stark white walls, and a long black and glass reception desk with a young woman behind it. "Hi there." She retrieved her badge. "I'm Detective Ellis, Bangor Police. This is my partner, Detective Fletcher."

"How can I help you?"

Ellis picked up on the woman's fearful tone and widened eyes. The reaction was pretty common. "Can you tell me if William Pierce is working today?"

"Uh." She fumbled around with papers on her desk before typing something on her computer. "It looks like he's out on an install but should be back soon."

"Soon? As in the next few minutes?" Ellis asked.

"Probably half an hour or so." The woman eyed the screen again. "I can call him and see if he can come back sooner."

Ellis and Fletch traded a knowing glance, and Ellis continued, "Would it be possible to give us his location?"

"I-I don't think I can," the woman replied. "He's at a client's house. I'm not supposed to give away client addresses."

"How about we speak to Mr. Pierce's manager? We have a search warrant that I'm sure your HR department is in receipt of," Fletch said. "How about you help us out here?"

"Sure. One moment."

Ellis and Fletch stepped away while the woman made the call. Ellis looked on. "I don't want to sit here for half an hour. We need to move on this."

"He doesn't have to talk to us without a lawyer," Fletch added. "If we go to the jobsite, it's not like we can arrest him."

The woman called out, "Detectives?"

Ellis and Fletch approached as she hung up the phone.

"Yes?" Ellis said.

"Mr. Pierce just returned and is in his office. His manager is on his way now and will take you back."

"Thank you," Ellis said, glancing with a nod to Fletch.

A moment later, a woman wearing dress pants and a button-down blouse approached. She appeared in her fifties with a thick waist and slim legs. "Afternoon, Detectives. I understand you're here to see William Pierce?"

"Yes, ma'am," Ellis said. "We'd like to ask him some questions."

"May I ask what it's regarding?" she pressed.

"It's in connection with the warrant sent to this office

yesterday afternoon," Fletch cut in. "And it's important we speak to him now."

The woman appeared reluctant, but finally nodded and waved her hand. "Follow me, please. I'll take you to his office."

Ellis trailed the woman with Fletch behind her. This could be it. The prints matched what was found on the tools near one of the homes in the neighborhood. And it was a logical conclusion to assume someone who knew the security systems had the ability to disconnect them and get inside his victims' homes.

The manager gestured at an office on her right. "Bill, I have some people here to see you."

Ellis and Fletch appeared in the doorway when Ellis continued, "Mr. Pierce, I'm Detective Ellis; this is Detective Fletcher. We'd like to ask you a few questions, if that's all right."

Pierce eyed his boss. She nodded. "Okay. Come in," he replied.

Ellis immediately noticed the look on his face. A deer in headlights sprang to mind. "Thank you. We won't keep you." She took a seat while Fletch sat next to her.

"We understand you've done work in the Woodland Heights neighborhood," Ellis continued.

"That's right. I've done some installs there," he replied. "Not in a long time, though."

"When would you say you were there last?" Fletch asked.

Pierce looked up in thought. "Well, I guess about six months or so ago," he replied. "Can I ask what this is about?"

Ellis set down the file on his desk and opened it to the photo of the tools. "Can you tell me if these belong to you?"

Pierce pulled the photo closer to him and examined it

through a narrow gaze. "Can't say for sure, but they're the type of tools I'd use." He looked at them. "Did you find this somewhere? I've been missing some tools, and I assumed one of my co-workers borrowed them."

Ellis glanced at Fletch and returned her attention to Pierce. "You're missing tools?"

"Yes, ma'am." He nodded. "It happens. We borrow each other's things on occasion. Usually no big deal, but now you got me wondering why it is you're asking."

"Sir." Ellis pushed another photo closer to him. "Those tools were found near the scene of a break-in about two days ago. In fact, we're certain it's tied to a string of break-ins in the area. And a recent murder."

Fletch shot her a look, and Ellis knew why. She hadn't planned on mentioning the murder, but when he claimed his tools were stolen, it was time to impress upon him the seriousness of the situation.

"Murder?" He swallowed hard. "Look, I haven't been to that neighborhood in months—like I said."

"Who might've borrowed this from you?" Fletch asked.

Pierce shook his head. "I don't know. Could've been anybody—"

"Do you know a man by the name of Joel Brooks?" Ellis asked.

"Brooks." He appeared to think on the question. "Doesn't ring a bell. Why?"

Ellis retrieved a photo of Jenna Brooks found in the woods and pushed it toward him. "This is his daughter. She was murdered about three years ago. Mr. Brooks and his family lived in Woodland Heights until she was killed. They moved on after that to New Jersey."

"Pardon my asking, Detective," Pierce began. "But what on earth does that have to do with me?"

"The people who live in that home now told us that their security system is from your company and that it was there when they bought the home," Ellis continued.

"Ma'am, I have to say that I cannot tell you why you found a set of my tools in that area or near that home. I promise you I wasn't there. I don't know this Brooks family." He seemed to choke back his nerves. "I have nothing to do with whatever it is you're thinking."

Ellis stood from the chair. "We'll need you to come in and make a statement to that effect, Mr. Pierce. Because your prints were found on a piece of evidence, you are considered a person of interest. I'll expect to see you first thing in the morning. If not, we'll be back for you." She eyed Fletch. "Let's go. We're done here."

ELLIS CURSED herself as they returned to the station. The entire trip had been a waste of time.

"It makes sense he'd deny it, Becca," Fletch said as they arrived in the bullpen. "We can't prove he's done anything wrong. Let him come in and make his statement. We'll check out his alibi, and it'll either clear him or not."

Ellis opened the file Seavers had put together and compared Pierce's image to the sketch and surveillance video. "I'm not seeing any resemblance."

Fletch leaned over her shoulder. "We just don't have enough detail, but Pierce does look older, wider. Regardless, we follow protocol for persons of interest."

"It does beg the question," she continued. "How the hell

did the intruder get Pierce's tools in the first place? He said he hadn't been back to Woodland Heights in months."

Fletch moved around and perched on the edge of Ellis's desk. "The guy could've been planning this for at least that long. Look, if he is who you think he is, meaning he killed Jenna Brooks, then I have to think he's been watching these people."

Ellis's phone rang, and her eyes lit up. "It's Rivera." She answered. "Dr. Rivera, it's good to hear from you."

"I have some information I knew you'd want to hear right away."

She glanced at Fletch and smiled. "I'm going to put you on speaker since I've got Detective Fletcher standing next to me." Ellis set down the phone and pressed the button. "Go ahead, Doc."

"Primary DNA transfer was obtained from Vicky Boyles's neck and arm. I entered it into NDIS—the National DNA Index System. A forensic hit was returned."

Ellis shot a look at Fletch. "Skin-to-skin transfer?"

"Correct, but of course, the identity remains unknown. The interesting part, I believe, is that the scene it matched to was that of a cold case out of Augusta—"

"Jenna Brooks," Ellis cut in.

"Yes, that's right. How did you know?"

"Call it a hunch." She glanced at Fletch. "This means that although the suspect's DNA isn't in the system, it's a match. Jenna Brooks and Vicky Boyles were killed by the same person," Ellis stated.

"It does appear to be the case," Rivera agreed. "I'll send over the report now. I hope this helps, Detective Ellis."

"More than you know. Thank you. I'll keep my eyes open for the email. Goodbye." Ellis pressed the end button and clenched her fist in triumph. "It's the same guy."

"Which was what you initially thought," Fletch said. "But that doesn't change the fact that this guy is still on the loose, and we have no idea who he is. And if Rivera entered it into NDIS and that was the only match he got? Then this killer hasn't murdered anyone else."

"Or maybe he just didn't leave behind a trace before," Ellis said. "Either way, this is something. And I'm wondering if we should get Pierce to submit a DNA swab."

Fletch pushed off the desk. "I don't think we have much of a choice."

THE ENTIRE NEIGHBORHOOD crawled with cop cars. Night had arrived, and he'd seen three pass him by in the last fifteen minutes. He'd wondered when they might step up their game. Fortunately, he was prepared.

The next house on his list was on Springville Road, which was about two blocks over from where he now stood. Would he get past the cops? Was it possible to get near the home, disable the alarm, and get inside before they made another round? Maybe. The other option was to wait it out. Wait for things to die down. But he didn't have that kind of time, not after Boyles' death.

He was on foot and had parked his car half a mile away. Weaving in and out of the streets of Woodland Heights was harder than it looked, even though he knew the place like the back of his hand. Avoiding the cops became the goal now.

Inside the community, paths diverged between wooded

areas that led to playgrounds. An elementary school was only minutes away. Behind the school were homes. A small buffer lay between the school and the homes. That was where he'd traverse. The cops probably had no idea it was there.

Dressed in black from head to toe, he made his way to the boundary of the school and arrived at the buffer zone of the residential street. The home he needed was at the end of this street.

With heightened senses, he moved through the shadows behind the homes, between iron fences and wooden pickets. Trees loomed large in the back gardens as he crept along toward number eight under cover of night. He moved quickly and efficiently, making his way toward the house.

Now he faced the rear yard fence of the home. He noted that it had a padlocked gate. Scaling the six-foot fence would be difficult since it was vinyl paneling and too slick to climb. He could bust the lock, but that would make too much noise. Only one choice remained; he would have to walk to the end of the street and make his way to the front, keeping a sharp eye out for the police patrol units.

Number eight's alarm system was outdated, and the panel was just inside the fence return. Son of a bitch. He was going to have to scale the fence after all. The clock was ticking, and a cop could roll by at any moment.

Just climb it.

Three attempts later, he'd made it over, falling to the ground with a noisy thud. He brushed off his clothing and walked to the side of the house where the security panel was located. It only took him moments to disable the system. Now, to get inside when he was certain every home in this neighborhood was locked up airtight.

His best shot? A bump key. The locksmith's go-to for accessing people's homes when they've locked themselves out. And he had one. With the security system disarmed, he made his way to the front door, keeping eyes out for the roving patrol units. He had but seconds to get inside before another one passed by.

Within moments, the deadbolt pulled back, and he was in, moving through the house with stealth-like precision. His target was an upstairs bedroom. For a moment, he considered that the owner could be in his bedroom, aiming a rifle at the door, just waiting for him. The risk of continuing on this mission had grown too great. Regardless, he would rather die than give up.

Down a short hallway lay two doors. Another lay at the opposite end. Simple enough. He walked inside the first of the two doors and noticed a teenager asleep on her double bed, half-curled up and uncovered. A faint light shone through the bedroom window, filtered through the wispy curtains.

He paused for a moment, taking in the sight of the figure before him. The soft rise and fall of her sleeping chest was almost hypnotic, and for a moment, he hesitated. But then he remembered why he was there and steeled himself.

He returned out into the hall and eyed the door that most certainly belonged to the parents. He reached out his hand and turned the handle. The door opened with a soft creak, which was enough to make him freeze in his tracks. He listened intently for any signs of movement or stirring, but there were none. Carefully stepping inside, he reached the bed. Kelly and Ted Holtz lay there, their breathing slow and steady. He would leave them a message. They would know he had been here tonight. He let go of the slip of paper and watched it float to the ground, landing where Ted would step first thing in the morning.

He turned around to leave, and the man shifted in his bed. His pulse quickened, and the handle on the knife tucked into his waistband pressed into his ribs. One swift move and this would all be over. Quick. Painless. Both would be gone before either could utter a sound.

As he waited, frozen, Ted seemed to settle again, so he stepped out of the room, pulling the door closed behind him. He made his way down the steps when he heard a noise from above. *Shit.*

And then he saw a man's figure cast in shadow.

"Hey!" The man—Ted—ran down the steps.

Is that a gun?

Peering over his shoulder, he knew Ted was armed. Reaching the bottom floor, he scanned the room, gauging whether he could make it to the front door before the man shot at him.

"Who are you?" Ted called out with the gun pointed ahead, gripped in his shaky hand. "My wife is calling the cops now!"

Mere feet lay between them, and in one swift move, he swung his arm, knocking the gun from Ted's unsteady hands. It fell to the wood floor with an echoing thump as it slid several feet away. He ripped the knife from his waistband and plunged it into the man's stomach.

Within milliseconds, the woman upstairs screamed. Her husband lay on the floor, clutching his gut, blocking the path to the front door.

"Stop!" Kelly shouted, hurtling down the steps.

As blood spilled around the dying man, he leaped over him, nearly slipping on the oozing pool. He dashed into the family room, where a sliding glass door was his only hope. The door was locked, and he fumbled with the latch for a moment as Kelly cried out for her husband.

Her distraction offered him valuable seconds to slip out into the backyard. He sprinted to the rear and scaled the six-foot wooden slats. His gloves tore open from the raw pointed tops, skinning the palms of his hands. Pulling himself over with all his might, he slipped beyond the fence and reached the wooded buffer between the homes and the school. Sirens sounded in the distance.

They're coming.

16

P atrol units with flashing lights lined the street of house number eight, belonging to Ted and Kelly Holtz. Neighbors stood outside in their pajamas. Some appeared to confront the officers with raised hands and raised voices. They were afraid now, and with another attack, Ellis knew they should be.

The situation had escalated beyond what she thought was possible. He had ramped up his efforts, and there was no telling when this would end, or whether they could stop him before he killed again.

She parked behind one of the police cruisers, with Fletch at her side, surveying the street. "We have a lot of eyeballs out here right now."

Fletch nodded. "I'll talk to these guys and have them set up tape and barriers for crowd control."

"Thanks." Ellis stepped outside. At two a.m., the early morning air was cool. Moss had sent Triggs to secure the scene, but on peering out over the grounds, she didn't see him. "I'm going inside. I need to find Triggs."

"Copy that. I'll see about barriers." Fletch carried on in the opposite direction.

Ellis approached the home where a few officers huddled. Glancing through the open front door, she spotted the evidence tech inside collecting what she hoped would identify their suspect. All she knew right now was that the homeowner, male, had been stabbed in the stomach and taken to the hospital. He was expected to survive, which could also be the break she needed if the victim could recall with better detail what his attacker looked like.

Right away, she noticed the gun lying on the foyer floor. "Hey?" she called out to an officer.

"Yes, ma'am?" He eyed the badge she wore on a chain around her neck.

"Get that off the ground and into an evidence bag before someone contaminates it."

"Yes, ma'am. I'm on it." He scurried away.

Ellis felt a hand on her shoulder and spun around. "Triggs, there you are. I just got here and was looking for you."

The young officer hooked his thumbs into his belt loop and looked out into the living room. "He got in again."

"And tried to kill the occupant," Ellis added. "Where was his point of entry?"

Triggs peered back at the front door. "Son of a bitch got past the security again. Looks like he used a bump key and got inside. Kelly Holtz is in the living room now. You want to talk to her?"

Ellis noticed the distraught woman on the sofa with a young teen girl, presumably the daughter, next to her. "Why didn't they go to the hospital with the husband?"

"That's on me. I asked them to stay and answer some questions."

Ellis shook her head. "They need to be with him. Questions can be asked later."

"Yes, ma'am. I'll let her know." Triggs veered off to speak to the woman.

Ellis glanced upstairs before climbing to the second floor. She reached the top and eyed the three bedroom doors. They were all open, and all the lights in the entire house had been turned on. To her left, she noticed the teen girl's room.

She stood at the entrance and examined the area. A double bed—unmade—in the center. White nightstands on either side. A dresser opposite and a small bench between the rectangular windows that flanked either side.

Ellis walked toward the windows and noticed a plush rug on the carpeted floor. She squatted low. "Shoe prints?"

She retrieved her phone and snapped a picture. "Could be Mom's or Dad's, though."

"You talking to someone, Detective?"

She shot around to see Triggs in the doorway. "Just myself."

Triggs drew in and squatted low to join her. "What do you see?"

Ellis aimed her flashlight at the corner where the carpet met the wall. "A scuff mark here. It's faint, but it looks like someone dragged their shoe across it. Don't know if it was already here." She returned upright again. "Let's check out the parents' room."

"The wife said her husband heard a noise, grabbed his gun and went out to see what it was," Triggs added.

"Guess he found out pretty quickly," Ellis replied. "Makes me wonder how the intruder managed to get out of the line of fire."

"According to Mrs. Holtz, Mr. Holtz never actually fired that gun before. I think he might've been too afraid to pull the trigger."

"Never a good idea to own a gun you don't know how to use or are afraid of." Ellis continued inside the parents' room. She studied the area for a moment and walked around the bed. "Wait. What the hell is this?"

Triggs caught up to her and examined the floor. "It's folded. Maybe it fell out of our suspect's pocket. Unless it belongs to the victim." He slipped on a pair of gloves and picked up the scrap of paper. "You want me to—"

"Open it. Yes." She waited while he unfurled it. "Looks like a piece of printer paper. We'll see if it matches the printer in the den downstairs." Ellis pinched her brow and leaned closer. "Does that look like a map to you?" She continued to peer at it. "Turn it over."

He did as she asked. "There's writing on here."

"'Why didn't you tell them what you knew?'" Ellis read.

"A torn piece of a hand-drawn map. And a message." Triggs eyed it closely. "What the hell does any of this mean?"

IT SEEMED that remaining unidentifiable was what this intruder was best at. With only a generic description offered by a frightened boy, corroborating that description with Kelly Holtz had been easy enough, but still offered no answers. Both had mentioned he'd been cloaked in a dark hoodie and seemed to be a large man. Mrs. Holtz's recollection of the night's events revolved almost solely around her husband falling to the ground after being stabbed in the stomach.

The family had been taken to the hospital, where Ted Holtz remained in stable condition. But once again, Ellis was offered the same ambiguous depiction. Holtz said the man had dark eyes and an unkempt, but light beard. That part was new; Ellis assumed he'd grown his facial hair to help further shield his identity. But Holtz had no better idea who had stabbed him than the others. She couldn't fault him. Life-threatening situations provoked primal survival instincts. Recalling in great detail an attacker's face wasn't one of those instincts.

Ellis and Fletch had parted ways so that they might find some sleep before the sun rose. But rather than sleep, Ellis had fixated on the latest find—this map.

The slip of paper lay flat on her coffee table. Several creases distorted the pencil marks, but they remained readable. A side lamp burned while she paced her living room; the rest of her home was cloaked in shadow except for the glow from the microwave clock in her kitchen.

The newfound evidence would have to be taken to Seavers for prints, but for now, she studied the small slip of paper not more than four inches by five inches. On it was a hand-drawn map of the homes inside Woodland Heights. However, it was clear this was just a portion of a larger map. In fact, what Ellis had was a map of the Holtz house, or as they called it "number eight," and their immediate neighbors. More importantly, there were the words the intruder had left for them. Once Ted Holtz was more alert, she would ask him about their meaning and hope that he could shed some light.

But what did the map mean? Why had the intruder walked inside the main bedroom, leave behind the scrap piece of paper, and then end up stabbing Holtz? Was it simply self-defense? Had he intended to hurt any of them? And this wasn't his first message. He'd left a message for the Madsens too.

Then she had to consider the Burnell murder. While Bevins still pieced that case together, it seemed logical to conclude the intruder had committed that crime as well. His MO was all over the place. Tracking down his next target would be as random as throwing darts blindfolded to see where they landed.

Ellis came to a halt in the center of the room. "There's nothing random about this at all."

<hr />

IF GIVEN THE CHANCE, Ellis would've insisted Abbott meet her at the station at four a.m. She needed to tell him how she'd figured out how to catch this man who'd terrorized a community. However, thinking on it a moment longer, she realized a couple of hours' rest would allow the idea to blossom into a full-fledged plan.

Now that morning had arrived, Ellis marched into the station, right on up the steps to see Abbott. Except, now that the time had come, Abbott wasn't alone.

"Becca?" Lieutenant Abe Serrano glanced over his shoulder as he sat across from Abbott. "Come in," he said, appearing to notice the look on her face. "Looks like you have something important to discuss. Don't mind me."

"Thank you, sir." She continued inside Abbott's office.

"As you know, Sarge, Fletch and I were called out to another attack by the intruder."

"I'm aware," Abbott replied. "How's the victim?"

"He'll be okay, but that's not why I'm here." She removed the scrap of paper from the evidence bag with a gloved hand and straightened it, setting it on his desk. "We found this inside the main bedroom, folded up on the floor, like the intruder intentionally left it there."

Serrano leaned over to view the paper on Abbott's desk. His thick gray hair was held back by a pair of reading glasses pushed up onto his head. The reedy man in his late fifties had been with Bangor PD a long time, long enough to have worked closely with Hank Ellis. "It's incomplete."

"Exactly," Ellis replied. "Like it was torn from a larger map." She pointed to the drawing. "That's the house we were called out to. He mapped it out. Marked them down. And he left the Holtzes a message, just like he did the Madsens."

"Why?" Abbott asked.

Ellis shrugged. "I'm not sure yet. But if I can decipher what this means, I think I'll be able to figure out where he'll go next."

Serrano pulled back and folded his arms over his narrow chest. "That's a hell of a tall order, Becca. What's your plan to decode this?"

She paced a small circle and kept her eyes on the floor. "There has to be a reason why he'd draw that street, focusing on three homes with an X on the target." Ellis raked a hand through her hair. "I'm still working out why he left that book at the Madsens', but it contained a message, and that's exactly what this is too." Ellis stopped and eyed them a moment. "This man has been precise in his every move. Ensuring his identity remained hidden, bypassing security measures, using locksmith's tools. This map—I think he had every intention of it being discovered."

Abbott slipped on his reading glasses and studied the paper. "I don't know, Becca. I'm not seeing how this penciled map is going to tell you anything more than what it says now, which is that X marks the spot, and he hit that house. End of story."

"Did he leave the knife?" Serrano asked.

"No, sir," Ellis replied. "He's smarter than that. He hasn't left us anything real except for that map."

Serrano rubbed his smooth, but lined cheek. "Maybe you're not entirely off the mark here. You could try to overlay that with a map of the area. You know the homes that have been hit so far. See if a pattern of movement shows up."

"I tried that already," Ellis replied. "There is no identifiable pattern—not that I can discern."

"You tried before, but without this." Serrano pointed at the evidence. "Look at it again with this in mind. See if something pops out at you. You say you want to see if you can decipher its meaning. There you go. Going through the steps is how you start. You've got nothing left to lose."

She carefully returned the paper to the evidence bag. "I'll make a copy of this and get it to Forensics for prints. Maybe he got sloppy enough to leave some. And then I'll see what happens when compared against the locations of the other victims. Thank you, both." Ellis turned around and headed back into the bullpen.

She returned to her desk after dropping off the original piece of evidence to Seavers in Forensics. Feeling less enthusiastic after the injection of a hefty dose of reality from her boss, she noticed Fletch head her way.

"Well, what'd he say?"

"The lieutenant was in there," Ellis began. "He suggested overlaying this map with the locations of the other victims and see if something stands out."

"We already did that," Fletch replied.

"Not entirely." She walked over to the board with a map of the area. "We've already tried to find a pattern among the known victims."

"Right." Fletch moved in next to her.

"So let's put this here and see if we spot anything new." Ellis pinned a copy of the hand-drawn map to the board where the home was located.

She and Fletch had been staring at it for several moments when McCallister approached them. "Hey, what are you guys looking at?"

Ellis glanced back at him. "Good morning. We found this last night on scene. We're certain it belonged to the killer and that he left it deliberately."

"So you're trying to make some sense out of it," he added.

"That's the goal." Fletch focused on the map.

Ellis let her eyes roam from one house to another, feeling a bead of sweat trickle down her forehead in the rising heat inside the stifling bullpen. Nothing stood out to her. This was her idea at four in the morning. She was certain it would all become clear in the light of day, but nothing seemed less likely right now.

McCallister tilted his head as he took a step toward the board. "Didn't you say you thought our intruder guy is the same one who murdered a girl from that neighborhood?"

"That's right. He was never caught. I feel like he's come back for them, but I don't know why," Ellis said. "Some of the people in these homes lived there at the time; some are more recent, like the family who moved into the victim's home. So we haven't been able to find a real connection among the neighbors yet."

"Hang on. What's this?" He pointed to the penciled map.

Ellis joined him. "What do you see?"

"This." He aimed his pinky finger at a small corner of the drawing. "That's another house, right?"

"Looks like it," she continued. "At least part of one."

"Has that one been hit?" McCallister pressed.

"No." And then Ellis saw it. "Wait." She narrowed her gaze. "There's a number written in pencil. I can hardly read it, but it looks like a nine." She regarded Fletch. "Do you see a nine there?"

Fletch stepped closer. "Looks like it could be. I mean, I can't say for sure, but it's damn close."

Ellis straightened her back with renewed confidence. "How did I not see that last night?"

"It's barely discernable," McCallister replied.

A wide grin pulled at her lips. "I knew there was a reason we needed you back. Only eight houses have been hit, including the Holtzes." She pointed to the map. "That must be number nine. His next target."

WILLIAM PIERCE WALKED inside the station, and he wasn't alone. On the advice of the owner of SafeHome, a lawyer accompanied him to make his statement. The whole thing was crazy, but the cops weren't messing around.

The lawyer led the way to the front desk. "Excuse me. My name is Ed Burgess. I'm here to represent my client, William Pierce. He's been asked to come in and make a statement."

Liz Varney was behind the desk, wearing her brown hair

in a tight bun. "You're accompanying your client for a statement?"

"Yes, ma'am. Detective Ellis insisted Mr. Pierce come in regarding a piece of evidence she discovered that may have once belonged to my client."

Liz typed on her computer. "The Woodland Heights case. I'm familiar. One moment and I'll have her come down."

"Thank you."

William waited only a minute or two before he spotted the detective descending the staircase. She was alone. The short one, nowhere to be seen. That was good. He didn't like her. She scared him.

"Mr. Pierce, thank you for following through on your word."

He shook her hand. "Like I told you before, Detective Ellis, I had nothing to do with any of this. So I'm here to make my statement."

She eyed the lawyer. "And you brought a friend."

"Ed Burgess." He offered his hand. "I'm only here to help guide Mr. Pierce."

"Fine by me." Ellis started ahead. "Right this way."

William followed the detective, walking by several police officers. The scent of coffee was heavy in the air.

The detective opened a door to a small room, and William walked inside.

"Why don't you take a seat, Mr. Pierce?" she asked.

As they found their places at the table, William did his best to appear stoic. "What is it you want me to tell you, Detective?"

"The truth," she replied. "I need to know how your tools got into the hands of a killer."

"Whoa, whoa." Burgess held out his hands. "That's a

little strong, don't you think, Detective? My client is here to clear up any misunderstanding. Now, the tools in question clearly had been misplaced when he was at a customer's house."

"I can tell you where I was. Who I was with when that murder happened," William jumped in. "I don't know if those tools are even mine."

"Your prints were on them," Ellis replied.

"Well, all I can think, then, is that whoever took them did so when I was in someone's house. I don't use those lockpick tools much, all right? I install security systems."

"There is one way we can help to eliminate you as a suspect, Mr. Pierce," she began.

"I'm innocent. I'll do what you ask."

"Within reason, William," Burgess shot back. "What are you asking, Detective?"

She appeared to be examining images in a file folder. One looked like a picture from a video, and the other appeared to be a drawing of a man's face. "Mr. Pierce, I believe you. I do. But the fact of the matter is, your prints are on a crucial piece of evidence. That said, we will verify your whereabouts, but we'd also like you to submit a DNA swab so that we can rule you out."

"Fine."

Burgess thrust out his hand. "Hold on. Why on earth would my client do that for you? He's under no obligation. You can't put him anywhere near your crime scene because if you could, he'd be under arrest."

William returned a sideways glance. "Ed, it's fine. Like I said. I got nothing to hide."

ELLIS RETURNED TO THE BULLPEN, wearing defeat.

Fletch looked up from her laptop. "What happened?"

She stopped at her desk. "Pierce isn't our guy. Not that I held out much hope anyway."

"What makes you certain?" Fletch continued.

"He offered to submit a swab despite protest from his lawyer."

"Okay, then we move on." Fletch leaned back in her chair. "He offered an alibi?"

"He did. And I took the file with me and had a chance to make a better comparison. Pierce doesn't look anything like the man in the sketch or the video. But we'll take the swab and see where it leads. He had no idea what happened to his tools. Claimed he didn't use them much anyway."

McCallister headed toward them. "Fletch, you mentioned that you thought the intruder could've been following this guy. Watching him?"

"If he knew SafeHome had installed some of the systems in the neighborhood, it would've been easy as hell for him to track down one of their trucks and steal the tools." She looked back at Ellis. "Makes us think it was a SafeHome employee."

"Shit." Ellis looked away for a moment. "And the employee records we looked at didn't give us anything either." She turned back to Fletch. "You were right."

"We had to see it through, Becca," Fletch said. "At least we can move on to the next thing."

"The stakeout," Ellis added.

"What are you talking about, a stakeout?" McCallister asked.

Ellis waited for Fletch's nod before continuing, "It's how we find him. We started kicking around the idea, and now that we're confident he has a number nine, we have to jump on it."

"We could use your help on this, Euan," Fletch added.

He drew in a deep breath. "All right. Nothing like jumping back in with both feet. You get Abbott's buy-off?"

Ellis wore a sheepish grin. "Working on it."

17

Abbott was a reasonable man, and Ellis felt confident he'd agree to the plan. With one exception. When civilians were involved, heavy precautions were taken. And with the family at number nine, that meant ensuring they were out of harm's way.

She and Fletch entered Abbott's office to find him finishing up a phone call.

He noted their arrival with some suspicion. "Why do I feel like I'm about to get heartburn?"

Fletch stepped forward. "Becca mentioned a lead based on the map found at the Holtz home last night." She glanced back at Ellis. "We think we know where the Woodland Heights killer might go next. And we could use the team's help."

Abbott crossed his arms and leaned back in his chair. "This based on that map the suspect left?"

"Yes, sir," Ellis replied. "I followed the lieutenant's advice. On closer inspection, we found another marking. This one showed a nine."

His gaze vacillated between the two, and then he slowly nodded. "Put something together and bring it to me. If it's a solid plan, I'll authorize it."

"Will do. We'll work on it right now. Thank you." Ellis tapped Fletch on the shoulder, and the two started into the corridor. "That went better than expected."

"Yes, it did," Fletch replied.

They returned to the bullpen to find most of the team at their desks. Lewis was in Forensics. And for Ellis, there was no better feeling. It was like McCallister never left.

Abbott wanted a plan, and now she had the means to present one with the help of her team. "Hey, guys. Fletch and I could use some input, if you have a minute," Ellis called out as she reached her desk. "We're drawing up a plan to present to the sarge about a stakeout." She turned to McCallister. "Euan's in on this with us. Connor? What do you think? I know Bryce is loaded down, and Gabby's got a case. You want in on this?"

"Absolutely." He rounded his desk and joined them.

The detectives huddled near the whiteboard and talked through the proposed options.

"We'll need to get the family out of the way," Ellis said. "So setting up a place for them to hole up will be important."

"You're assuming they'll cooperate," Bevins said. "Do you think this guy will still show up if he figures out no one's home? His entire MO is to terrorize the residents."

"All right. Fair point," Fletch replied. "But we all know they can't be used as bait."

"No," Ellis cut in. "But I can."

McCallister shot her a look. "What are you saying?"

"I'm saying Connor's onto something. If we want this guy

to think the family is home, then someone needs to be there. And that someone should be me."

"Wait, you want to stake out the home from the inside?" he continued.

"Not just me. I'll need eyes out there," she replied.

Bevins narrowed his gaze. "What are your plans for surveillance?"

Fletch walked toward the board. "We'll set up cameras at the front and rear entrances to the home. The garage included."

"And the streets?" Bevins continued.

"No, we won't have that kind of time," Ellis said. "But there's an elementary school behind this street. We'll need someone in that area because I can almost guarantee he thinks we don't know about that spot."

"I'm happy to throw my hat in the ring for that," Bevins said.

"Okay. That'll work."

"Euan and I can stake out the property from a location out of view, but one that still allows us to reach you quickly if things go south," Fletch added.

"You'll have to control the entire perimeter," Pelletier called out from his desk. "Sorry for the interruption." He stood up and walked toward them. "If this guy gets inside with Becca and somehow bypasses all of you, then she's going to be in trouble."

Ellis considered his idea. "How would he get past Connor at the back and Fletch and Euan at the front?"

Pelletier fixed his gaze on her. "He's managed to remain hidden from Moss's patrols. He's been able to get inside his victims' homes—through the front doors in some cases—completely undetected."

"Dude's right," Bevins said.

"You don't think he has the ability to slip by our team?" Pelletier cocked his head. "You have to consider the possibility, Becca, or you're leaving yourself vulnerable."

THE WHOLE THING was falling apart. He'd barely escaped with his life last night, and now he contemplated how much Ted Holtz had been able to tell the police. Could they identify him now? Would those sons of bitches finally piece it together and find him?

His only saving grace was that they hadn't busted down his apartment door yet, so maybe there was still a chance to finish this. It was the final part of the plan, and he would have to formulate it with meticulous precision. Each home had led him to the next and then the next until, finally, he was ready to end this.

His focus was on the pinboard that lay on the table in his bedroom. The curtains were drawn as the day reached its peak, and only the light above his unmade bed shone. He hadn't slept in two days, fearing the police would find him, and exhaustion weighed down his thoughts.

And now, a knock came on his front door. Perhaps they'd found him after all. He entered the hallway that led to the living room and carried onward to peer through the door's security lens.

"Hey, yo, anyone home?"

The knock came again. It wasn't the police. Far from it. It was his neighbor from upstairs, Anthony Larkin. He'd never met the man but had seen him a couple of times and knew his name from the nearby mailboxes. He unlatched the deadbolt and turned the handle, slowly pulling open the door just a little. "Yeah?"

The guy pinched his brow. "Dude, why is it so dark in there?"

"What do you want?" he asked.

"Sorry, man. I was heading out and figured I'd stop and give you a heads-up. The cops have been sniffing around here, so don't be surprised if they come knocking."

"Why?" he asked.

The kid raised his brow. "You didn't hear what happened?"

"No, which is why I asked the question."

"Oh, right. So that dude who lives next door to you—he's dead. Like, someone killed him. So the cops have been asking a bunch of people around here if they knew anything. They came and talked to me. Course, I didn't know shit, so I told them to come see you."

His heart dropped into his stomach as he opened his mouth to speak.

"Don't know if they knocked on your door. So, anyway, I figured if you heard shit going on in Taylor's apartment, or whatever, that's why. They're trying to figure out who snuffed him out."

"Thanks for the heads-up." He started to close the door when the kid thrust out his hand to stop him. He looked at the hand.

"Sorry, man, but you know, did you see any weird shit going down next door?"

"No. I work nights, and I sleep during the day. That's why it's dark in here right now."

"Oh, dude. I'm sorry, man." He raised his palms. "I'll let you get back to sleep. Just thought I'd ask."

He closed the door in Larkin's face, and the hall was cast in darkness again. The pounding in his chest started to slow. His impulsive decision might just cost him everything. The asshole deserved to die after getting nosy, but now the cops were asking questions around here. It was a mistake, but too late for regrets now. He only needed a few more days and he'd be gone.

This, however, would take better planning. That started right now. He marched into his bedroom and grabbed a baseball hat and sunglasses. It was time to do some recon to see what the cops had up their sleeves. No more underestimating them. As he returned to the door, he peeked through the lens again, noting that his neighbor was long gone. He placed the cap on his head and the glasses on his face before stepping outside into the afternoon sun.

His gold Toyota Camry was near the front of the parking lot, and he slipped inside. Within moments, he was on his way, heading into Woodland Heights to see firsthand what the cops had in mind.

As he entered the neighborhood, two patrol units rolled by. It was the first of who knew how many. He was surprised they hadn't stopped him, though he wasn't going to press his luck. If they caught sight of him again, pulling him over would likely be the first thing they'd do.

He'd perfected his story should that come to pass. He was just out looking for a home to buy and had heard this neighborhood was in a good school district. Chances were good they'd ask for his ID, which he would produce without hesitation. The ID was fake, and unless they ran his plates, he'd be in the clear. However, banking on that might be a mistake.

The house down on the next block over. That was the

place. He drove along that street, scoping out the surroundings and looking for any potential weak spots in the security. Knocking out the internet to this area would be the easy part.

About ten years ago, a fiber-optic line had been installed that now provided service to the neighborhood. Through a request to the city authorities, he'd obtained a set of plans showing him where it had been installed. Going to the nearest connection point, he'd only have to dig three feet deep and ram a shovel hard through the cable. That would do enough damage to partially sever it.

Scrambling cell towers was almost second nature to him. An EMP device would take care of it, but only for a short time. Minutes, really, but it would be enough.

Of course, cutting power to the home only required a look inside the electrical panel in the garage and pulling out a couple of the fuses.

He wondered whether people knew just how easy it was to completely shut down their access to the outside world. All the modern devices taken away with a snap of his fingers. And that would be the least of their worries.

"LET ME GO IN WITH YOU," Pelletier said. "Euan and Fletch can keep watch out front. Connor at the back, just like you said. But it means you won't be in there alone should something go wrong."

"I agree with Bryce," McCallister said. "Someone else needs to be there with you."

"No, Euan. It's going to be me. Bryce is working a case. And it seems to me you both are forgetting that I'm a trained officer." Heat brewed under her collar. "Look, you and Fletch will be the first line of defense. He won't get the opportunity to get inside the house."

"And if he does?" McCallister pressed.

"I'll be ready. As far as we know, this man doesn't have a gun. He's used a knife in his attacks. I need you and Fletch on the outside, keeping eyes out. Connor will be alone in the back, so it's really no different to what I'll be doing. Unless you both think Connor needs a partner too?"

"Last I checked, I was a trained officer too," Bevins replied.

"The plan is solid. No question," McCallister said. "But if this guy gets in—no matter how small the odds are of that happening—you can't be alone with him. So, you and me? We wait inside. Fletch and whoever else she wants with her can be eyes on the ground."

Ellis pressed her lips into a white line.

"Better to be safe than sorry, Becca," Fletch said. "I'll be fine inside a car. Connor will be good at the back. We still have several patrolmen in the area. We won't be alone, but you will."

"Yeah, all right. Fine." Her curt response was anything but, and she'd just felt for the first time McCallister's weight being tossed around. This was still her department.

"Okay. So what's the plan for getting the family out, then?" McCallister continued. "Where are they going to go? And we'll have to make sure they don't utter a word of this to their friends, co-workers, anyone. We can't afford for this to leak out and the killer somehow get wind of this. We still don't know whether this guy lives in the community or not."

"I'm going to the home first thing in the morning, before the couple leaves for work," Ellis replied. "I'll explain everything, and I have no doubt they'll cooperate. No one in that neighborhood wants to be there. I don't think I'll get pushback."

Fletch nodded. "What about tonight? Who's watching out for them?"

"Moss has two unmarked units parked nearby," Ellis added. "He'll keep up additional patrols, but eyes will always be on that house. I won't risk another attack."

Pelletier cleared his throat. "Not to beat a dead horse, but he's gotten past them already. Why would tonight be any different? And what's your level of certainty he'll show up tomorrow night when you want to execute this thing?"

"I have zero certainty of that," she shot back. "We have no choice but to assume he'll push on with his plan, making adjustments along the way, given the fact he's murdered two people and stabbed a man. He's proven what lengths he'll go to in order to do whatever it is he's doing. And he also has to know we're going to step this up." She eyed the team. "He'll take his shot, and he'll do it soon."

AFTER THE DETAILS WERE SET, equipment authorizations completed, and a thorough retelling of the plan to Abbott, Ellis was done. She respected her team's concern for her, but this was her plan. She'd given in to McCallister's request and felt some measure of resentment. He'd challenged her, and maybe it was just her bruised ego, but she was kind of pissed at him. Now, if it had come from her superiors, like Abbott or Serrano, she'd follow orders, but McCallister was her equal —or so she thought.

Ellis drove on to Hank's house, wondering if he'd ever

gone through something like this. Had he ever dated another cop? Hank never talked about his personal life, and she didn't pry. Maybe she was a little too much like him in that way. But after June, her stepmom and Carter's biological mother, passed away from cancer, Hank had closed himself off to love. She was sure of it.

Was there hope for the old man to find it again? Is that what he even wanted? These were questions never to be answered because Hank would never entertain the suggestion. He was who he was, and she wasn't going to change him now. Ellis realized she was more like him than she thought.

She arrived at his house and pulled up behind his truck in the narrow driveway. The street was lively with neighbors, people playing basketball in their driveways, chatting on their front porches, listening to music. The warm summer night brought them all out into the open. This was her favorite time of year. Life. Warmth. Happiness.

Ellis turned the handle and opened the front door, announcing herself as she always did. She closed the door behind her, the loud television drowning everything else out. "Dad?"

"In the kitchen, kid," he shouted his reply.

This late and he was in the kitchen? Interesting. Ellis carried on and noticed him snacking on a sandwich. "Is that supposed to be your dinner?"

"No, I ate earlier." He set down the lunchmeat sandwich. "You know, I've been taking care of myself for longer than you've been alive."

"I know that, Dad. But I could've brought you something. You should've called."

He swatted away the idea while taking another bite. His round face appeared even rounder as he chewed.

"You remember what your doctor said, right?" she asked.

"That I could eat and drink to my heart's content?" He laughed.

"Not exactly." Ellis pulled out a barstool and sat down at the kitchen island. "Euan's back. Full duty release."

"Is that so?" He swallowed down a bite. "When?"

"Monday, officially, though he got caught up in a bunch of red tape for a while. The guys and I put together a plan to draw out the Woodland Heights killer."

"You have, have you?" He set down his food and turned serious. "Abbott sign off on it?"

"He did," she replied.

Her dad raised an eyebrow. "Well, all right then."

Ellis couldn't help the smile tugging at the corners of her lips. Hank rarely displayed his approval, but it was there.

"So what's the plan?" he asked, leaning with his elbows on the island.

"Bait and switch, I guess you could say," she replied. "I'll be there instead of the family he'll be coming after."

Hank frowned. "Not sure I like the sound of that."

"We've got it handled, Dad. Euan and I will be inside the house," Ellis said. "Fletch and Connor, maybe Bryce too, will be the eyes outside."

He nodded slowly, raising his gaze to the ceiling as if in thought. "I've been where you are, kid. This isn't like anything else you've done. This isn't a game. You confront this guy, and it won't be like that man you arrested for what he did to me. This guy won't just go along with you because you said so. He'll fight back, I guarantee you that. Just promise me you'll be careful, okay?"

"You know I will," she promised. "I always am."

18

Derek and Lorna Cannon lived in the house marked by the intruder as number nine. Ellis now sat at their kitchen table, with McCallister beside her, informing them that it was believed they would be next. While they processed the news, she noticed that their home was unadorned. It lacked warmth and appeared basic in design with outdated finishes. Oak cabinetry, black appliances, and wallpaper patterned with various fruits covered the kitchen.

The childless middle-aged couple had lived in Woodland Heights for years. And Derek Cannon seemed in disbelief, raking a hand through his full dark hair. His cheekbones were underscored by a well-defined stubbled beard. The sharp lines of his face and the downward tilt of his nose lent a harsh exterior that now appeared to soften under worried brown eyes. "Why would he target us? I don't understand any of this. I was at the community meeting when Russ said that the cops were handling all this. Then Vicky was killed..."

Lorna placed her hand on his while smoke drifted from the cigarette she held in the other. Her warm features were in stark contrast to her husband's. Plump cheeks and full lips. Her age was apparent around her eyes and her thinning dirty blond hair, but she appeared kind. "I know how much you cared about her. We all did."

"And then Ted gets stabbed." He set his sights on Ellis. "How the hell is this actually happening? And now you're saying he's coming after us and that we have to leave?"

"I'm sorry, Mr. Cannon, but this is the best and safest plan for you and your wife. We know what this man has done to your community," Ellis said. "Trust me when I say that this will come to an end if we're allowed to put this plan in place."

"He has to be stopped, and this is our best chance to do that," McCallister added.

Lorna puffed on her cigarette before letting it dangle between her fingers. "And what happens when the neighbors start asking questions about where we're at?"

"Unfortunately, they can't know you're away," Ellis replied. "Word reaches social media or other neighbors that you're not home, and that same word might reach the intruder. He's getting information about all of you, and we don't know how, so it's best to keep this quiet."

"And what if this doesn't work?" Derek asked. "He doesn't take the bait? What if he figures it out and then comes back for us long after you and the rest of the cops have left?"

"That won't happen." Ellis noticed McCallister's sharp gaze. She'd gone a step too far; she had no way to guarantee the safety of these people if this plan didn't work out. "There is something I'd like to ask. You've lived here a long time. Did you know Joel Brooks well? The man whose daughter—"

"I know what happened to his daughter, Detective," Derek shot back. "Of course I knew him. Everyone knew Joel. That was the kind of guy he was—before—" The couple traded a forlorn glance. "Still can't get over how that all went down. Such a tragedy."

"I don't understand why us," Lorna pressed. "We don't have kids. We don't talk to Joel anymore. Are you saying you think the person who killed his daughter is connected to what's been going on here?"

"I don't have that answer for you, but it's something we're considering." To admit Ellis had no idea why any of this was happening would've been the honest answer, but after the couple had already questioned the legitimacy of the plan, was it the right response? She glanced at McCallister, whose eyes confirmed her decision. "I do know that what we've discovered along the way suggests he is coming here, and that he's coming for you both. So the best that I can offer is a chance to catch him in the act. But that means you can't be here."

"Okay." Lorna flicked ash into the ashtray. "We can stay with my sister. I don't know what you'll do about work, Derek."

He rubbed his eyes. "I'll take some time off. Just find this asshole and arrest him, would you? This neighborhood has been through enough. Whoever this is needs to pay for what he's done."

"Then we're in agreement. Thank you." Ellis got up from the table, and McCallister joined her. "We'll exit through the back, the same as we entered, and use the wooded path behind your house. I want you two to pack enough for a few days. Use small duffel bags. No large suitcases. We don't want it to look like you're taking an extended trip. A day trip at best, all right? Head to the station. Leave your vehicle. One of our people will take you where you want to go, and I'll return your car this evening. It'll look like you're home."

As the Cannons showed them out, Derek stopped at the rear sliding glass door. "Is all this cloak and dagger really necessary?"

Ellis squared up to him. "Yes, it is."

SETTING up an operation like this took planning and cooperation from more than just CID. Sergeant Moss's officers, who had patrolled Woodland Heights for more than a week, would also play a part.

While the day reached its end, the detectives' work had only just begun. They convened inside the bullpen to review the details.

Ellis studied the board. "We know that the intruder likely escaped the other night through the back woods behind the homes. So that will be where Connor will set up. It's a broad area, but if he comes for the Cannons, he'll come from that way, and you'll probably spot him long before any of us."

"Copy that," Bevins replied.

Ellis then turned to Fletch. "You'll keep watch from inside the vehicle, which will be parked over here." She pointed to the location.

"Got it," Fletch replied.

"Euan and I will hole up in the house with eyes on the front and rear entrances. We want him to think the Cannons are home, so their cars will be parked in the driveway. We'll take the one they left here this morning. The porch light will be on, and we'll keep one or two lights on inside the home as well."

"Fletch, you'll hear from one of us on the hour, every hour," McCallister added. "If you get radio silence—"

"I'm grabbing Connor and we're going in," she cut in.

"And you'll call whoever's closest on patrol. They'll stand a chance of getting there before you do," Ellis replied.

"What if he goes after a different house?" Bevins asked. "I don't mean to be the asshole here, Becca, but what if you're wrong?"

"We can't afford to be wrong," she replied.

Bevins tipped his head. "Got it."

They gathered their things, checked their weapons, and headed downstairs. The lobby had settled down in the evening hours, but that would change sometime around midnight. The worst shift was twelve to four a.m. Ellis remembered it well from when she worked in Patrol.

The operation was solid, as far as she was concerned, but Abbott remained a question mark. He'd signed off on the plan, but his hesitation spoke volumes. And with Bevins voicing his uncertainty, she'd begun to second-guess herself. That was the point at which things tended to go downhill.

Fletch and Bevins jumped into Fletch's charcoal gray Nissan Pathfinder. A subtle, non-showy SUV that cemented the practical side of her character. Fletch didn't put much stock in things, only rank.

Ellis and McCallister stepped into the Cannons' Mercedes SUV, a luxurious ride she would never be able to afford. They drove onward toward Woodland Heights as the hour reached eleven p.m. The idea was that the streets would be quieter. People would be inside their homes.

Ellis grabbed the radio. "Fletch, make a right up ahead.

The school is down this street. You'll drop off Connor, and he can walk toward the back of the Cannons' house."

"You got it."

Ellis watched Fletch make the turn and disappear while they continued into the neighborhood toward the home. She grabbed the radio again. "Stay in contact with Patrol. Moss authorized us to use his guys as necessary. You're going to be out there on your own. If things get hairy, call for backup."

"Copy."

Ellis and McCallister pulled up into the Cannons' driveway just as the radio sounded again.

"The package is out the door."

Ellis reached for the receiver again. "Copy that. We've arrived and are preparing to enter the home. Let's keep this line clear."

Ellis pulled down the ballcap on her head and opened the passenger door of the Mercedes. McCallister stuck close by and followed her until they reached the front porch. With the key the Cannons had provided, she unlocked the front door, and they walked inside the dark, empty home.

All the windows were shuttered, and the only light came from a thin stream between the living room curtains. They had been here only this morning, but now it felt ominous. And the hairs on the back of her neck stood.

Ellis reached under the lamp on the living room table and turned the switch. "If he's keeping to his MO, he'll show up sometime after he thinks they're in bed."

McCallister scanned the room. "Could be anywhere from now until two or three in the morning. Plenty of time to set up."

Ellis surveyed the home. The Cannons were ninth on the list, and so far, they hadn't discovered the possibility of a tenth. If this was to be the killer's final stop, would murder be on his agenda? She'd banked on him being armed only with a knife. But if he intended to kill, then they needed to be ready for anything.

———

FLETCH KILLED the engine and the lights, parking at the end of the street from the Cannon home. She reached for her phone and made the call.

"Yeah, Fletch, what's up?" Bevins asked.

"What's it like back there?"

"Dark. Damp. Generally unwelcoming." He laughed. "Nah, it's all right. I'll be good for a while. You?"

"Just getting settled in now. Becca and Euan are inside, so I guess we wait."

"That's all we can do."

She noticed he'd gone quiet. "Connor, you there?"

"Yeah, I'm here. I hope this isn't a colossal waste of time."

"Me too. We just have to trust Becca's hunch pays off," Fletch said.

"Listen, uh, I'd better go. I'll contact you in an hour," Bevins added. "Good luck and stay safe."

"You too, Con. Bye." She ended the call and reached for a bottle of water from the back. She twisted off the top and took a long drink. With a pinched brow, she pulled it away and examined how much she'd just gulped down. "Better ration this unless I want to spend the night peeing behind a tree."

This was the first time Fletch had been on a stakeout. She'd been so eager to climb the ladder, but right now the humbling reminder that she didn't know even half of what was necessary to be a great detective was staring her in the face.

Passing her detective's exam on the first try and at her age made her a little bit of a phenom, at least inside Bangor PD. Outside the department? She didn't have much of a life. No boyfriend. Only a few friends, and they were primarily those she worked with. Policing was her life, and maybe someday, she'd run a department. This one or another. The idea of leaving these people was one she didn't relish; however, her ambition was the driver.

A small part of her could admit that the push for Abbott to put McCallister on leave had been a test. Did she have the clout to pull it off? Turned out, she did. Manipulating the sarge wasn't the goal, but it sort of felt like that was exactly what had happened.

And now, sitting here alone with her thoughts, a part of her regretted convincing Abbott to punish McCallister for something that had happened before he arrived at their department. It was easy to tell Ellis that it was for her own good.

But maybe—maybe it was for the good of Fletch and her career.

ELLIS HAD BECOME accustomed to being alone; in fact, she often preferred it that way. This, however, was an entirely new feeling. She felt responsible for McCallister's safety. He was a veteran detective who knew his way around, but because this plan was hers, that responsibility lay squarely on her shoulders.

The daughter of legendary detective Hank Ellis didn't get

scared, but with McCallister here, that was exactly how Ellis felt. Vulnerable to the idea something might happen to him. And Fletch had called it right. When she'd gone to see him after he'd been shot, the notion she could lose him scared the hell out of her.

"You okay?" McCallister returned to the living room with bottles of water. "We're ready when he comes. The doors, windows. We have everything covered. You can take a breath for a minute."

"Yeah, I'm fine." She took one of the bottles from him as he dropped to the couch next to her. "I have to say there is a part of me unsure whether this is going to happen. I realize that I could actually be wrong here."

"Keep that kind of talk to yourself. Don't let your team know how you're feeling because it'll make them doubt not only you, but themselves too." He grabbed the remote and turned on the television. "Let's make everything appear completely normal, as if the Cannons are the ones on this sofa. He might be watching."

While their years of experience were similar, McCallister had the advantage of having worked for a big-city department. Not to mention that he'd been a homicide detective for much longer. Regardless, she'd seen a different side to him now. His insistence that she not be left alone here gave her a glimpse of who he was, and that had gotten under her skin. And now, he'd instructed her on how to handle the team. The team she knew best.

"Can I say something?" she asked.

"Of course." He muted the volume on the television and surrendered his attention.

"Do you trust me?"

He pulled back in surprise. "Of course I do. Why would you ask that?"

"I know I just voiced my doubts, and maybe I was wrong to do that. But I thought you and I were on equal footing."

"We are, Becca," McCallister said. "Where is this coming from?"

"Just because we're sleeping together doesn't mean I suddenly forgot how to be a detective. Even if I am wrong in this case, I need to know you have my back. It's the only way this works."

He gazed at her for a long moment before he nodded. "Understood."

The hours ticked away with an awkward silence as the two sat in virtual darkness. No more television. No more lights on inside the house. Everything suddenly felt very much all business. She couldn't regret laying it on the line as she had, but now her conviction waned.

Bevins still monitored the area behind the houses. Fletch sat in her car. Police cruisers rolled by every so often. And here she was, waiting for her suspect to just waltz right in and hold out his hands ready to be cuffed.

Her phone lit up beside her on the sofa, and she looked at the message. "It's Connor. He's asking how we're doing."

"Probably better than he is," McCallister replied.

"Outside in the bushes?" She laughed, feeling a slight crack in the tension. "Yeah, you're probably right." Ellis typed her reply.

> No sign of anything yet. We keep at it.

It had been three hours, and if the intruder was going to show, it would have to be soon.

Abbott had given her the rope, and now it had begun to tighten.

———————

DAYLIGHT HAD BROKEN with no sign of the intruder. McCallister wouldn't say this out loud, but the possibility existed that their suspect had noticed something off inside the Cannon home and figured this was a setup. The other option? Ellis was wrong. And after their conversation last night, he reminded himself that he had her back, even now.

As he got up from the sofa and walked into the kitchen, he noticed Ellis peering through the front window. "I know what you're thinking, but you have to understand this wasn't going to be easy."

"Nothing." She rubbed her eyes and joined him. "Absolutely no sign of him anywhere. Patrol got nothing. We got nothing."

"Yeah, well, that's part of the gig," he added. "The good news is we can go home and get some sleep and do it all over again tonight, assuming that's your plan."

"I don't think I should leave," Ellis said. "I can't risk him coming here today."

He closed the fridge door and set his eyes on her. "Becca, this guy has never come to a house in broad daylight. Why would you waste your time here when we still have a case to solve? We can keep working the clues."

She looked right past him, gazing through the kitchen window. "No, I don't think so."

McCallister's phone rang. He answered the line. "Fletch, you all right?"

"All good. Tired as hell. You guys?"

"About the same," he replied. "Listen, Becca wants to keep watch here today."

"I thought the plan was to stake out at night when he was more likely to turn up," Fletch said. "I just picked up Connor. I thought we were done."

"Becca, let's get the hell out of here." Bevins' voice sounded on the line. "I need to get some sleep."

"You three should go back," Ellis said. "There is a lot you can do from the station. Connor, you still need to finish questioning Burnell's neighbors. Something could break our way there. Look, I forced this family out of their home. And who knows? Maybe the intruder figured it out. And if he did, what are the odds he'd come back in the light of day, break in and wait it out?"

McCallister felt uncertain about her reasoning. "You need sleep."

"I'm not sure she's wrong," Fletch cut in. "Hey, Becca, you might be onto something. This guy is smart, and we can't afford to underestimate him. Staying there might be the best plan of action."

"Thanks, Fletch," Ellis said. "You three go back, do what you can to work with what we have, come back here tonight, and we'll do it again. But I would suggest you get some sleep."

"I couldn't agree more," Bevins said.

McCallister was the one who'd insisted he be there with her in the first place. It wasn't her idea. She knew she could handle this on her own. So why had he pushed her to do this his way? *Because it was the smart way.* But was it? Fletch and Bevins were out there on their own. She was right to question him. To call him out last night. Did he have the same confidence in Ellis as the others, or was he too close to her now?

For years, he'd sworn off dating anyone he'd worked with for this very reason. But then she came along. Ellis was her own person, and if he didn't work on this flaw, that would be the end of it. "Then we keep Patrol fully informed so they can back you up."

"I do know what I'm doing," Ellis insisted. "So I'll see you guys tonight. Fletch, Euan will meet you at your car. Don't come here."

He ended the call and kept his eyes on the floor. "I'm sorry, Becca. This is your operation. I have no right to tell you how to run it." He felt her hand on his shoulder and looked up again.

"I know I don't have the experience you do, and I appreciate your concern. But like you said, it's my call, Euan. If it's the wrong one, then so be it."

19

M cCallister was well aware things hadn't gone as expected. The team had spent another night at the Cannon house and still no sign of the intruder. Ellis had chosen to stay, yet again, holding onto hope her plan would work. For all anyone knew, the man could be in the wind, having figured out their plan.

While it felt great being back, this situation gnawed at him. Something about this entire deal felt off. Like they were missing an important piece of the puzzle. He noticed Bevins approaching his desk and considered that maybe the Burnell murder was that piece.

Bevins wore an air of exhaustion as he carried on with his hands in his pockets. "I just got off the phone with Rivera. He got the labs back on Burnell."

"And?" McCallister asked.

"No dice. If it was the same suspect, he didn't leave anything behind."

"Damn."

"I asked him to send me the specifics regarding the knife used to stab Burnell." Bevins opened an image on his phone. "Take a look here."

McCallister leaned over for a better view of the screen. "Details on the type and length of the knife." He looked up. "Does this match Ted Holtz's wound?"

"It does." Bevins grinned. "We have a connection. And since Burnell had no ties to Woodland Heights, I gotta think that the killer knew him from some other place."

"Makes sense." McCallister considered this new, concrete link between the two. "He's targeted specific people, numbering their homes. We know now that they weren't random attacks. His MO isn't to commit random murders."

"So he targeted Burnell too," Bevins added. "I need to go back to the apartment complex where Burnell lived and finish questioning the neighbors. I'll check out his work-place too, just to cover my bases. Burnell knew this guy. I have to find out how."

"Good. Get on it." McCallister peered at his desk, which was covered in paperwork. "Fletch and I will pore over the details on the Brooks murder. There could still be something there." He reached for the Jenna Brooks file. "I'll reach out to Joel Brooks and see if I have better luck than Becca did. If the Cannons are the killer's final target, and Brooks knew them, we stand a shot at getting to the heart of this guy's motive."

Fletch outstretched her hand as she approached them. "While you're on the phone, let me start digging into this file." She turned to Bevins. "Keep us posted on your progress."

"Thanks, guys." McCallister retrieved the phone number in the file and made the call. A man's voice answered. "Yes, sir. My name is Detective Euan McCallister with Bangor PD. Is this Mr. Joel Brooks?"

"Christ, what the hell are you people calling me again for?" he asked.

"Sir, I don't mean to disturb you, but I know you spoke to my colleague regarding a new investigation she believes is tied to your daughter's murder."

"Yeah, I'm aware, Detective. Are you aware I told her everything I knew? And that what's in the file is all Naylor ever found?"

"I am, sir." McCallister sensed the man's agitation. He would have to handle this guy carefully. "I'd like to know if you're acquainted with Derek and Lorna Cannon. They live in Woodland Heights."

"Why are you asking about them?" Brooks snapped.

"Just trying to cover our bases. Were you and your wife friends with the couple?"

"I wasn't, no. And I'm afraid you can't ask my wife. She's dead."

The news took McCallister by surprise. "Oh, I'm so sorry, sir. My condolences."

"Don't bother," Brooks shot back. "My daughter's murderer has roamed free for the past three years. You really think you'll be the one to catch him by asking about my former neighbors? Good luck and leave me out of it." He ended the call abruptly.

McCallister looked at his phone. "Shit." Brooks' response was interesting. And why had they only just learned that his wife was dead? When had she died, and how? These were things he had to find out. Maybe a clue lay hidden in there somewhere. "Hey, Fletch," he said, standing up from his chair. "We should probably follow up on this."

She looked up from her computer, her eyes bloodshot and tired. "On what?"

"Joel Brooks' wife is dead. We need to find out how and when."

"What, now?" Fletch asked. "Why is that important?"

"The man's daughter was murdered. Her killer never caught. And his wife is dead too? Was it suicide? Was she overcome with grief at the loss of her daughter, or maybe she felt guilty about something. Something she might've known and couldn't reveal. Brooks is pushing back a little too hard. I want to know why."

ELLIS NEEDED to make sense of this case. She stared at the coffee table, where papers and file folders were strewn about haphazardly. But, in fact, each pile had meaning.

She looked back at the people who'd lived in the neighborhood at the time of Jenna Brooks' murder. The Cannons were seemingly no more than acquaintances of the Brooks family. But Joel Brooks seemed to be liked by many in the neighborhood. If the Cannons were the last on the list, what had they done to draw the attention of Jenna's killer—a man who Ellis was now certain was the same person terrorizing this community?

"If this is all random, then I'll be out of a job soon." Ellis hovered over the table, staring at the papers. The crime scene photos. All of it.

"What about Jenna Brooks?" She shifted the papers until homing in on the autopsy photos of the girl. "Here it is." She reread the report and then focused on the girl's neck. Multiple stab wounds and a slashed throat. Boyles had been strangled, so there was no way to look for a pattern between the two killings. "Damn it. What the hell am I missing?"

Her phone bounced on the table as the vibration of an incoming call brought it to life. She noticed the caller ID, and her shoulders dropped as she answered the line. "Detective Alcott. Hello."

"I believe you and I had a scheduled call yesterday morning, Detective Ellis," he began. "You missed it. Here I am willing to help you out and yet—"

"Please accept my apology, Detective. I was caught up in an investigation."

"Aren't we all," he replied.

"Of course. But I have time now, if you'd like to discuss Myra Cook."

"Well, I'm glad I could fit into your busy schedule." Alcott unleashed a heavy sigh. "What is it you want to know about this investigation?"

Ellis sat down on the sofa inside the Cannons' home, then placed the call on speaker. "I suppose I'd like to understand whether you or the feds have obtained sufficient evidence to bring charges against her. And if so, what those charges might be."

"This is an ongoing investigation into securities fraud on a state and federal level," Alcott began. "I can say this much. Ms. Cook faces a great deal of legal trouble."

Ellis rubbed her forehead and closed her eyes. "So you're confident about moving forward with charges?"

"In due time. Now, I understand you're the ex-wife of Ms. Cook's current fiancé."

She figured he would've looked into her, and he had. "I am, yes. Andrew Cofield came to me with concern. I told him there wasn't anything I could do for him as a Bangor police detective."

"You're right. You can't. But if you want to help your ex-husband, I suggest you tell him to get himself a very good lawyer."

Her lips parted, and her face blanked. "Why is that?"

"Because, Detective Ellis, Mr. Cofield has been implicated as well."

FLETCH HELD up a document as she approached McCallister's desk. "I got her death certificate. Because Jenna Brooks was a cold case, the file was sealed. I eventually cut through the tape after mentioning the current investigation, and New Jersey Vital Records gave me a copy."

McCallister read the certificate. "Cause of death, bone cancer. And this was after their daughter was killed, and they'd moved."

"Yeah." Fletch nodded. "I'm not sure what you want to do with that information…"

"It does help explain why Brooks isn't willing to talk about any of this," McCallister said. "His daughter was killed, and then his wife died of cancer. I don't think I'd be open to offering help either if I was in his shoes." He looked at Fletch. "You're right. I don't know how this helps us, except that we know she didn't kill herself out of guilt. So maybe she didn't know any more than her husband did about their daughter's death."

"Let's not forget, this is the same guy who pointed the finger at his neighbors. At least, according to Detective Naylor," Fletch added.

McCallister narrowed his gaze. "What are you saying?"

Fletch shrugged. "I'm saying maybe he was onto something, but Naylor squashed it, so he gave up. And what's happening now? I guess Brooks figures it's karma."

20

Ellis pushed back the curtain on the front window and peered out. A clear, dusky sky came into view. The front garden's lush greenery shielded the home from the glaring rays of a setting sun.

The team would arrive soon and get themselves into place. It was hard to maintain focus after the conversation with Alcott. What the hell was she going to tell Andrew? Was he truly guilty, or had he just gotten tangled up with this Myra Cook in a way he couldn't escape?

The distraction was unwanted. She was after a killer, and something like this situation with her ex-husband could cause her to make a mistake. One she couldn't afford in light of the fact that nothing about her plan had panned out as of yet. Andrew's problems were not hers. Hank would tell her the same thing. Nevertheless, she had loved him once, and she wouldn't wish that kind of trouble on her worst enemy.

Ellis spotted Fletch's Nissan drive by. It was her signal that they were getting into place now. Bevins was probably already at the back, and McCallister would be here in just minutes. The curtain was about to rise, and the show about to start.

She waited for the knock on the side door. And when the faint echo resonated through the kitchen, she made her way there and opened it. "Oh, I thought you were the pizza guy."

"Pizza does sound good. I should've brought one with me." McCallister grinned and stepped inside. "Everyone's at their post and ready to go. How are you holding up?"

He knew nothing about Andrew's return or his troubles. And she wasn't prepared to tell him. Not yet. She closed the door and headed back into the living room. "I keep staring at the same information, hoping something new will pop out at me. Doesn't seem to be working, though." Ellis stopped and turned to him. "What's the temperature among the others?"

McCallister dropped onto the edge of the sofa. "They're feeling the frustration, but they're behind you. And so am I."

He was making up for his overstep. It didn't go unnoticed.

CHAIN-LINK FENCE SURROUNDED the substation of the fiber-optic cable that had been installed to service Woodland Heights, among other communities. Just outside the fence, the cable ran only about three feet deep, connecting at various points where it could be accessed and serviced.

Sitting behind the wheel of his gold Toyota sedan, he spied the maintenance station. Three lights were mounted around the facility, illuminating it as shadows spread across the wooded landscape. All he had to do now was walk out to the connection point, outside the fence. Out of view of the cameras.

Cloaked in black, he raised the hood of his jacket to further obscure his identity. No one was out here. Nothing but woods surrounded him, along with the two-lane road that traversed it.

He stepped outside, his boots squishing the soft damp earth as he walked around his car and opened the trunk. A short-handled shovel lay inside. He picked it up and walked ahead to the connection point as it appeared on the plans. The cable was thick and wouldn't easily be severed. However, he only needed to damage it to knock out the internet connection to thousands in the area, including the home he was about to visit.

Clearing away the earth, the cable was revealed. It lay inside a conduit next to other lines that were most likely electricity and telephone. Taking out the telephone line might be a good idea, even if most people didn't have land-lines anymore. No point in going through all this effort to be foiled by a phone call.

He raised the pointed shovel high and slammed it into the conduit. The plastic broke away, revealing the line inside. Again, he raised it high, thrusting it into the line. Luckily, he thought, he knew the difference between the electrical and the fiber-optic cable, or he would be on the ground right now, dead by electrocution. Fiber-optic cable wasn't electri-fied, but it was a bitch to repair.

He examined his handiwork, feeling confident it would do the trick. Returning to his car, he turned the ignition and headed onward to Woodland Heights. Further increased police presence was a certainty, so he would watch and wait to count how many and how often they made their rounds.

The wooded buffer zone around the back was likely to have been discovered after he escaped the other night.

However, on the far side of the elementary school was a walking path for the kids in Woodland Heights. He would come in from there. One thing was certain; tonight, he would not be chased out. Tonight, he would get his target.

THE TELEVISION HAD BEEN on for background noise, to make it appear that the Cannons were home. However, when the screen went blank, McCallister took notice. "That's odd."

Ellis had been studying the Jenna Brooks case files spread out on the table and glanced up. "What is?"

"The TV just went out." He looked at the Alexa device next to it. "So did that."

"Guess the internet's down," she replied. "I'm sure it'll be back on in a minute."

He pushed off the couch. "I'm going to go find the router and see if I can pinpoint the problem."

"Is it really that important?" she pressed.

He stopped and turned back. "It is if the entire neighborhood's just been cut off. It could be intentional." He made his way to the Cannons' home office, which would be an obvious location for a router. And there it sat on a shelf under the large oak desk near the window.

McCallister squatted low and examined it. "Okay, what's wrong with you?" The lights on the side were out. It appeared to be down. He pressed the button to reset it, but only the power button illuminated. "Shit." During the previous two days' stakeout, nothing had happened—until now. Coincidence? He wasn't a big believer in them.

He stood up again and returned to the living room. "I need to check this out. Something doesn't feel right to me."

Ellis regarded him. "What are you going to do?"

"Go outside and have a look around for the cable and internet hub."

"I'll come with you," she said.

He raised a hand. "Don't. You need to stay here. Keep your eyes open."

"Yeah, okay," she replied.

McCallister headed into the garage from the kitchen and walked through the side exit door. No point in drawing attention to the front door because he didn't know who was watching. The hour had passed eleven p.m. Still early. The sound of cars driving by proved it. People were still up, meaning the intruder would probably wait it out until later.

He carried on outside to inspect the perimeter. Was this the only house to suffer the outage? It was impossible to know. Had someone damaged the hub? Well, that was what he was about to find out.

HAVING PARKED OUTSIDE WOODLAND HEIGHTS, he had stepped out of his car, taking the rest of his journey on foot. The internet and phone lines were down. It wouldn't go unnoticed, so timing was critical. Gauging the comings and goings of neighbors, he also calculated how many cop cars drove by and how long it took them to complete a round. About five minutes and four cruisers. They were out and in full force.

He reached the elementary school and walked onward to the path that led inside the community. Upon reaching the wooded area behind the homes, he glanced down the swath of trees and shrubs, listening for movement. No sound emerged, but the risk the cops waited for him there was too great.

Instead, he scanned the dimly lit pathway, noting only the sounds of crickets, frogs, and the occasional snapping of twigs as he walked. His senses heightened as he continued this dangerous game. In hindsight, would it have been better to go after the one instead of the many? *No.* His reasons were plentiful, and they would be revealed tonight.

As he kept to the shadows, the Cannon home came into view. He was merely steps away, close enough to see the light through the front-room window. *Shit.* They were still awake.

A contingency plan didn't exist, but the realization they were still up would force a change in tactics. For a moment, he considered turning around, executing this on another night. But underestimating the cops was a bad idea. If this went on for much longer, he would be caught. He couldn't risk discovery.

Too late to turn back.

He pressed on and identified a weak point near the entry —a blind spot obscured by overgrown foliage that would allow him to move onto his target. He maneuvered through the underbrush, evading thorny branches and damp soil, inching closer to his destination under the moonlit sky.

Without hesitation, he withdrew his EMP frequency jammer from inside his jacket and pressed the button. The lights on the security cameras posted around the home went out. The cell towers would cease to receive signals as well; he had but moments.

The once watchful eyes of the police force that rolled through the community would be momentarily blinded, and their voices drowned in a sea of static.

Swift and silent, he continued his approach toward the

side of the house, knowing that the window of opportunity would soon close. But the sound of a voice stopped him in his tracks. He listened, hearing only his own breath for a moment, and then he heard it again.

"Hello? Hello?"

The male voice was unrecognizable. Was it Derek? Was he outside? With the EMP device deployed, the call would've instantly dropped. Was it the cops? Did they know he was there?

His mind spun with various scenarios as to how this would play out. This couldn't be the end. Not yet.

He moved toward the voice with muted steps on the soft ground, armed with his knife. A gun might've been preferable in this moment, but gunfire would draw out the police, and he would end up dead or in cuffs before the job was finished. But if he could sneak up on whoever this person was, knocking him out cold was his best option.

"You there?" the voice called out.

The jammer would only work for five, maybe ten minutes at best. He had to get inside before the signal returned, so he followed the voice and spotted a shadow near the corner of the house. The man's back was turned. His identity obscured. One sound and his presence would be revealed before he was in position. He steadied his hands but couldn't control his rising pulse. Steps away, he raised the knife high, the handle ready to strike hard.

The man spun around, the whites of his eyes revealed as he reached for a weapon.

Hit him.

He brought down the handle of the knife, hammering the man's head, forcing him to collapse to the ground. He hovered over him. Was he out? It appeared so, but for how long? And what he knew for certain was that this man wasn't Derek Cannon.

The badge made it clear he was a cop.

With seconds ticking away, he had two options. Take the risk that Cannon was inside, and he could get what he came for, or flee knowing Cannon would never pay for what he'd done. Prison, death, or revenge?

He grabbed the downed cop's gun from his holster and ran back to the power box nestled against the outside wall. He withdrew a pair of wire cutters and snipped, severing the main power line.

If this was to be the end, then so be it.

ELLIS JUMPED to her feet as the house plunged into darkness. Light from the moon streamed through the gap between the curtains on the front window. The air took on a purple tint. Her pulse quickened as she brandished her gun, training it on the darkness. "Euan? Euan, are you in here?" She listened for any sound, for any movement and was met only with silence and a strange stillness that infiltrated the house.

But when a noise echoed in the open space, she firmed her grip on the gun. A gentle tap sounded on the wood floor as she zeroed in on the source. *The kitchen.* A door led to the garage and another to the backyard. Someone was here. Someone was inside.

With slow, measured steps, Ellis moved closer to investigate. McCallister would've called out if he could. The idea something had happened to him sent a flush of heat to her chest as anger rose. "Who's there?"

She crept toward the kitchen and noticed the side door

was ajar. *It's you.* Despite all her planning, the intruder had found a way inside, and now she was alone with him.

Her defenses raised, she knew McCallister had been hurt or worse. Could she get word to Fletch or Bevins? Anyone who could do something. But diverting her attention for even a moment could give him the advantage. Her life was on the line, and she felt it in every breath, every beat of her heart.

A figure darted across her line of sight. Ellis raised her gun. *There he is.* "Stop! Bangor PD."

———

IT WASN'T SUPPOSED to go down like this. Get in, take out the son of a bitch, and leave this godforsaken city. Instead, some cop waited for him, and now he was pressed behind the door to the den, the cop's gun ready at his side.

Taking a deep breath, he stepped out from behind the door, pushing it farther open to reveal an impenetrable darkness that engulfed the home. He stepped into the hall, every nerve on edge.

Silence pervaded the house, broken only by the sound of his footfalls. He ventured deeper when a faint noise caught his attention. *She's close.*

With each step, his heartbeat grew louder, pounding in his ears. The scant moonlight that shone through the window revealed a flicker of movement, a fleeting glimpse of a shadow vanishing around a corner. He quickened his pace, determination fueling the pursuit.

Entering the hallway, he caught a faint scent, a mixture of fear and the light floral trace of a woman's perfume. She must've been mere inches away, her face obscured, yet her presence felt.

"You won't get out of here alive unless it's in cuffs," her voice called out. "In this darkness, you're lost. Now, show yourself."

IT WAS five minutes past the hour, and Fletch made the call to Bevins. "Hey, you hear from them yet?"

"No. Nothing," he replied. "I haven't seen anything either. What do you want to do?"

She turned the engine. "I'll make a drive around and check that everything's okay."

"Copy that," Bevins replied. "Keep me posted. I don't like this."

"Neither do I." Fletch ended the call and drove on to the next block over. The Cannon house was less than a minute away, and she'd seen two patrol units pass her by. *Everything's fine. They seem to think it's fine too.* Rolling by, she noticed the house was dark. It was beyond midnight, and most of the homes were dark. Maybe this was just them blending in.

Or maybe something's wrong.

Fletch killed the headlights. She pulled to the side of the road a couple of houses down from where her team waited. She grabbed her phone, ready to call Ellis. "What if they're in trouble?" Making the call could put them in jeopardy. They knew the plan. Every hour on the hour. So to miss the call meant the plan had gone south.

She typed a succinct message to Ellis.

Are you OK?

She stared at the phone, praying for an answer. "Come on, Becca, answer the damn message."

Fletch tried McCallister, typing the same message. "Please, God." She let out a shaky breath. But seconds passed and still nothing. Her eyes were glued to the house, hoping to see movement, a light, something.

She called Bevins again.

"Yeah?"

"Conner, we have to go in after them. Now."

TIME BECAME irrelevant as Ellis weaved through the house, shadows battling against the flickering light. Her mind raced, analyzing every sound, every footstep, trying to anticipate his next move. She had to outwit him; she was relying on her instincts and training to survive. *Where the hell are you?* What was worse was that she had no idea what had happened to McCallister.

A crash echoed from down the hall. He must've been in a bedroom and knocked something to the ground.

Ellis marched ahead, her flashlight resting above her gun as it aimed into the shadows.

He stepped into view, the beam from her light briefly illuminating his face.

She flicked off the safety on her gun and saw the flash of terror etched across his shadowy features. "Stop!"

A round went off. It wasn't hers.

The fiery light of the bullet whistled through the air and

finally extinguished, and so had he, vanishing somewhere into the depths of the house. "Fuck!"

Silence descended once more, broken only by her heavy breathing. He was there, hiding, waiting for her.

In that pitch-black house, her resolve burned. Her fear that McCallister was hurt propelled her. The game of cat and mouse continued, the stakes growing ever higher.

Ellis stood still for a moment, regaining her bearings. He was there, in the blackness. She only needed to find him. Her flashlight illuminated the hall, the doors, the approaching staircase. But no sign of the killer.

He watched her. She felt his stare. *Where the hell are you?* Ellis turned around, shining her flashlight on every corner of the room. Empty.

Footfalls sounded on the landing. With her gun trained, she rushed to the steps and ran up. The footsteps grew louder as she climbed, leading her to the second floor.

His steps ceased, and silence returned.

Her eyes widened to absorb as much light as possible, while her aim trailed her movements. She wasn't the only one afraid. The scent of his desperation hung in the air. He was close.

As Ellis inched down the hallway, she noticed a faint glow coming from under a door at the end of the hall. She moved toward it and could hear the killer's breathing: ragged and uneven.

Ellis braced herself before pushing the door open, her gun at the ready. Her eyes were drawn to the corner of the bedroom. He was crouched low, her light bouncing off the gun in his hand.

She recognized the gun. Police issue.

No.

"Drop your weapon," Ellis called out.

He fired a round, and she whipped back, pressing against the wall outside the room. The bullet struck the door, flinging it wide open. And as she regained balance, she swung around to fire back, but he was there and knocked the gun from her hands.

Turning sharply sideways, she rammed her elbow into his jaw, and his gun slipped away, sliding across the hallway floor.

Both unarmed, the two tumbled to the floor, grappling for control. He was a large man, and despite her strength, he pinned her down. She eyed a gun just inches away and outstretched her hand. *Come on. Come on.* Her fingers spread out like tentacles, hoping to grasp just enough, but he rammed his knee into her bicep.

Ellis howled as her arm felt like it snapped in two. She kicked and thrashed, trying to break free from the killer's grip.

He tightened his hold on her as he went for his gun. But a sudden burst of strength surged through her body. She twisted her hips and knocked him off balance. With one swift movement, Ellis flipped over on top of him and straddled him while she reached for her gun.

He screamed at her, and she looked down at his face, seeing it clearly for the first time. She gasped. "What the..."

21

She'd hesitated too long. Ellis was thrown from the man, and once again, she lost control of her weapon as it slammed against the wall. The killer lunged at her, but Ellis was already on her feet. She dodged his attack and tried to land a punch, but he was too fast. He grabbed her arm and twisted it behind her back, causing her to cry out in pain. She struggled to break free from his grasp.

Ellis gritted her teeth and kicked out at him, connecting with his shin. He stumbled backwards.

A voice yelled out.

They both froze for a split second as Ellis shouted, "Over here!" She knew it was McCallister's voice and that Fletch was probably with him. He was okay. He was alive.

Her eye was drawn to the killer as he reached again for her weapon. "No!" Ellis leaped toward it, landing hard on the floor, and clutching the gun between her hands, pulling it toward her chest.

He spun around and sprinted out of the hall.

"Stop him!" Ellis scrambled to her feet. Still in the dark,

she hurried out. "I'm coming out. It's me. Don't shoot!" In the dark, it would be too easy to make that mistake. "He's trying to escape."

McCallister and Fletch stood at the front of the hall, guns aimed.

Ellis raised her hands. "It's me. It's me."

"Jesus, are you okay?" McCallister asked.

"He's getting away." She pushed onward. "We have to stop him."

Ellis took off down the hall. She heard McCallister and Fletch following close behind. She burst through the back door in time to see him disappear over the fence at the edge of the property.

Without a second thought, Ellis took off after him, her feet pounding against the soft grass as she ran. She gained ground quickly, her heart racing as she closed the gap.

The sounds of footfalls hurrying behind her meant McCallister and Fletch were close. She wondered if Bevins was nearby. Would he hear the commotion and cut off the killer before he slipped away?

Ellis noticed him look back at her. He veered off course and headed toward the thick brush that surrounded the property.

She followed him, using her instincts to guide her through the darkness. She could hear the rustling of leaves and branches as he pushed his way through the thick foliage, and she forced herself to move faster, refusing to let him escape.

Ellis could feel her breath coming in short, sharp gasps as she ran. The branches and shrubs stung her skin, making her even more awake and alert. She was gaining on him.

He darted off to the side, disappearing into a dense cluster of trees.

Ellis cursed under her breath and tried to follow him, but it was too dark for her to make out his path. She slowed to a stop, doubling over and gasping for breath. Recovering her strength, she listened intently when a branch snapped ahead. That had to be him.

Ellis took off again, following the sound until she burst out of the trees onto an open road. She scanned both sides frantically for any sign of him, but there was nothing. He was gone.

A gunshot rang out inside the woods, and her heart skipped a beat. *Who fired?* She pushed through the brush again and saw him.

Bevins stood poised, gun aimed at the ground. "He's down. I got him."

"Thank God." Ellis rushed over and saw the killer in a heap on the ground, a pool of blood forming around him.

Within moments, Fletch and McCallister joined them.

They hovered, gazing down at the dead body.

Ellis should've felt relieved. But, on looking at his face again, the realization of his identity took a moment to fully sink in. "It's him."

"Who?" McCallister asked.

"Joel Brooks."

BEVINS RETURNED his gun to his holster. "I ran into that son of a bitch at the apartment where Burnell lived. I remember his face. Did he kill his own kid and then come back here for more?"

"I don't know." Ellis shook her head in disbelief. "I don't know why he's here. Or why he's done these things."

Fletch holstered her weapon. "We have to get this body out of here. People are coming out of their homes. Everyone would've heard the gunshot."

McCallister grabbed his phone. "I'll call for the ambo now." He stepped away.

"How did you recognize him?" Fletch asked.

"I saw photos from Jenna Brooks' case file," Ellis replied. "Why would he do this? I thought he was in New Jersey, but he was here the whole time."

"But where?" Fletch asked. "Where the hell was he staying?"

Ellis looked out toward the school. "He was running that way. He could have a car over there. We should go check it out."

"I'll stick close to the body," Bevins said. "Make sure no one gets nosy. You two go."

The two walked on until they reached beyond the elementary school and made it back out onto the neighboring street outside Woodland Heights.

"You sure you're okay?" Fletch asked. "You were alone with him for a while."

"I'm fine." She looked at Fletch. "What happened to Euan?"

"The guy cold-cocked him. When you guys missed your call, I drove over to check things out. Saw the lights off. Knew something was wrong. I searched the property and found him in the back corner. He was already starting to come around."

"And then you came inside. Thank God," Ellis replied. "I'm so glad you're both okay. I don't know that I would've been able to hold him off much longer. I just can't believe it was him." Ellis wiped the sweat from her forehead. "I don't get it."

"Maybe he did murder his own kid," Fletch said. "But you got him, Becca. You stopped the killer."

"Connor did," she replied.

"It was your plan." Fletch stopped cold and squared up to her. "You put this plan into action, and it paid off. I know you weren't sure after a while. Hell, none of us were, but you persevered."

They started on again, and Ellis spotted a gold sedan parked in front of a small patch of open space. "There." She pointed ahead. "Let's check out that car."

As they approached, Ellis peeked inside the windows while Fletch kept watch from a distance. An open bag on the passenger seat. She checked the door, and the driver's side was unlocked. She reached in and shone her flashlight inside. "Tools. Shoes. Some clothes."

"Unlock this side, would you?" Fletch moved in and stood at the passenger door. When the lock clicked, she used her shirt to grab the handle to open it. "This is a rental. I see the sticker on the windshield. But where is he staying?"

"The apartment where Burnell lived," Ellis said. "That's where Connor recognized him from. It's safe to say he killed Burnell, but I'll bet we'll find the knife, and it'll be the same one he used to stab Ted Holtz." Ellis aimed her flashlight inside and popped open the glovebox. Papers spilled out onto the seat, and she rifled through them with a pen, careful not to touch anything. "Here it is."

"What'd you find?" Fletch asked.

"The rental car agreement." She held up the document. "Yeah, that's the place. That's where Burnell lived."

ONE CASE HAD BEEN SOLVED, but it had left many unanswered questions about another.

They'd returned to the Cannon home to secure the scene and wait for the ambulance to take the body of Joel Brooks.

Officers controlled the crowd that formed as neighbors emerged from their homes. It was almost two in the morning, and now the team prepared to search the place where Brooks had been holed up.

Ellis approached McCallister as they stood out front and examined the lump on his head. "You should probably go to the hospital to get checked out."

"She's right." Fletch joined them. "You took a hell of a hit, Euan."

"I'm fine," he insisted. "We need to get inside that apartment."

Ellis knew she wasn't going to change his mind. "I guess Fletch is driving. Let's go."

A quick stop to see Moss, who'd just arrived on scene, and Ellis briefed him on where they were headed.

"Let me know if you need anything," he said. "I'll make sure we're buttoned up here."

"Appreciate the help." Ellis nodded and trailed the team as they walked to Fletch's car. She climbed into the front passenger seat. After the others stepped inside, she regarded them. "I just want to thank you guys for what you did."

Fletch pressed the ignition. "We did our job, Becca." She pulled away and headed along the road toward the apartment complex. "All of us did."

On their arrival, Bevins scoffed. "Son of a bitch. He was here the whole time, and I didn't even know it."

"How could you have known?" Ellis asked. "I talked to him on the phone and had no clue."

"Same here," McCallister said. "He'd probably planned this out for a while. He knew what he was doing, which was why he was able to get around the neighborhood unseen."

Fletch parked in front of the building. "How are we getting in?"

"Break a window," Bevins replied as he opened the door. "Let's go."

Ellis stepped out. "Management won't be here. Maintenance might, though."

"Becca, we aren't waiting for someone to come and unlock the door," Bevins insisted. "The guy's dead. We can get inside."

They followed him to the first-floor apartment.

"This is it," Bevins said, eyeing the front window. "I guess we get in through here." With his elbow, he smashed the glass. The sound echoed throughout the space.

"Well, that ought to bring out the cops," Ellis replied.

Fletch picked up her phone. "I'll call the station and let them know."

Bevins cleared away the glass and climbed over the window frame and into the apartment. "Jesus, I was just across the way. How the hell did I miss this guy?"

McCallister followed him inside. "Let it go, man. No way you could've known. Not without evidence pointing to him." He helped Ellis inside.

"Thanks," she replied.

He offered his hand to Fletch, but she crawled through without his help.

Ellis flipped on the lights. The walls were a drab, yellowing color, and the peeling wallpaper revealed patches of damp. The curtains and furniture were both worn and stained. In fact, the sofa looked like it had been scavenged from the side of the road. The carpet was faded and matted, and the air was stale.

"Nice place," Ellis said. She continued inside, turning on the lights as she entered each space. And when she reached the only bedroom, and the lights flicked on, her mouth fell ajar. "What the hell is this? Uh, hey, guys. You might want to come in here."

The rest of the team joined her.

She glanced at them. "What the hell do you make of this?"

Names, faces, pretty much everyone who had been attacked was on the board. Some with an X on their photos.

"Take a look here," Ellis said, indicating a map that had been torn. "This is where the map was ripped off. I still have no idea why."

As they examined the pinboard, McCallister appeared to notice something on the desk. "What's this?" He reached for a black leather journal and flipped through the pages. "He wrote in this. It looks like details about each victim."

Ellis moved toward him and examined the book. "Brooks documented how he had planned to execute each assault." She turned to Fletch. "He'd only planned on scaring them."

"That didn't work out so well for him, did it?" McCallister set down the journal as they studied the pages.

"Anything in there about the bar?" Bevins asked. "Why the hell did he go after that guy?"

"I don't know," Ellis replied. "I don't see anything here about it." She looked back at him. "In your interviews, did anyone mention seeing those two talking?"

"Not a one. And when I came here to talk to him, he

wasn't home." Bevins walked away, appearing angry with himself.

"Best guess is Burnell got in his way somehow," McCallister continued. "I think we've found enough evidence to connect him to the attacks."

"But it doesn't tell us why," Fletch added.

"And was he responsible for the murder of his daughter?" Ellis asked. "The DNA from Vicky Boyles' and Jenna Brooks' murder scenes matched. Was it his, and did he kill them both?"

BY THE TIME the apartment had been taped off and the evidence removed, the sun had risen. Ellis and the others hitched a ride with Fletch back to the station, where they parted ways for a few hours of rest.

Now, as her eyes popped open, Ellis realized she'd fallen asleep on her couch. "Shit." With her elbow, she propped herself up in search of her phone. It lay on the floor, and she quickly retrieved it. The screen displayed the time. Ten in the morning.

And a text from Abbott appeared.

Come in as soon as you can.

Ellis stood from the couch and raised her arms in a long stretch. Within moments, she jumped in the shower and got dressed. A quick cup of coffee, and she was out the door.

As she drove onward, she called McCallister.

"Morning," he answered.

Peering out at the road ahead, she replied, "Back at you. How are you feeling?"

"The same as I did last night. I'm just fine. You manage any sleep?"

"Some. Then I saw a text from Abbott. Said to come in right away."

"I think we all got it," he said.

She made the turn onto the highway. "I'm on my way now. Where are you?"

"Already here."

Ellis rolled her eyes. "Am I going to be the last one to the party?"

"Yeah. Sorry about that. But none of us had to fight off an attacker, so we'll cut you some slack."

A smile tugged at her lips. "Thanks for that. I'll see you soon." Ellis ended the call and began to think about how Joel Brooks had managed to do what he'd done. And more importantly, why he'd done it. Evidence waited, and maybe more would be revealed. And there was still the Burnell murder. Had that man been involved in the planning of all this? Who was he?

She believed that after the end of this operation, the case would be over. But it was far from over. The people of Woodland Heights would have questions, and right now, she had no answers.

The stationhouse appeared in the distance, and Ellis drove onto the parking lot. She took a moment to clear her head and prepare to deal with whatever might happen today. One thing was certain, Joel Brooks was a killer. But the question they kept all asking themselves was, had he murdered his own daughter?

She walked inside and was climbing the steps when a voice called out.

"Detective?"

Ellis turned back to see Triggs. "Hi."

He jogged to meet her. "I heard about what happened last night. Are you okay?"

"Yeah, of course. Thanks for asking."

He crossed his arms and widened his stance. "So, uh, you guys need any more help going through all the evidence? I hear you brought in tons of stuff."

"I don't know yet. Maybe. I'll be sure to give you a heads-up. I appreciate all the work you've done on this case, Triggs. Might be a good idea to talk to Moss and see what you guys can do to meet with the neighbors. I have a feeling they'll all be here soon."

"Me too. Hey, I'll catch up with you later, then?"

"You got it." Ellis carried on upstairs and entered the bullpen. "I am the last one to the party." She looked around. "Did any of you sleep, or was it just me?"

"Just you, Becca." Bevins laughed. "No, it's all good. How you doing, anyway?"

She continued to her desk and nodded to McCallister. "All right. Thanks."

Pelletier walked around and made his way to her. "I hear things went nuts last night."

"Yeah, they did. Nothing went down like we expected."

"But you're good?" he pressed.

"I'm good."

"Glad to hear it. Let me know if I can do anything to help you guys out."

"Will do, Bryce. Thanks." Ellis sat down and looked at

McCallister, who was already at his desk. "Has the sarge said anything to you guys?"

"Not yet. I think he was waiting for you to get here." He looked out at the team as Lewis walked inside.

"Well, well, well." She sat down at her desk. "Sounds like I missed a whole lot of action last night. Everyone okay?"

"All good," he replied.

"We came out with a few bumps and bruises," Ellis cut in. "And Connor got our guy, so we're doing okay."

"Thank goodness for that," Lewis added.

McCallister turned back to Ellis. "We should probably go brief the sarge."

"Yep." Ellis looked at Fletch and Bevins. "Let's be sure our ducks are in a row, people. The sarge is waiting for us."

The team headed into Abbott's office, and Ellis wasn't surprised at all that Serrano had decided to join him.

"Morning, everyone." Abbott removed his reading glasses. "So, who wants to start?"

"I will." Ellis thumbed over at her team. "These guys saved my ass last night. Connor took down our suspect, Joel Brooks, and we learned he'd been living in an apartment nearby. The same one where Taylor Burnell lived."

"You probably already know, Sarge, that Brooks is almost certainly Burnell's killer. I'll be working to wrap that up today," Bevins added.

Abbott and Serrano traded a glance before Abbott pressed on. "So, what's next?"

"Well, sir," Ellis said, "it seems we've solved one problem but found another. According to the file given to me by Detective Naylor in Augusta, Joel Brooks lived in New Jersey."

"And yet he had an apartment here," Abbott said.

"That's right," McCallister replied. "And we've collected all the evidence we found there."

"So here's what I think needs to happen next," Ellis jumped in. "We'll find the answers we need there."

"In his house in New Jersey?" Serrano clarified.

"Yes, sir." She regarded him. "We have to go to New Jersey."

22

The lobby was inundated with the residents of Woodland Heights. Not only the victims, but the community as a whole had gathered in search of answers. Word had spread quickly as to the identity of the man who'd terrorized them.

Ellis and the others emerged from Abbott's office when she stopped and gazed down over the railing. Sergeant Moss, alongside Triggs and Yearwood, attempted to calm the rising unrest among the crowd.

It was plain to see they wanted more answers. Why had he come after them? Why had he murdered one of their neighbors and let others live? These were questions Ellis also had, but they were not going to be answered here.

McCallister placed his hand on her shoulder. "You doing okay?"

Ellis glanced at him. "It's a madhouse down there."

He peered out over the railing. "Patrol has a handle on it. Let them do their jobs. We should get a move on if we want to coordinate with the Jersey police."

With her gaze still outward, she began, "Do we have to get them involved?"

He wore a puzzled frown. "Is that a real question?"

"Right." She turned away from the railing and noticed Bevins and Fletch returning to the bullpen. "How about we keep them here to review the evidence found in the apartment? You and I can head to Jersey and check out the house."

"Abbott gave us his nod, so let's get moving," McCallister replied.

They returned to the bullpen, and Ellis stopped at Fletch's desk. "Euan and I are going to Jersey. Can you assist Connor with the evidence from the apartment?"

"Yeah, of course." Fletch glanced over at him. "What do you think you'll find at Brooks' house?"

"A reason for why he did what he did would be great," she replied.

Fletch appeared to study her a moment. "You think you'll figure out what happened to Jenna Brooks?"

"If the answers to that cold case present themselves..." Ellis shrugged. "Then all the better."

THE NONSTOP FLIGHT to Newark had arrived without delay. Now, Ellis and McCallister headed to Westfield PD for a courtesy meeting to discuss Joel Brooks. The question was, why had Brooks returned to Woodland Heights? Much still needed to be considered, and speaking with the local authorities for a clearer picture on just who they were dealing with would show cooperation on their part in the hope they would get the same in return.

The drive to the upper-middle-class suburb took about forty minutes. When they finally arrived, Ellis and McCallister approached the admin desk with badges in hand.

"Good afternoon," Ellis began. "We're with Bangor PD, and we'd like to speak with someone regarding one of your residents who unfortunately has died in our jurisdiction."

"Where at, Detective?" the officer asked.

"His address here was 1279 Shoreman Drive."

The officer keyed in the information. "District two. I have it here. Uh, why don't I get our lieutenant to speak with you?"

"That would be fine. Thank you." When the officer walked away, Ellis turned to McCallister. "Did you see the look on his face?"

"Sure did," he replied. "I have a feeling Mr. Brooks may have a history with this department."

They'd waited only moments when a man in a navy suit with a badge on his belt approached. His hair was thick and black and heavy with product, making it appear stiff. He was younger than Ellis expected. Possibly only in his late thirties —young for a lieutenant.

"Hello, Detectives. I'm Lieutenant John Graves. I understand you've come down from Bangor." His wide brown eyes shifted between them. "How can I help you?"

"We're investigating the death of a man named Joel Brooks," Ellis began. "We understand he has ties to Westfield, and we were hoping to speak with someone who could offer insight into him."

"Of course." Lieutenant Graves nodded, his expression unreadable. "Can I ask the manner of his death?"

Ellis's mind flashed back to the moment when Brooks

had her pinned down, his eyes filled with rage. "My team and I were in pursuit. He was gunned down by one of us."

Graves hesitated for a moment before speaking. "I see."

"We've uncovered some troubling details that we think may have contributed to Brooks' return to his former neighborhood," McCallister said. "What can you tell us about him, Lieutenant?"

"Why don't we discuss this in my office?" Graves turned around and headed into a lengthy corridor. He glanced over his shoulder as they followed. "How long have you been after him?"

"About ten days or so," Ellis replied. "It started with him breaking into the homes of his former neighbors, and escalated from there."

The lieutenant gestured toward his office. "Come on in and take a seat." He followed them inside and closed the door.

His office was lined with file cabinets, and a desk was centered between two windows, topped with notes and paperwork. A bulletin board was mounted on the wall, with mugshots pinned to it, along with an array of maps and files.

Graves walked around to his desk chair and sat down, entering commands on his keyboard. "I'll pull up what I have on Joel Brooks. How did you track him down here?"

Ellis took a seat. "I'd actually spoken to Mr. Brooks at the beginning of our investigation. We knew that he lived here in New Jersey, and believed he'd been here the entire time, until we learned otherwise. We'd like to search his home in connection with a cold case involving his daughter as well as the multiple murders he committed in our jurisdiction."

"Jenna Brooks. I'm aware." Graves stood from his desk.

"Let me grab the report from the printer. I'll be back in a moment."

He left the office, and Ellis turned to McCallister. "He's aware?"

"Yeah, I caught that too," he replied. "If he had to print a file, it must be sizable. I'm not sure what that says about Joel Brooks, but I'm anxious to find out."

When the lieutenant returned, he handed a copy to Ellis and one to McCallister before sitting down again. "The Brookses moved here about two and a half years ago. Mr. Brooks has been alone for the last six months or so."

Ellis perused the file. "We're aware the wife passed away from cancer."

"That's right. But as you can see from the file, Mr. Brooks grew increasingly unstable shortly thereafter."

She continued to read the details. "How many times did he come in here asking for help?"

"About the investigation into his daughter's murder?" Graves asked. "At least three times a month. Each time, he was certain he had sufficient evidence."

"Did you assign the case to anyone?" McCallister asked.

"How could I?" Graves shrugged. "It wasn't even in our jurisdiction. We helped him as much as we could. Sent the information to Augusta, but apparently nothing ever came of it."

Ellis sighed. "And so, after his wife died, he figured he had nothing left to lose and took matters into his own hands."

Graves steepled his fingers. "That is how it appears. If you want to search his home, I'm happy to assist."

"We could use help with gaining entry," Ellis said. "And then I think we can take it from there."

As they drove out to Brooks' home, Ellis couldn't help but feel a sense of unease. The notion that Brooks had played a part in his daughter's death diminished with the lieutenant's new details. However, she felt something darker still lay ahead.

McCallister appeared to notice her apprehension and reached over to place his hand on hers as it lay on the gearshift. "We'll get in and find what we need to end this."

"I'll take your word for it." Ellis offered him a small smile.

Within a few more minutes, they'd arrived at the middle-class neighborhood with its older homes clad in wood siding and brick facades. Wide, tree-lined streets and narrow sidewalks spread as far as the eye could see. In the late afternoon sunshine, kids traversed the street on bikes and skateboards, dressed in T-shirts and shorts. Some played catch, and others jumped through sprinklers in their front yards to cool off.

Graves had sent along one of his officers, and he followed closely behind Ellis's rented car. She pulled curbside in front of the modest tri-level home with a single-car garage.

"This is it," Ellis said, cutting the engine. "No signs of life inside, from what I can see."

"Let's hope it stays that way and we aren't in for any surprises." McCallister stepped out and waited for her on the sidewalk.

The Westfield police officer caught up to them as Ellis and McCallister started on toward the front door. "If we need to break a window, I'll do it," he said.

"I've got no problem with that, Officer." Ellis climbed the

front steps and reached the door. She gestured to him. "I'll leave this part up to you, then."

The young officer, who wore his hat low on his face, searched for an easy point of entry. Checking the door and windows, he found that all were locked. "Okay, I'm going in." He busted the side window next to the front door and reached inside. Quickly disengaging the lock, he turned the handle. "Not as hard as I thought it would be."

"Thank you." Ellis stepped inside and turned back to the officer. "We've got it from here."

"Yes, ma'am. Just let the lieutenant know when you're finished, and he'll make sure someone comes out to secure the place again." The officer took his leave.

The house was quiet, and they could hear the sound of their footsteps echoing in the empty hallway. Board and batten lined the entry that led to the oak staircase. Beige square tile lined the floor until it met with a light wood from the hallway and living room. The décor was sparse. A few pieces of cheap-looking floral art hung on the walls. No personal pictures. Older furnishings. And the damp summer air that hung inside the house made it seem that it had been locked up tightly for quite a while. They made their way inside, checking each room carefully. It felt like it had been abandoned.

"I don't think he ever intended on coming back here," Ellis said as she reached one of the bedrooms. "This must be where his wife stayed at the end of her illness," she observed as she noticed a hospital bed and some medical equipment.

McCallister joined her, his face masked in sympathy. "I can't imagine losing a child and then your wife not long after."

"No doubt it's what led to his unraveling," Ellis said. "She died more than six months ago, and the bed is still here. That's not the sign of a man who has started to recover from his grief." She carried on down the hall. "I don't see anything more down this way. I noticed a set of stairs in the kitchen. The place has a basement."

"Let's check it out," McCallister suggested.

They continued through the unremarkable home. In its lack of any color or warmth, it reminded Ellis of a furnished rental home.

The kitchen was outdated. White melamine cabinets and a laminate countertop with a cast-iron sink. A small dinette set in the center. And then, an open door with a staircase inside that must've led down into the basement.

Ellis took the lead and walked down the steps, flipping on the light switch on the wall. "It's cold down here."

"Imagine what it must be like in the winter," McCallister replied.

The basement was carpeted with some kind of commercial-grade covering. The masonry walls were painted, but no drywall installed over the top. Probably why it was so cold.

They stood in an open area. Off to the right was a small bathroom with only a shower and toilet. Toward the left appeared to be a bedroom. And as they surveyed the unsettling room, Ellis saw the table. She aimed toward it. "Over there."

Ellis walked ahead while McCallister followed. "Banker's boxes." She opened the lid to the box on top of the table and eyed the contents. "What the hell is this?"

Photos. Witness statements. Timelines. It was all here inside. But that wasn't everything. Ellis reached into one of the boxes, retrieving a few pieces of paper. She scanned them before looking up at McCallister. "These are the old police reports from Augusta."

McCallister moved closer, his brow furrowing as he read over the documents in Ellis's hand. "Jenna Brooks."

Ellis continued to sift through the pile of evidence. "He collected everything Naylor had. Jesus." She viewed the notes and more photos. Three years' worth of evidence that had led nowhere.

Ellis continued to sort through the many files inside several boxes. "He collected every single news article. Every snippet of information about his daughter's murder."

"This was what Graves talked about. Brooks coming to him and asking for help," McCallister said.

She picked up what appeared to be a notebook. "This is like the book you found in the apartment." Flipping through the pages, she noticed penciled scribbles that seemed almost chaotic in their expressions. "Are these theories?"

"Could be," he said with a nod.

"He was putting together theories about who, where, and why his daughter was taken." Ellis peered at him.

"He didn't kill her," McCallister pressed.

"No, he didn't." She furrowed her brow. "And these theories, they're detailed. He has names, places, motives. It's like he's been investigating the case himself." She looked at him. "I think he was trying to figure out who did it, and that's what led him back to his old neighborhood."

23

Rebuilding a three-year-old cold case took time. Ellis and the team compiled the information they'd gathered in New Jersey in hopes they could draw a conclusion as to why Brooks had returned to his old neighborhood.

Comparing that information to what had come from the Westfield police as well as from the basement in Brooks' home was a monumental task. Brooks had clearly learned a connection was there, but now they had to find it.

As it reached nearly eleven o'clock at night, Ellis and McCallister remained in the bullpen, poring over the details of the case.

Abbott ambled toward them. "Why are you two still here?"

Hunched over her desk, Ellis looked up at him with glazed eyes. "Sarge? I didn't know you were here too."

"It's my job to be." He eyed McCallister. "I see you're making up for lost time."

"I'm trying to, sir," he replied. "Becca's onto something here. We could solve this case."

"You solved your case already," Abbott insisted. "What you're working on now is the responsibility of the Augusta police, not us."

Ellis rubbed her eyes. "If we don't do this, then Jenna Brooks died for nothing. Joel Brooks was searching for his daughter's killer, and he believed it was someone who lived in his old neighborhood. If we let this go, no one will look at it again."

"It's not your responsibility to solve cold cases in another jurisdiction, Becca," Abbott insisted. "I appreciate what you're both trying to do here, but your investigation is over. I don't know how to justify two of my detectives—one of whom has only just returned to duty—spending so much time on this. Bangor has its own problems."

Ellis raised her chin. "And if Jenna Brooks' killer lives here? Lives in Woodland Heights? Doesn't that make it our business?"

Abbott folded his arms over his broad chest and lowered his gaze. "At least go home and get some sleep. It's late. Start fresh in the morning with a clear head. Maybe something will click."

Ellis looked over at McCallister. "Maybe he's right. We've been at this all day."

"I'll follow your lead," he replied.

"Good," Abbott said. "Both of you get out of here, and I'll see you in the morning." He turned around and headed back to his office.

McCallister started packing up his things, and it seemed he noticed Ellis watching him. "What?"

"Nothing. It's just really nice having you back. I didn't realize how much I missed you being here."

"It does feel good being part of the team again," he said, holding her gaze. "I hope to get back to the way things were, you know?"

"They will in time." She closed her laptop. "You ready?"

"Yeah."

The two headed toward the staircase and walked down into the first-floor lobby. The station was quiet with only a few officers on staff.

McCallister held open the door for her as they prepared to walk outside into a warm, humid night. When she hesitated just inside the entrance, he called out, "Are you coming?"

Ellis shook off the lingering thoughts about the case. "Yeah, sorry."

"It's not easy to stop, is it?" he asked, walking beside her into the parking lot.

"No, and I'm sure I'll dream about it too, if I'm lucky enough to sleep," she replied.

They arrived at their vehicles, and McCallister pressed the remote to unlock his Ford. "You feel like coming over for a nightcap?"

As much as Ellis wanted to be with him, her thoughts were on anything but their relationship. It seemed she struggled to find balance in her personal and professional lives, and now, as always, the professional side was winning out. "Raincheck?"

His face wore mild disappointment. "Sure. Yeah. Good-night, Becca."

NOT ONLY HAD they to sort through the information from Brooks' apartment, but they also had to review every document from the Westfield police as well as what Brooks had amassed on his own. With the new day, and some much-needed sleep, Ellis was ready to get to the bottom of who had murdered Jenna Brooks, and why her father had homed in on the residents of Woodland Heights.

As Ellis enlisted the help of her team, one detail had immediately emerged. Joel Brooks had developed an obsession with finding his daughter's killer. They learned that after his wife died, his behavior became more erratic. Something Lieutenant Graves had also confirmed. Brooks had lost his job and soon spent most of his time searching for answers—until two months ago. That was when he'd signed a month-to-month lease on his Bangor apartment.

Ellis scrolled through documents on the flash drive and came across a file named HOA. Inside were several documents, but one held particular interest for her. "This is a newsletter from his old homeowners' association."

"How'd he get hold of that if he'd moved away?" Fletch walked over to view it. "What's it say?"

"Best guess is that it could've been available online." Ellis briefly scanned it before landing on an interesting piece of information. "Says they're cutting back on their security contract."

"They had security?" McCallister asked as he sat at his desk.

"Apparently so. Rent-a-cops, by the look of it," Ellis replied.

"Why would they cut back on that?" Bevins asked.

"Lack of funds to pay for it, I assume. And given the area, they probably felt it was unnecessary." Ellis continued to read. "This decision happened shortly before the break-ins started." She eyed McCallister. "Brooks knew about it and used it to his advantage."

Fletch set her hands on her hips. "Was that his reason, or could it have been the catalyst? He spotted an opportunity and seized it."

Ellis regarded her. "That's a fair point. But how and why he chose those particular neighbors, I still don't know." She glanced through the window on the back wall as the sun climbed in the sky. "Brooks took extra measures to ensure he could execute his plan for the Cannons." She turned back to them. "He took out phone, internet, power."

"He learned from his mistakes," McCallister said. "Vicky Boyles and Ted Holtz. The Dobson's boy and even the dog. I don't think he'd planned on any of them. Figured he could keep sneaking around completely unnoticed because he'd been successful at it the first time or two."

Ellis considered McCallister's notion. "I'd tend to agree with that except that we think the Cannons were the last on his list."

"True. We haven't found a number ten," Fletch said.

"Right." Ellis opened her drawer and snatched her car keys. "I'm going to take a harder look at that family."

"You want company?" McCallister asked.

"I appreciate the offer, but we need as many eyes as we can get on all this information in case something turns up." She glanced at the team. "I won't be long."

As Ellis made her way downstairs, it was noticeably quieter than yesterday. She spotted a reporter approaching, but averted her gaze and pushed through the exit as he shouted questions at her.

Not a chance she was authorized to speak to reporters,

nor had she any desire to. Instead, she carried on under a sunny, muggy day until she reached her SUV.

Inside, she pressed the ignition and turned the air on full blast. The polyester blend of her pants suit clung to her skin. The time showed eight thirty in the morning. It might be too late to catch Derek Cannon heading into work, but maybe not. She wasn't sure what she would learn, but the only way to find out was to tail him.

Ellis drove back to that house, noticing both vehicles still sat in the driveway. Turned out, she didn't miss him after all. So where would he go? Work? A friend's house? A family member?

As she sat parked across the street, Ellis watched Derek emerge from his house and make his way to his car. The Cannons had returned to their home just days after Brooks had been killed. After a debriefing, the couple claimed to have no idea why Brooks came after them.

Ellis was here now to find out whether that was true.

She followed Derek's shimmery silver Mercedes SUV as he drove on to what appeared to be his place of work. In the rush to protect them, a thorough background hadn't made its way through the pipeline. After all, she had no reason to suspect them of anything, in much the same way their neighbors hadn't either.

Ellis noted the sign on the exterior. *Premier Marketing.* The modern building with sleek lines and dark colors was offset with lush greenery all around it. She drove past as he entered the parking lot, making sure to keep out of sight. Confident he'd gone inside, Ellis returned and parked on the outskirts of the lot.

She grabbed her laptop from inside her shoulder bag. A quick Google search and she learned it was a mid-sized advertising firm. And now, it was time to start asking questions. Derek Cannon's background was what interested her most. She scoured social media and public records. Having already run a criminal background, she knew he was clean. He had attended a state university and had been working at the advertising firm for seven years. In his spare time, he volunteered at a local animal shelter, according to his Facebook page.

Other than that, nothing stood out about this guy. Nothing she found involved Brooks either, which was the real problem. So far, no ties to him, which meant that maybe her hunch was off.

And then the door to the office building opened, and she noticed him step outside. He slipped on his sunglasses, which was odd considering the sun was buried under heavy clouds.

She hunkered down onto her seat, watching him enter the parking lot and stepping into his Mercedes. He drove off in an apparent hurry, and Ellis jumped into action so she wouldn't lose sight of him. Where was he going when he'd only arrived an hour ago? A meeting? She was about to find out.

He led the way through Downtown and ended up on the north side, heading along the I-95. Ellis kept her distance. He wasn't going home, that was clear.

After more than an hour, he arrived at his destination— the Augusta Police Department. He pulled into a parking lot while she stayed out of view. When he stepped out, she noticed he had a bag slung over his shoulder. Something that must've already been inside his car because he hadn't taken it into his workplace with him.

Her gaze focused on him as he strode across the lot and

walked inside. "What are you doing here?" Was this just a strange coincidence, or did Cannon have something to do with Brooks' last stand after all?

Ellis stepped out of her car, determined to find answers. She crossed the street quickly, hoping not to draw attention from anyone exiting the station.

After he'd gone in, she took a moment before walking in herself. Ellis stopped short when she caught sight of Cannon standing in front of an officer at one of the desks. "What the hell?" she whispered. Obscured by a column in the corner of the lobby, Ellis watched Cannon, who shifted his weight from side to side. And then Detective Naylor arrived. Her face deadpanned. Why was Cannon here to meet with the detective in charge of Jenna Brooks' murder investigation?

The two were in conversation for a while when the detective motioned him back.

Confusion swirled in her mind. What had happened to bring Cannon here? Did he have new information about Jenna Brooks?

When they disappeared into the hall, Ellis approached the officer who'd initially helped Cannon. "Excuse me," she said, holding out her badge. "I'm with Bangor PD. Can you tell me why Detective Naylor was meeting with Mr. Cannon?"

The officer gave her a once-over before responding, "I'm sorry, Detective, but I can't say. If you want to speak with—"

Ellis raised her hands. "I'll reach out to him later. Thanks." Disappointed, she waited inside the lobby, around the corner from the hall.

Several minutes passed before Cannon emerged and pushed through the lobby doors. He was leaving. Now was her chance.

Ellis got up from the chair and walked ahead, bypassing the front desk, holding out her badge. "I need to see Detective Naylor. I know where his office is," she called out to them, carrying on while one of the officers asked her to wait. "Call him," she yelled back, refusing to stop.

She eyed the names on the doors and recalled his office was near the end of the hall. There it was. Ellis opened it without so much as a knock. "Detective Naylor, you mind telling me what the hell Derek Cannon was doing here?"

Was it just McCallister who wondered why Ellis hadn't been in contact after attempting to hunt down Cannon? It had been hours, and no one had heard from her yet. He was growing concerned.

It seemed Fletch picked up on his worry. "She'll call if something's up."

Meanwhile, the crime board was filled with photos and information. What the hell was he missing? McCallister stared at the board as Pelletier approached.

"I'm guessing nothing's opened up on this yet?" He stood beside him, staring at the same board.

"No, not yet," McCallister replied. "What do you have going on?"

"Found our restaurant thief. He's in Booking now, and I was just about to head downstairs," Pelletier replied. "Where's Becca?"

"Good question."

"Anything I can do to help?" Pelletier asked. "I know you have Connor and Fletch jumping in, and as soon as I wrap up this other thing—"

"I appreciate the offer, Bryce, really. But, uh, Abbott made it clear to us last night he doesn't think this is something our team should be working on, and I've already got too many department resources on it as it is."

"Then why are you?" he pressed.

McCallister laughed. "Ask Becca. We'll see how long we can keep this up before Abbott shuts us down. But I'll let you know if there's anything we need." He watched Pelletier head out of the bullpen, and noticed a text had arrived on his phone. "Becca. What the?" He typed back.

> Why was he there?

I'll tell you when I get back. Driving now.
See you soon.

McCallister returned to his desk and reviewed the file she'd just emailed. It was information on Cannon. They'd performed a cursory look into the neighbors early on in search of a connection to each other that had made them targets. So what had shown up on here that she wanted him to look at before her return?

He opened the file and read through it, noting Cannon's employment history. Nothing out of the ordinary. His wife didn't work. That much, they'd already known.

As he read on, Ellis referred to the fact that Cannon had made a big stink at the community homeowners' meeting before everything turned to shit. Insisting they bring back the security, even though nightly patrols had increased. Why did this matter to her?

And why had this guy gone to see Detective Naylor? That was the real question. He continued to review the information and came upon the one piece that stood out. "Hang on."

He zoomed in on the file and read it again. "Volunteered?" He furrowed his brow a moment, then stood from his desk, walking over to the board again. "Fletch?" he called out.

She walked over to him. "Yeah? What's up?"

"Becca sent over more info on Derek Cannon. She's in Augusta—"

"Augusta?" Fletch cut in.

McCallister raised his hands. "Long story. Anyway, I started looking at it, and I saw that this guy volunteered at an animal shelter."

"Okay. How does that help us?" Fletch pressed.

He moved in closer to the board and grabbed a marker. "Here. This was in Brooks's files, the ones we brought back from Westfield." McCallister circled a note that Brooks had written.

Fletch joined him and eyed the note. "Jenna worked part-time at an animal shelter." It seemed to take her a moment to pick up on the connection. "Oh my God. Cannon volunteered at one too." She pulled back, shoulders raised, and head cocked. "Do we know if they were the same?"

McCallister perched on the edge of his desk. "We sure as hell better find out."

24

On the drive back to Bangor, Ellis thought about what Naylor had told her. Cannon had gone there to ensure his name wouldn't be brought up in connection with Jenna. Why? Well, according to the detective, he'd once been considered a suspect, but was later cleared. That information would've been useful earlier, and she recalled how Naylor seemed to jump at the opportunity to point out that he'd done everything he could in the investigation. Maybe not, and he was simply covering his ass.

Ellis arrived at the station and hurried inside. She climbed the stairs to the second-floor CID and entered the bullpen. She noticed McCallister standing beside Fletch at the whiteboard. "I'm back."

They turned to her, and McCallister called out, "We found something."

Ellis set down her bag on her chair and walked over. "What's that?"

"I looked at the file you sent on Cannon. When I noticed

that he'd volunteered years ago at a local animal shelter, I recalled something similar in Brooks' information."

Ellis raised a brow. "Similar?"

He retrieved the file. "This is what Brooks had. Jenna worked at this very same shelter a few months before she was taken."

Ellis's face masked in disbelief. "Why the hell didn't we know that? Why wasn't that part of Naylor's case file?"

"Maybe because Naylor didn't ask the question, or because Cannon only volunteered and there was no employment record," McCallister replied. "Becca, do you know what this means?"

"It means there's a direct connection between Jenna Brooks and Derek Cannon. More than their being neighbors or that he was a friend of Joel Brooks," she continued. "They knew each other. And Brooks had figured that out too."

THE DNA that had been found on Vicky Boyles matched what was found on Jenna Brooks. So that meant, if Ellis was on the right track, that it was DNA that belonged to Derek Cannon. It flew in the face of her idea the DNA belonged to Joel Brooks, as the man ultimately responsible for killing Boyles. So where the hell did Cannon fit into the murder of Vicky Boyles?

Rivera had Brooks' body and was running labs now. It would take days to identify Brooks' DNA. She didn't have days. If Cannon murdered Jenna Brooks, and he'd run to the Augusta police as a pre-emptive measure, then there was no telling how long he'd stick it out if he believed he was under Ellis's microscope.

Ellis needed to be certain about this as the web of deceit grew larger. How Cannon connected to Boyles was something else to consider. And it stood to reason why Joel Brooks would go after him. But why had he gone into the others' homes first? Was it a process of elimination? Had he been searching for a clue to lead him to the truth?

The unknowns numbered far too many; they made her head spin. For now, Ellis had to keep working the case, and that started by paying a visit to the animal shelter where both Jenna and Derek had once volunteered. The question remained: would anyone remember them from three years ago?

The shelter was just ahead, and McCallister called out to her, "Becca? You're about to drive past it."

"Oh." She shook out of her thoughts and made a sharp right. "I wasn't paying attention."

"I see that."

She drove into the parking lot of the small red-brick building. "Yeah, sorry. Just letting the wheels spin for a minute. Didn't you see the smoke?"

McCallister opened his door. "Are you kidding? Thought it was a five-alarm fire."

Ellis stepped outside, wearing a grin. She peered at the building for a moment, waiting for McCallister to join her. "Who else knew those two volunteered here at the same time?"

"Probably a question we should ask the neighbors. The ones still alive, anyway."

Ellis started ahead toward the entrance. "Could be why he went after them."

McCallister pinched his brow. "Brooks makes the

connection between Cannon and his daughter, assumes he's the one who killed her, then blames his neighbors?"

"Sounds strange, but maybe not so much." Ellis stopped at the doors. "Think about it. If Cannon is some kind of predator, and others knew or suspected it, that would be enough to motivate me to make them suffer for it."

He pulled open the door. "Fair point, Detective."

Ellis walked inside and spotted a young blond woman behind a counter. Her hair was pulled back, and she wore a green T-shirt with the name of the kennel embroidered on it.

"Good afternoon. How can I help you?" she asked, smiling warmly at them.

"I'm Detective Ellis. This is Detective McCallister. We'd like to speak to the manager?"

The young woman looked at them with some uncertainty. "Uh, yeah, sure. I'll go get her. One second."

As she stepped away, Ellis spied the dogs in the nearby kennels. Her heart broke a little at the sight of them. Three huddled together in a cage. They looked like some kind of lab mix. Hank wasn't big on dogs, and Ellis had never had one. The thought of it had crossed her mind on occasion, but then the pragmatic side of her kicked in, reminding her that the job would get in the way.

The young woman soon returned with another beside her. Older, more skeptical in appearance. She offered her hand to Ellis. "I'm Angie. How can I help you folks?"

"About three years ago, a young teenaged girl volunteered here. Jenna Brooks. Does that name ring a bell?"

"Course it does," Angie replied. "She was a great kid. Smart. Sweet. Loved the animals." She lowered her gaze a moment. "Terrible what happened to her."

"Yes, ma'am, it is," Ellis replied. "A man also volunteered

around that same timeframe. Derek Cannon. Do you recall him as well?"

"Yeah. Yeah." Angie looked up as if thinking on the matter. "I do, actually. He came around on the weekends. Twice a month or something like that, if I recall correctly."

McCallister glanced at Ellis when he began, "Would Jenna have crossed paths with him?"

Angie raised her shoulder. "Probably. He stopped coming around not long after what happened to Jenna. I believe he lived in the same neighborhood as she did." Her face deadpanned as her gaze vacillated between the detectives. "Oh, dear Lord. You don't think—"

Ellis glanced at one of the dogs who'd made a yelping noise. "Don't know, but it's why we're here looking for answers."

"Okay, then. What can I do to help?"

"Any records you might still have..." McCallister pressed.

"You mean like when Mr. Cannon came in?"

"When he was here, yes," Ellis began. "And when Jenna was here. Whatever connection we can find between the two would be very helpful."

Angie scratched the side of her head. "I'll do some digging. We have to track volunteer hours for tax purposes, so we should have that information, certainly going back the past few years. Let me see what I can find."

Ellis handed her a card. "Please call me with whatever you turn up. You've been very helpful. Thank you for that."

As they headed out, Angie called to them, "I hope you do find whoever killed Jenna. The world was a better place with that girl in it."

Ellis wore a closed-lip smile. "I don't doubt that at all."

THEY RETURNED TO THE STATION, where they continued to review the files and documents so thoroughly put together by Joel Brooks. Nothing else pointing to Cannon had emerged.

Getting a warrant to search someone's home or computer without mentioning to that someone they were a suspect definitely wouldn't fly with the judges. But that was the best way to learn whether Derek Cannon was responsible for the murder of Jenna Brooks.

Talking to the other neighbors who were victims could lay the groundwork, but it was impossible to know whether any of them would warn Cannon. Without sufficient evidence to bring him in, Ellis wasn't going to get very far in discovering the truth. And the evidence they had was woefully inadequate.

Abbott made his way inside the bullpen as everyone else seemed ready to leave for the evening. He approached Ellis. "Still working on a case that isn't ours, huh?"

She turned around. "Hi, Sarge. Well, we think this could be ours after all."

"We are making progress," McCallister added.

"Oh yeah?" He eyed the board. "Show me."

Ellis relayed the details she'd learned from the visit to the animal shelter as well as the connection Joel Brooks had unearthed between his daughter and Derek Cannon. "We're still laying all this out, Sarge, but there seems to be a fair amount of circumstantial evidence pointing to Cannon."

Abbott was quiet for a moment as he studied the board. "All right. Then you need to find a way to make it concrete."

"What are you saying, sir?" Ellis pressed.

"I'm saying you might be onto something. So do what you have to do to make it stick." He turned around and walked out of the bullpen.

Ellis couldn't help but grin. "Okay. Guess he's on board now."

"Thanks to you finding a connection." McCallister checked the time. "Not much more we can do tonight. Listen, I'm starved. You feel like grabbing a bite to eat?"

"I did tell Hank I'd bring him some dinner. You want to tag along?" she asked.

"It'd be my pleasure."

Within minutes, they'd grabbed their things and headed out into the parking lot. The sun had dipped below the horizon, casting a purple-orange hue among the clouds that had only partly thinned over the course of the day.

Ellis didn't say much on the way to Hank's, feeling more comfortable with McCallister after their disagreement.

She pulled up into Hank's driveway after having stopped for food. A car was parked out front and caught her attention. The sun had all but disappeared behind Hank's house as she stepped out under a dusky, steel-blue sky. McCallister walked around to join her, and they headed inside.

Whose car is that?

"I brought food and company," she called out from the foyer. "Euan's here, and we brought dinner." The smile on her face disappeared the moment she walked into the living room.

"Becca." Andrew got up from the couch. "I thought it'd be nice to stop in and see Hank. Hope that's all right."

"Course it is," Hank said from his recliner. But the look on his face as he peered at Ellis said otherwise.

This was it. The collision course she was desperate to

avoid. She hadn't spoken to Andrew yet after getting the news from the detective. And now, here he was, no doubt looking for answers after not hearing from her. "Andrew. Hi."

"Aren't you going to introduce me to your friend?" he asked.

Ellis was certain that were she to look up the definition of "awkward," she'd find a picture of this very moment. "Andrew, this is Detective Euan McCallister. Euan, this is my ex-husband, Andrew."

McCallister offered his hand. "Good to meet you."

"Likewise." He spied the bags of food.

Ellis noticed his gaze. "I'm sorry, but I didn't know you'd be here. I'm afraid I didn't bring enough for everyone."

Andrew swatted away the idea. "This was a last-minute stop, and Hank was good enough to let me say hello. I don't want to intrude more than I already have."

"Nonsense, Andy," Hank cut in. "Stick around. I can rustle you up something."

Ellis glared at her father when she felt McCallister's hand on her shoulder. She peered over at him.

"Maybe I should go wait in the car," he whispered.

"No, it's fine. Stay," Ellis said, continuing into the living room. "I'm pretty sure Andrew has to leave anyway, right?"

"Uh, actually, I was hoping to talk to you about what we discussed."

Strike two. Yet another thing Ellis had failed to mention to McCallister.

"But I'm sure we can talk tomorrow. I probably should go." Andrew patted Hank on the shoulder. "It was really great to see you, Hank. I'm glad we got a chance to catch up."

"Me too, son. You take care of yourself, yeah?"

"I will." He walked between Ellis and McCallister on his way to the door.

"I'll see you out." Ellis handed the food to her father. "I'll be right back, Euan."

"Sure, yeah. Take your time." McCallister waved his hand. "Nice to have met you, Andrew."

"And you, Euan. Take care." He stepped outside.

Ellis joined him on the porch. "What are you doing?"

"I've called you five times. Why haven't you called me back? Look, I'm sorry to do this, and in all honesty, it was nice to see Hank—"

She folded her arms tightly together. "I was on a case, all right? You knew that. You have no idea what the past few days have been like for me."

"You're right. I don't know," Andrew said. "That's not much of a surprise, though, is it? You never talked about your work. I was left to just pray you made it home every night."

Ellis turned away a moment. "For God's sake, Andrew. Look, I did what I could for you, okay? I talked to the detective." She rested her arms on the porch railing and looked out over the darkened street. "I don't know what your fiancée did, but he said they have enough to bring charges."

"What?" He paced a tight circle. "Are you sure? That can't be right."

She reached for his shoulder to stop him. "I'm sure. And Andrew, I—I have to tell you something else. This detective, he says they have something on you too. And that you ought to think about getting a lawyer."

"Oh my God." His face screwed up in confusion. "What are you talking about? I haven't done anything wrong. Neither has Myra."

"She did, Andrew. And it looks like she brought you down with her."

He stopped cold. "No. You're wrong. She would never do anything to hurt me. She didn't take that money. I didn't take it."

"They think you did," Ellis whispered.

"Well, what am I going to do, Becca? You have to help me. I need you."

In that moment, she saw the man she once loved. His vulnerability. His kind nature. Her eyes reddened. "I'm sorry, Andrew. I can't do anything for you. I have no jurisdiction. I can maybe help find you a good lawyer. If you're innocent, then you have nothing to worry about."

"Right, because innocent people never go to jail." He rubbed his temple. "I can't believe this is happening." Andrew peered at the front door and was quiet for a moment. "So he's the guy, huh?"

Ellis glanced at the door. "Euan's a good man. A great detective."

"Do you love him?" He raised his hands. "Never mind. I don't want to know. I just feel lost now. I thought I knew Myra." He gazed out over the yard. "I'm sorry, Becca. I'm sorry for everything. For not understanding who you are. For not realizing the job is and will always be your first love." He turned back to her. "I hope that guy in there sees that too. Otherwise, he doesn't stand a chance."

ANDREW LEFT, and Ellis considered that it might have been the last time she would ever see him. She'd let him down. He could face prison, by all accounts, and the idea brought heavy guilt. But what could she do? She knew he'd done nothing wrong. Myra? Well, that was another story. Regardless, it was something she couldn't deal with now, as cold as that was.

McCallister would be full of questions, wondering why she never bothered to tell him Andrew had come to town. He waited inside, probably chatting with Hank about the good ol' days on the force.

The Band-Aid was off, and it stung. But the secret was out, and she would accept the consequences. However, as Ellis returned inside, McCallister only smiled at her.

"All good?" he asked.

"Yeah. All good."

The evening hadn't gone as Ellis had planned. But McCallister didn't push. He didn't say a word, and she didn't offer any. Shoving it under the rug probably wasn't the best way to handle it, but it was done now. Though the day would come when a deeper conversation would take place. Maybe she would be ready to be honest with him and herself by then. Maybe.

As she'd arrived home, stretched out on her sofa at the late hour, Ellis reached into her laptop bag that lay against the couch below her. More work needed to be done if she hoped to prove her hunch about Cannon. It had been Brooks' hunch first, but she wasn't about to let it go.

There had to be more out there about Cannon that would point to the idea he was who she thought he was—a predator. After spending days in the man's house, nothing stood out to her as unusual. Then again, she wasn't exactly looking. That was about to change.

The Woodland Heights social media pages could hold more than she realized. Having only taken a brief look previously, this was now her last-ditch effort to uncover the truth, or at least enough truth to get a warrant.

Access had been authorized last week when she and Fletch hoped to find the same kind of information Ellis searched for now. She pulled up the Facebook page and scrolled through every single post.

Picnics, fundraisers, fun runs. All of it was there. She'd seen photos and posts of every one of the people who'd been a victim of Joel Brooks, including Vicky Boyles, the woman he'd murdered.

Regardless, her focus had to be on Derek Cannon. Could she learn anything about his behavior? Could she find any interaction between him and, say, another girl in the neighborhood? Who was he? A playboy? A flirt? A creep? Or was he a killer? Ellis had no idea right now, but she prayed the truth would reveal itself if she looked hard enough.

Lorna Cannon didn't work, and it appeared from the contents of this page that she was heavily involved in the community and its activities. But Derek Cannon?

From what Ellis had seen from her scrolling, he hadn't been nearly as involved as his wife. Stood to reason, but he had appeared at some events. This one here. Ellis clicked on the post. A Halloween block party last year.

Inside a cul-de-sac, tables lined the sidewalk, where kids would grab treats and move on to the next table. A movie screen was set up in the center; it showed a kids' film. Ellis studied the pictures. Ten in all.

That was when she noticed Derek Cannon alongside a

couple of teen girls. She didn't recognize them, but then again, they were dressed in heavy makeup and wore somewhat skimpy costumes. Typical for girls that age, Ellis had come to understand, experimenting with their blossoming sexuality. It was up to the adults, the parents, to give them that breathing room while reminding them to respect themselves and their bodies. It was also a time when grown men took the opportunity to leer. Ellis had seen that side of some men on too many occasions. And now she saw it in the eyes of Derek Cannon.

The hairs on the back of her neck stood on end. This was the start of it. Now, she needed to find more. Jenna Brooks was dead, and if Cannon was responsible, then there could be others who'd drawn his interest, like those two girls.

Compelled to find out, Ellis pushed on until she found something else. Cannon had posted a comment about the high school bake sale that the neighborhood had hosted. He'd shared the post to his page and captioned it.

Our girls have the creamy goods just for you.

But it wasn't just his words that could have easily been misconstrued. He'd posted lewd GIFs alongside the photos. "Why did no one call him out for this?"

That was it. Ellis had enough to bring up the question. Between this and the fact he'd volunteered with Jenna Brooks, as confirmed on a voicemail yesterday from Angie at the shelter, it could be enough to convince a judge to issue a search warrant for Cannon, his home, his laptop, everything. If she was wrong, then so be it. But nothing about what she'd just seen posted by a middle-aged man, or any-aged man, was innocent. Not in her experience.

25

The judge had sided with Ellis, and the search warrant for the Cannon home had come through. It was almost noon when Ellis walked out of city hall with the signed original in her hand. She drove back to the station, which was only blocks away.

There would be no need to convince Abbott. A judge was convinced, and Abbott would be too. She walked into his office, waving the warrant in her hands. "Sarge, hear me out."

He raised his hand. "If Judge Russo agrees, then so do I."

"Thank you, sir. I'm going there now, and I'll keep you posted."

"Not alone, you're not," he cut in. "Take Fletch or Euan with you. We don't serve warrants alone. You know that."

She nodded. "Yes, sir." Ellis headed back into the hall and returned to the bullpen. McCallister was at his desk with Fletch standing beside it; both turned their gaze to her.

"Well?" McCallister asked.

Ellis held up the warrant. "Who wants to go with me?"

"I'll go," Fletch said. "We've been on this together since the beginning."

"She's right," McCallister said. "I can take Bevins, and we can be backup if necessary."

"Then let's go." Ellis grabbed her bag from her desk chair and slung it over her shoulder. "I don't know if the Cannons are home, but I know where Derek works, if the wife isn't around."

The team headed out into the parking lot. Taking two vehicles, they started out toward the highway.

Navigating through light traffic, Ellis took a moment and glanced at Fletch. "I wanted to let you know that I appreciate everything you've done to help with this investigation."

"Hey, you didn't think I was going to let you take all the credit, did you?" Fletch laughed. "I'm your partner on this one. It's my job to be here."

"I don't know what we'll be looking for exactly," Ellis continued, with a nod to her partner. "The warrant covers electronics, personal devices, and other potential evidence."

"Other? That's broad," Fletch replied. "Russo must have been feeling generous today."

"Maybe so. I'm just glad she thought I had enough." Ellis hesitated a moment. "This guy, Cannon, I can see why Joel Brooks homed in on him. And if we do find something relevant to Jenna Brooks' murder, I have to think Cannon could be targeting other girls in that neighborhood."

"But we still haven't figured out why Brooks went after his other neighbors or killed Vicky Boyles," Fletch added.

"No, but I have a feeling if we nail Cannon, it'll shed light on some pretty dark places inside Woodland Heights."

The detectives arrived in front of the house they'd staked out only a week earlier under very different circumstances.

McCallister and Bevins parked on the street while Ellis and Fletch pulled into the driveway.

Ellis stepped out of the SUV, preparing for what awaited them. An angry wife. A combative husband. There was no telling how this would go down. "Let's go."

She carried on to the front door and raised her hand to knock. But before she could, the door opened.

Derek Cannon stood in front of them, his face confused and apprehensive. "Detective Ellis. What are you all doing here?"

"I thought you might be at work, Mr. Cannon." Ellis held up the papers. "We have a warrant to search your home."

"What the hell for? I've been cooperating with you the entire time. You stayed in my house." His face heated with anger as his voice rose. "What the hell is this shit?"

Ellis took a deep breath, steadying herself to avoid escalating the situation. "This is about Jenna Brooks and your relationship with her before she was murdered."

"What?" Cannon's face turned almost purple, and his chest puffed out. "My relationship with her? Are you insane? Why would you even suggest something like that? I'm the victim here. Joel Brooks came after me and my family. You said so yourself."

"We're not accusing you of anything, Mr. Cannon," Fletch said calmly. "We're just following up on leads."

"I don't know what kind of leads you think you're going to find here." He started to close the door.

"Sir, step aside," Ellis instructed as she thrust out her hand to stop it. "This warrant gives us the right to enter your property with or without your cooperation."

"Fucking bitch," he whispered under his breath before backing up.

Ellis led the way, her eyes scanning the room. She'd spent days here already and hadn't seen anything then. What had she expected to find now? Except that now she believed Brooks had been onto the truth about his daughter's murder. He had taken his own meticulous measures to confirm which of his former neighbors it had been.

And then Cannon had lied, or rather, he hadn't divulged that he'd known Jenna Brooks. Ellis wasn't going to back down. Not now when they were so close.

"Why aren't you at work, Mr. Cannon?" Ellis asked, still scanning the living room. "And where is your wife?"

"Not that I have to tell you anything," he began, "but after I allowed you to stay in my home so you could catch a madman who murdered my neighbor, my wife has gone to purchase some new items the police were good enough to destroy. That *you* destroyed."

She squared up to him while Fletch remained close with her hand on her pistol. "You've kept secrets from us, Mr. Cannon, and that was the catalyst that brought us back here."

"What the hell are you talking about?" he asked, hands firmly on his hips.

"We know you knew Jenna Brooks from your time volunteering at the animal shelter," Ellis began. "Funny how you stopped shortly after she died."

He looked up as if recalling a long-forgotten memory. "Wait, the shelter?"

"Yes," Fletch jumped in. "We know you were there and crossed paths with Jenna Brooks. Do you have anything else you'd like to say about that?"

"Good God, that was so long ago. I can hardly recall even being there," he replied.

"You know what, Mr. Cannon," Ellis began, "maybe it's best if you wait outside while we do our jobs in here. Detectives McCallister and Bevins are waiting out there if you'd like to have a talk with them."

His face turned to stone. "Fine. I'll step out while you violate my home once again." Cannon brushed past her. "Guess the first time wasn't enough."

She turned around. "Oh, we'll need your phone."

He stopped cold. "What?"

"Your phone, Mr. Cannon. It's included in the warrant."

He slammed it against her outstretched palm. "Fine."

"You can give us the passcode, or we'll have Forensics contact the manufacturer. Trust me when I say that they will grant us access."

He scoffed. "Have at it, Detective."

After he stepped outside, Ellis grabbed her phone and called McCallister. When the line picked up, she began, "You should see Cannon outside. He was pushing back, getting confrontational, so keep eyes on him."

"You got it. Anything yet?" he asked.

"I have his phone, no code. But we're just getting started. I'll keep you posted." Ellis returned her phone to her pocket and looked at Fletch. "I'm pretty familiar with this place now."

"So where do you want to start?" she asked.

Ellis thought back to the night she'd fought off Brooks, barely escaping with her life. "Everywhere."

"Understood."

Ellis made her way to the living room, where she sifted through the various knick-knacks that adorned the shelves. She ran her fingers over the smooth surfaces of porcelain figurines and considered how easily they could be used as murder weapons. But she already knew Jenna's throat had been sliced. To hope to find the knife that slit her throat after three years was unrealistic, so she had to search for Cannon's concealed fetish. A possible desire for young girls. Something she would likely find on his computer. But nothing would be overlooked.

As Ellis moved through the room, she noticed few photos of the couple. They were childless, and the occasional picture of the two of them on vacation dotted the room. "I'm going to search for laptops. There's an office down this hall."

"I'll check out the attic," Fletch said. "I noticed a scuttle in the ceiling. If someone was going to hide something, that'd be the place to do it."

Ellis aimed a finger gun at her and winked. "That's the Fletch I know." She made her way to the office while Fletch climbed into the attic.

Farther down the hall, Ellis flipped on the light in the office. A large oak desk sat between two windows on the back wall. A tall black leather chair behind it. On the right were two bookshelves, with mostly junk on them. And on the left, a couple of tall filing cabinets.

And right on top of the desk, just as she suspected, was a laptop. Cannon must've taken it with him when she'd been here before, because she couldn't recall seeing it then. Of course, she hadn't considered him anything but a victim at the time. Now, this laptop could hold the answers to everything.

With gloved hands, she placed the laptop in a box along with a CPU that lay under the desk. Then Ellis went to work searching through the desk drawers and the filing cabinets. Most of it was old papers, tax forms, and receipts, nothing out of the ordinary. But then, in the bottom drawer of the desk, tucked in the back, she found a small black notebook.

Ellis sat down in the chair and flipped through the pages. "Oh my God." They were filled with entries, each one detailing, with horrible accuracy, the movements of girls whose names she didn't recognize. And as she carried on, Jenna's name appeared. He must've followed her every move, noted her outfits, who she was with, where she was going. As Ellis read on, she felt sick to her stomach. "You're obsessed with them. All of them."

She snapped the notebook shut and dropped it into the evidence box. She had to tell Fletch.

The ladder for the attic had been extended to the hall floor. Fletch was still up there. Ellis climbed up and peered into the dimly lit space filled with boxes, an old file cabinet, and several plastic storage bins full of Christmas decorations. The air was thick with the smell of old wood and dust. She spotted Fletch hunched over a small wooden chest a few feet away. "How's things going in here?"

Fletch turned back. "Come check this out."

Ellis walked over to her and peered inside the chest. "Looks like old party decorations. Summer stuff. Fourth of July."

"That's what I thought until I saw this." Fletch reached in and pushed away some of the decorations until the item she'd noticed was within reach. "It's a picture." She pulled upright again and showed it to Ellis. "What do you make of this?"

Ellis moved in closer to view the photo. "That's Jenna Brooks, there by the pool. She looks really young."

"She's standing in between her parents," Fletch said. "I recognize Brooks at least."

"Right, and take a look over here. See off in the far corner?"

"Exactly. That's Cannon." Fletch shot her a glance. "And he's looking at Jenna like she's about to be his dessert."

"That makes perfect sense with what I found," Ellis said. "What was that?"

She set her gaze on Fletch. "The nail in the coffin."

MCCALLISTER KEPT his eyes on Cannon. "Is it me, or does this guy look nervous to you?"

Bevins peered. "Hard to say, but the way he's pacing, he's either pissed or guilty."

A moment later, McCallister noticed Fletch and Ellis step outside. "Oh, shit. I think they found something. Look at them." He watched while they discussed something with Cannon, something that seemed to agitate him.

"Oh boy, he's gonna run." Bevins placed his hand on the door handle. "Should we back them up?"

"Hang on." McCallister raised his hand. "Give them a second."

Ellis displayed a black book, and Cannon's face deadpanned.

"Now he's gonna run." McCallister flung open his door, and they both jumped outside, guns ready.

Cannon bolted down the street.

McCallister and Bevins took off after him, yelling for him to stop, while Ellis and Fletch sprinted too.

Cannon kept running until he came to a cul-de-sac the next block over. He turned around, his eyes wide with fear as the detectives closed in on him.

"Put your hands up!" McCallister yelled, training his gun on Cannon.

He slowly raised his hands, his body trembling. "I didn't do it," he stammered. "I swear I didn't kill her."

"Why are you running, then?" Ellis shouted, her gun aimed at his head. "Mr. Cannon, you're under arrest for the kidnap and murder of Jenna Brooks."

***

BEVINS TOOK Cannon into custody and drove back to the station while the rest of the team searched the home. More evidence and more names could be uncovered. And as the minutes ticked by, Ellis didn't discover any more details regarding Jenna or any other girl. The black book was a crucial piece of evidence, but it still hadn't proved anything. Regardless, Cannon was going to be left with no choice except to submit a DNA swab. That could solidify the entire case.

It wasn't until Ellis opened the door to Lorna Cannon's closet that she noticed the shoeboxes. It appeared the woman liked her shoes. But on peering into the back of the dark closet, her flashlight aimed down, she noticed two boxes in the far corner stacked on top of one another. Small, square. Definitely not shoes.

Ellis dropped onto her knees and crawled under the hanging clothes, pulling out the boxes.

She wiped off the light layer of dust that covered the lid of one and opened it. Inside were several sheets of paper folded to fit the box. "What is this?" Ellis grabbed one of the pieces and unfurled it. It took a moment for her to realize what this was, but soon it became clear.

Text messages. Emails. They were printouts of messages Derek Cannon had sent to Jenna Brooks, along with her replies.

The messages were mildly sexual, growing more graphic as they went on. The girl seemed to have gone along with Cannon's flirtation at first, but soon it appeared that when the flirtation turned more insistent, the girl had tried to back off. And then the messages took on a more violent tone when Jenna asked him to stop.

So many times Ellis had dealt with cases like this. A young girl getting caught up in something with a man, usually older. The fear of what her parents would do was often enough to keep them quiet. And that fear and shame was something the adult male counted on.

"Why do you have these?" Ellis wondered. Why would Cannon's wife keep proof of some kind of relationship her husband had had with a girl who'd been murdered?

McCallister rounded the corner. "Becca?"

"Down here." She pulled out from inside the closet and stood. "I think I might have been wrong."

He joined her. "About what?"

She handed over one of the printouts. "I found this in Lorna Cannon's closet, inside a box next to her shoes. Two of these boxes are filled with folded sheets of paper like this." Ellis waited a minute while McCallister read the exchange.

"Holy shit." He looked at her. "And the wife had these?"

"Yeah. What the hell do you think that means?" Ellis asked.

"That we now have two suspects in the murder of Jenna Brooks."

26

E llis thought she'd solved one crime after taking down Joel Brooks. Now, she had enough evidence to get Cannon to submit a DNA swab, and when it matched what had been found on Jenna Brooks, then it would be game over. Even if the question hung in the air as to Vicky Boyles. If there was a DNA match there to Cannon's too, then had he played a part in Boyles's death?

But what part had Lorna Cannon played in all this? The copies of text exchanges, emails. Why had she kept them? And why not go to the police with them when Jenna was murdered?

She needed to get to the bottom of this, and that would mean talking to the wife of her suspect. It seemed Lorna Cannon had just arrived at the stationhouse. Ellis approached her as she entered the lobby.

"Detective Ellis, what's going on?" Lorna asked, her voice shaking.

"Before you see your husband, could I have a word with you?"

"Yes, of course," she replied.

"If you wouldn't mind following me, then?" Ellis carried on into the hall, past the Patrol bullpen until she reached one of the interview rooms. Next door was where the woman's husband sat. "Please take a seat, Lorna." Ellis gestured for her to enter, and then she closed the door.

She walked to the table where the two boxes had been placed in the center. "I wanted to talk a little bit about Jenna Brooks."

"All right," Lorna said, and then her face shifted slightly as she noticed them. "I don't know what I can help you with. But I'll try."

"As you know, we obtained a search warrant for your home."

"I'm sorry, but I actually didn't know that," she began. "Today? You were in my house today?"

"Yes, ma'am. Your husband was there. Unfortunately, things took a wrong turn, and now, as you know, he's here. But getting back to Jenna Brooks." She opened the lids of the boxes. "Do you mind telling me why you had copies of text messages and emails from your husband to Jenna in these boxes, which were found inside your closet?"

Lorna stared at them and was quiet for several moments.

"Ma'am, did you understand my question?" Ellis pressed.

"I kept them as proof," she whispered. "Proof of what Derek was doing."

"And what was your husband doing?" Ellis asked.

Lorna looked at Ellis with a hardened gaze. "He was trying to get that girl to have an affair with him. After Jenna was taken, her father went on a rampage. Not that I could blame him. So I asked Derek some questions because, well, I'd seen things. Things I thought were innocent enough at the time, but maybe not in light of Jenna's disappearance. Of course, he denied everything."

"And you didn't believe him?" Ellis asked.

"I was skeptical. It wasn't the first time I'd suspected he was cheating. And then when I looked at his laptop one night, I found the emails and texts. This was after Jenna had disappeared, and I wondered if he'd done it."

"Why didn't you go to the police?" Ellis asked. "When you realized your husband might have been involved in the abduction of a young woman?"

"I don't know." She looked away, twisting her fingers nervously. "I didn't have proof, I guess."

"But these messages would've led the police to look into your husband a lot more than they did." Ellis struggled to understand how this woman could've had all this information and not act on it. "Why would you protect him?"

Lorna's eyes reddened. "Because I loved him. Because I didn't want to face the reality of what he was capable of."

Ellis leaned forward. "Have you spoken to him yet?"

"No," Lorna shot back. "I got the call he was here, which is why I'm here now."

"Then I have some news for you. He's been playing dumb. Denying any involvement in Jenna's murder," Ellis said. "And given what I discovered in your closet, I think we both know there's a lot more to this situation than how it appears on the surface."

Lorna shrugged. "I'm not sure I know what you mean."

Ellis tipped over the boxes, the papers spilling out onto the table. "I mean that your husband may have been trying to have an affair with Jenna, but I don't think he killed her. Not anymore. Not after finding these." She spread out the papers. "I think you did. You had motive, you had access to

Jenna, and you had a lot of evidence to suggest your husband was guilty. I think you used that to control him."

"No, you're wrong." Lorna shook her head, tears streaming down her face. "I didn't do it."

"Then why did you keep all this evidence?" Ellis asked. "Why did you go to the trouble of printing out and keeping those text messages and emails if not for your own insurance?"

"I don't know," she cried. "I was scared, okay? Scared of what he was capable of. And when Jenna was murdered, I just didn't know what to do. I didn't want to believe that my husband could do something like that, but the evidence was there, staring me in the face."

Ellis leaned forward. "And where were you the night Jenna was killed?"

"I was at home," she shot back. "With my husband."

"Can anyone attest to that?" Ellis asked.

Lorna brushed the tears from her face, defiant now. "No, we were alone. But I swear I didn't do it."

Ellis had grown tired of these two people lying to her. "Excuse me for a moment, would you?" She stepped out of the interview room and reached for her phone.

"Detective Naylor, it's Ellis with Bangor PD. Listen, I have Derek and Lorna Cannon in custody, who I think could be responsible—either individually or as a couple—for the murder of Jenna Brooks. You feel like making the trip over? I could use your insight."

"I'm on my way."

ELLIS WAITED UPSTAIRS IN THE DETECTIVES' bullpen for Naylor to arrive. She stared at the whiteboard and the files, wondering what else she might have overlooked. But by now she was convinced that Lorna Cannon had either murdered Jenna or helped her husband do it. How to prove one or the other of these scenarios was the question now. Because, while DNA could prove Derek Cannon was guilty, it couldn't prove his wife was innocent. She checked the time on her phone. Naylor would arrive soon, so she headed downstairs again.

As she waited in the lobby, McCallister walked toward her.

"How's it going down here?" he asked.

"Not great. I'm waiting for Naylor. He should be here any minute." Ellis sighed. "What I still can't figure out is why Brooks hit all those neighbors? What the hell was he looking for? What the hell was he trying to achieve?"

Detective Naylor entered the lobby. "I might have an idea."

Ellis turned to him. "Detective, thank you for coming."

"Thank you for making progress on my cold case." He offered his hand.

"This is Detective McCallister." She gestured toward him.

"Good to meet you." He returned his attention to Ellis. "So, you think it's the Cannons who are responsible?"

"I do," Ellis replied. "One or both. That's what I'm not certain of."

"Well, here's what I think," Naylor said. "Based on the information you've given me, I think Brooks truly believed it was Derek Cannon who killed his daughter. He also realized that his neighbors knew all about the man's penchant for pretty young girls. Yet they said nothing. We know that

Derek was particularly close to Michael Madsen, who, I believe, was one of your victims."

"And a book with a telling message was left at their home." Ellis raised an eyebrow. "How do you know this?"

"Despite what you might think, Detective, I did work this case. I talked to the neighbors. While no one pointed at Cannon to say, 'This guy's a creep,' there was an underlying theme that I picked up on."

"And did you pursue it?" she pressed.

"Brooks had accused Cannon of stalking his daughter, that much he did say to me. And I think he was trying to find evidence to support that claim," Naylor began. "I found no evidence to suggest Cannon was guilty of his daughter's murder. Nor did I find proof of any stalking activity."

"And regarding his suspected behavior?" Ellis continued. "His penchant, as you put it."

"Well, that was cleared up after I'd had a look at messages exchanged between Jenna and her friends, including Gladstone's daughter, who was Jenna's closest friend. It seemed the girl was enamored with Derek Cannon. And she wasn't the only one. Hardly his fault."

Ellis lowered her gaze, disgusted by the lack of interest this man had displayed when it came to the nature of these messages.

The sound of officers and other people walking by as they stood in the lobby dissolved, leaving her clear to think about all he'd said. A moment later, she regarded Naylor again. "Is that what the fight was about?"

"Oh yes." He nodded. "The fight between Brooks and his neighbor Johnson. When I spoke with Mr. Johnson, he said Joel Brooks attacked him out of nowhere. Claiming he was close with Cannon and knew all about him. Course, Johnson had no idea what he was talking about."

Maybe he had known.

"So, the other eight families," Ellis began. "You're saying Brooks believed they all knew what a slimeball Cannon was, but said nothing when Jenna disappeared? He'd taken trinkets from some of them, which we found in his apartment. Why do that? And why murder Vicky Boyles?"

Naylor raised his hands. "I understand you got a lot of questions, Detective Ellis, for which I have no answers, hence the reason this case went cold. Best guess regarding Boyles? I think she got in his way. Simple as that."

"Excuse me for a moment, would you?" Ellis stepped away with a brief nod at McCallister. The unspoken exchange was understood to mean she had an idea and needed him to keep Naylor occupied while she pursued it.

Vicky Boyles and Jenna Brooks had traces of the same DNA. How could that have been possible when Ellis knew, without a doubt, that Joel Brooks had murdered Boyles?

She stopped cold in the hallway just outside the interview room. "Oh my God. He was her father. Of course his DNA was found on her. It was secondary transfer." Ellis looked back down the hall and watched McCallister hold a conversation with Naylor. "Why didn't you rule out the father by obtaining a swab from him then?" If she was right about this, and no other DNA was found on Jenna, she couldn't prove that either of the Cannons killed her.

Ellis opened the door to the interview room where Derek Cannon was speaking with his attorney. "Pardon the interruption, but can I speak with you, Mr. Padilla?"

The lawyer nodded to his client. "Sit tight for a minute, Derek." He rose from the chair. "After you, Detective."

Ellis returned to the corridor, where Padilla joined her. "Lorna Cannon is here, and you should know that she has evidence to prove your client was involved with Jenna Brooks."

The lawyer remained stone-faced. "Does this evidence prove my client murdered Ms. Brooks?"

"No, sir," Ellis replied. "But it does contradict what Cannon told investigators at the time of Miss. Brooks' death. What she has is damning and, if shown to a jury, would virtually ensure a conviction."

"What is it you're saying, then, Detective?" He raised his chin. "Are we talking about a potential deal?"

"That would depend on what your client has to offer." Ellis had no idea which of these people murdered Jenna Brooks. But based on what Lorna had, Derek Cannon would find himself in prison for the rest of his life. The only problem with that was if the real killer was his wife.

"You want me to get Derek to turn on his wife," Padilla said.

Ellis didn't respond, but simply waited for a reply. This was all she had in her bag of tricks—and it needed to work.

Padilla appeared to think on it for a moment. "Let me see what I can do." He returned to the interview room.

Getting the couple to turn on each other was the first part of the plan. Now, Ellis had to implement the second, which wouldn't come so easily. She returned to the room where she'd questioned Mrs. Cannon.

Inside, Ellis noticed her, unwavering in her position. "Sorry to have kept you waiting." She made her way into the room and sat down. "Your husband is still speaking with his lawyer."

"And when is it my turn?" Lorna asked.

"To speak to a lawyer?" Ellis shrugged. "You're not under arrest. You can walk out that door right now if you want to." She raised her finger. "But you should know that Derek is hashing out a deal with his lawyer that would see you behind bars instead of him."

Her eyes flickered for a moment. "You're lying."

"You'll find out soon enough." Ellis leaned over the table. "You don't have to say another word to me without a lawyer, Mrs. Cannon. But if you want to stop all of this, then now is the time for you to come clean."

"I already told you that I didn't kill Jenna Brooks. Her father was crazy. You know that. Look at what he did to our community," she pressed. "He murdered Vicky Boyles, for Christ's sake."

"It does appear that way, Mrs. Cannon, but this case isn't over. Joel Brooks came after the people of Woodland Heights because he knew what your husband had done with his daughter," Ellis said. "It was too late for her by the time he found out, so he took out his revenge through other means." She pulled back in her chair. "But the matter of who murdered his daughter remains. This will get ugly very fast, Mrs. Cannon. So if you know more, now's the time to say so."

INSIDE THE INTERVIEW ROOM, Derek Cannon clenched his jaw while his hands balled into fists in his lap. His knee bounced under the table. "You're telling me my wife is claiming I killed Jenna?" He scoffed. "That's complete and utter bullshit, and she knows it. Why would she say something like that, huh?"

"Because the police found the emails and text messages

you exchanged with the girl," Padilla replied. "Did you know she discovered them on your computer and printed copies to keep in case she needed them later?"

"What?" His face screwed up. "No, I didn't know that. What emails and texts?"

"Derek, come on. I'm your lawyer, and I need to know what we're up against, you get that, right?"

"What am I up against?" Derek asked.

"Well, that depends on what your DNA swab turns up," Padilla continued. "Which, by the way, you have no choice but to submit. What will they find, Derek? Will they find a match to the Jenna Brooks' crime scene? And what about Vicky Boyles?"

"I didn't kill Vicky. I was at her house the night she died, but I didn't kill her," Derek shot back. "Joel did. He was insane."

"You'd be surprised what grief can do to someone, Derek." Padilla sighed. "Now, I need you to tell me what you did with that girl. The truth, please. Then we can talk about a potential deal."

"A deal?"

"Again, it depends on what you have to say right now. So, what is it? Did you or your wife murder Jenna Brooks?"

Derek closed his eyes a moment. "Look, I'll admit that I was attracted to Jenna, okay?"

"And how old was she at the time?" Padilla asked.

"Sixteen." He lowered his gaze. "I started DM-ing her on Instagram. Soon, she responded. We both volunteered at the animal shelter a few miles away."

"Did she volunteer before you?" Padilla asked. "Was she the reason you did?"

He swallowed hard. "Yeah, she was already there, and I knew it. Anyway, things sort of grew from there."

"Did you have sex with her?" Padilla asked.

Derek raised his hands. "No. No, it wasn't like that."

"Did you want it to be?"

Shame masked the man's face. "Of course I did. I tried, okay? I tried to convince her no one would ever know. Especially her parents."

"Was she the only one?" Padilla firmed his gaze, his tone cold. "The only young girl you tried to groom?"

"Jesus." He looked away. "Grooming? That's—that's not even..."

"Were there others, Derek?" Padilla pressed.

He hesitated, licking his lips, raking a hand through his hair. "Yeah, there were others after Jenna. But I didn't kill that girl. I promise you."

"What can you tell me about that day?" Padilla asked. "The day Jenna was taken?"

Derek thought back to when he'd gotten the call from Joel's wife. She'd called all the neighbors when Jenna hadn't returned home for dinner. "I just remember the panic. Everyone searched the community. The parks, the elementary school. Joel and his wife tried to track Jenna's cell phone, but it was shut off or something."

"And where were you?" Padilla asked.

"Work. I came home early to help. And that was when I saw my wife's face. The look on it. She was talking to Vicky and Sydney and a couple other neighbors. They were just standing in our driveway, huddled together, crying." He looked away. "I—I guess I'd never seen that kind of grief before. And that was before anyone knew Jenna was dead."

"Your wife's face. What did you mean when you said you saw the look on it?"

Derek rubbed his forehead. "I saw that she knew."

"Knew what?" Padilla pressed.

"She knew about Jenna and me."

"And so that's why you're telling me you think she killed Jenna? Why didn't you say something at the time?"

"I figured if she knew, then she would tell everyone. And the others—the other girls—they'd say something too."

Padilla narrowed his gaze. "You were protecting your reputation."

"I guess so."

"And why do you think it was your wife who murdered Jenna?" he continued.

Derek's mouth turned down as he stared off into the distance. "Because when I pulled up at our home that day, and I saw the women talking, including my wife, I got out and walked straight inside the house. Didn't say anything to them."

"And?"

He set a firm gaze on Padilla. "I was changing out of my tie and saw the necklace on top of our dresser. I knew it belonged to Jenna because I'd given it to her." He let out a long breath. "And it had originally belonged to my wife."

27

The deal was offered. It was for Derek Cannon to turn on his wife with a sworn statement about what he knew and what he'd done. While he was innocent in the murder of Jenna Brooks, he was guilty of grooming underage girls. That, alone, was a ten-to-fifteen-year sentence. However, murder would've seen him serve twenty-five years to life. Either way, Derek Cannon's life, as he knew it, was over.

The reasons as to why Lorna Cannon had killed a sixteen-year-old girl left Ellis enraged. An innocent in all this, Jenna Brooks had been enticed by a sick man. It was no wonder Joel Brooks had sought revenge.

Lorna knew her husband, and she knew what he'd done, yet she'd taken it out on Jenna Brooks. However, it came as a surprise to Lorna that Derek had groomed other girls—at least, she claimed not to know about them. That was something the DA was going to have to flesh out during the trial. The worst part about it? Derek Cannon had kept his mouth shut about all of it during the investigation into the murder of Jenna Brooks, simply to save his own skin.

While Ellis sat at her desk, she considered what might've happened had she let Joel Brooks come for Derek Cannon, rather than stop him before he had the chance. But even Brooks hadn't known the truth, not in its entirety.

Abbott walked into the bullpen, and Ellis noticed him heading her way. He wore a look of submission. After pushing hard against her and the others working on the final leg of this investigation, he'd come not to apologize, but to admit he'd been wrong. Was it the same thing? No, not really. Not for Abbott and not for her either.

"You got the husband to turn on his wife," Abbott said.

"Yes, sir. I dangled a carrot, but the lawyer convinced him to do it," she replied. "He'll still serve time regardless. That's what's important."

"Yes, indeed. Just not as much." Abbott scanned the bullpen. "Looks like everyone's gone for the evening, huh?"

"Not everyone," Ellis replied. "Euan's still here."

He grinned. "Why does that not surprise me? Congratulations on closing both cases, Becca. I'm glad you didn't listen to me."

Abbott seemed to notice her holding back her relief. "It's okay to smile about this. You got Joel Brooks off the streets. Don't forget that he was still a killer, regardless of his reasons. You caught Jenna Brooks' killer. Listen, go home. In fact, take tomorrow off. You need time to reset."

"Thank you, sir. But if it's all the same to you, I'll see you in the morning."

Abbott smiled and shook his head. "Of course you will."

AFTER STOPPING by to see Hank to fill him in on the results of her investigation, Ellis returned home. The sun had set. The night air was warm. And it felt great to sit on her front porch with a bottle of beer in her hand, staring at the stars.

But one thing still gnawed at her—the way she'd left things with Andrew. Now that the investigation was over, she'd had a minute to think about what lay ahead for her ex-husband. Could she really sit idly by while he faced a potential prison sentence just for his association with his fiancée? Was there anything she could do?

Ellis grabbed her phone from the table in between the two Adirondack chairs. She pressed Detective Alcott's contact, and the phone rang. He answered.

"Detective Alcott, this is Rebecca Ellis, Bangor PD. Good evening."

"Evening to you, ma'am. How can I help you?" he asked.

"I don't know how much progress you've made on the Myra Cook investigation since we last spoke," she began, "but I think I'd like to make that trip to New Haven to sit down and figure out what it means for Andrew Cofield." She noticed that he'd gone quiet for a moment. "Sir?"

"Yes, I'm here. What is it you think you can do for him, Detective?" Alcott asked.

"He says he's innocent. I'd like to help prove that." Ellis noticed McCallister as he stepped out the front door, but she continued with the conversation. "Is that something you'd be open to discussing?"

"I'm open to just about anything, Detective. So long as you remember who's in charge and whose jurisdiction you're in."

"Then I'll clear it on my end and plan to see you in the

next day or so," Ellis replied. "Thank you. I realize you don't have to do this, so I appreciate that you are."

"It's Mr. Cofield who should appreciate what you're doing. Good night, Detective."

When the call ended, Ellis watched McCallister set down a plate of cheese and crackers on the table.

"For the lady," he said before taking a seat next to her. "So, who are you planning to see?"

"Thought I'd meet with the detective in New Haven and see what it is the feds have on Andrew," Ellis replied. "I can't let him face this on his own."

He pressed his lips together in a thin smile. "I know you can't."

Ellis reached for a piece of cheese and plunked it into her mouth. "Delicious. Thank you."

McCallister took a drink from his beer. "It really is nice out tonight."

"Even nicer when a case is over, right?"

"That it is." He took a sip from his bottle of beer. "I know I wasn't there for you when the investigation started, but I'm glad I was able to come in and offer some help—not that you needed it."

Ellis turned to him, wearing a grin. "I'm glad you were there, too. And thanks for the backup." It was his way of apologizing for stepping on her toes, going against what she'd wanted for her investigation. But she owed him one, too. "I'm sorry I didn't tell you about Andrew earlier."

"You don't owe me anything, Becca." He raised a preemptive hand. "It was none of my business. We both have a past."

She picked at the label on her bottle. "You should know that I have no feelings for him anymore."

The corner of his mouth ticked up. "Well, that's a relief."

Ellis noticed a car rolling up to her driveway. "Who's that?" But then the car came into view under the streetlight. "Connor?"

McCallister peered out. "Yeah. What's he doing here?"

"I have no idea." She waited while Bevins stepped out of his Mustang and started toward them. "Oh, I don't like the look on his face. Something's happened."

"Yes, it did," McCallister replied.

As he drew near, Ellis pulled up to the edge of her chair. "Hey, Connor, what's going on? I wasn't expecting to see you tonight. Everything okay?"

"No. Everything's not okay, Becca." He leaned against the porch railing, shaking his head.

"Hey, man," McCallister said. "Just spit it out."

"Someone knows." Bevins crossed his arms tightly over his chest. "Someone knows what happened at West Point."

Ellis's expression was one of confusion as she glanced over at McCallister. And the look on his face suggested he knew exactly what Bevins was talking about. "What's going on? What am I missing?"

Bevins rubbed his nose with the back of his hand. His legs shifted, and his breaths sounded labored.

Ellis stood up. "Con, you're scaring me. What the hell's going on? Who knows what about West Point?"

He glanced at McCallister before retrieving his phone. "Watch." He opened the screen and pressed play on a YouTube video.

McCallister stood up to join Ellis as the two peered at the screen.

The video began with a young man sitting at a desk wearing headphones. He looked at the camera. "For those of you who still think justice is blind, check this out." A photo appeared on the screen of an older man.

"That's my dad," Bevins said.

The video returned to the young man in the head-phones. "This man, Jack Bevins, is a top aide to the chairman of the Joint Chiefs of Staff. A West Point graduate—with honors. And do you want to know what I learned?" he continued. "It all started when that shit went down about that bad cop. You remember, right? Some piece-of-shit Boston detective shot that kid, and the family just won their civil case against Boston PD." The guy laughed.

Ellis glanced at McCallister, who didn't appear amused.

"So I started digging around into that piece of shit. Come to find out, he's not the only bad apple at Bangor PD, which is where this genius is at now, by the way. Oh yeah. I looked into all them guys. Took me a minute, but when I came across the name Bevins, well, I found all sorts of stuff. Like ol' Jack has a son. And that son went to West Point too. Only things turned out a whole lot differently for him."

Another image appeared of a wrecked car in a ditch. And when the guy returned to the screen, he raised his brow. "Can you say Chappaquiddick? For those of you who don't get the reference, look it up, you ignoramuses."

"What?" Ellis covered her mouth.

Bevins ended the video, his whole body shaking, and his eyes red. "How the hell did he find all that?"

Ellis glanced between them. "Why doesn't someone tell me what the hell is going on? Because I have a feeling I'm the only one in the dark about this."

McCallister opened his mouth when Bevins stopped him. "No, it's my story to tell." He turned to Ellis. "What can I say, Becca?" He drew in a long, steadying breath. "I thought this might happen after what we went through with Euan. But I didn't think any of this was out there, you know?"

Ellis grew heated. "Any of what?"

"If my dad was good at one thing, it was hiding shit. And he hid my accident well, or so I thought. But with this out? It won't just be me who goes down. He'll go down too."

"Christ, Connor, will you just tell me exactly what the hell is happening right now? I know what happened at Chappaquiddick. Everyone does. Are you trying to tell me that car in the ditch was yours and that whoever was in there with you died?"

Bevins cast down his gaze, tears dropping onto the concrete porch. "Something like that." He looked up at her. "And now it's out there on the internet for everyone to see." He glanced at McCallister.

Ellis picked up on the exchange and turned to him. "You knew about this?"

"I asked him not to say anything," Bevins cut in. "Becca, what the hell am I going to do? It was an accident, but my dad—he said we had to keep it from coming out. And now it has."

Ellis was pissed that she'd been kept in the dark. Now they'd been blindsided in much the same way as McCallister had been. "I don't have an answer for you, Connor. I don't know what we're supposed to do now."

She cast up her gaze at the stars once again, catching her breath from what felt like yet another sucker punch to her gut. "This department, this team, we only scraped by after the Boston thing. But this?" Anger heated her face as she headed to the front door. Gripping the handle, she turned back to them. "I don't know how you recover from this." Ellis walked inside and slammed the door behind her.

WE HOPE YOU ENJOYED THIS BOOK

If you could spend a moment to write an honest review on Amazon, no matter how short, we would be extremely grateful. They really do help readers discover new authors.

ABOUT THE AUTHOR

Robin Mahle has published more than 30 crime fiction novels, many, of which, topped the Amazon charts in the US, Canada, and the UK. Also a screenwriter, she has adapted some of her works into teleplays, which have gone on to place in film festivals nationwide. From detectives to federal agents, and from killers to corruption, her page-turning tales grab hold and refuse to let go. Throw in tense action and thrilling twists, and it becomes clear why her readers come back for more. Robin lives in Coastal Virginia with her husband and two children.

www.robinmahle.com

ALSO BY ROBIN MAHLE

Detective Rebecca Ellis Series

No Safe Place

A Frozen Grave

The Dead Lake

Leave No Trace

No Way Back

Printed in Great Britain
by Amazon

52652662R00187